KISSING IN MISTY HARBOR

Ned moved a step closer, crowding Norah against the side of the car, but he didn't touch her. "Do you have any idea how hard it is for me not to kiss you right now?"

"What's stopping you?"

"I don't want to frighten you."

"You don't frighten me."

"You're so tiny."

"You're so big," she fired right back while looking up. Way up. She could feel the heat of his body warming the cool evening air.

"We're back to size, are we?" The corner of his mouth kicked up into a small smile as he inched closer. His chest was nearly touching her chin.

"You started it."

Ned slowly put his hands on the roof of the SUV. One on either side of her body. "So I did." He studied her face as he blocked her in. "Can I kiss you now?"

His tempting mouth seemed a long distance away. "Can I stand on my tippy toes?"

"You can do anything you want, as long as you kiss me back," Ned said as he slowly lowered his mouth and kissed her . . .

Books by Marcia Evanick

CATCH OF THE DAY

CHRISTMAS ON CONRAD STREET

BLUEBERRY HILL

A BERRY MERRY CHRISTMAS

HARBOR NIGHTS

Published by Zebra Books

Harbor
Nights

Marcia Evanick

ZEBRA BOOKS
KENSINGTON PUBLISHING CORP.
www.kensingtonbooks.com

ZEBRA BOOKS are published by

Kensington Publishing Corp.
850 Third Avenue
New York, NY 10022

All Kensington titles, imprints, and distributed lines are available at special quantity discounts for bulk purchases for sales
promotion, premiums, fund-raising, educational, or institutional
use.

Special book excerpts or customized printings can also be
created to fit specific needs. For details, write or phone the
office of the Kensington Special Sales Manager: Attn. Special
Sales Department. Kensington Publishing Corp., 850 Third
Avenue, New York, NY 10022. Phone: 1-800-221-2647.

ISBN 0-8217-7708-4

First Printing: September 2005
10 9 8 7 6 5 4 3 2 1

Printed in the United States of America

This book is dedicated to the newest light within my heart.
There is always room for one more.

Welcome to the world, Logan Aldrich.
Love, Grandma

Chapter One

Over the years, Ned Porter had encountered many things in his parents' backyard, but never once had he discovered a woodland nymph under his mother's prize rosebush. It wasn't much of a rosebush, considering his mother's thumb was more brown than green. The same thing couldn't be said about the nymph. From the shadows in which he stood, he had a clear view of the tiny woman and her pert, little jean-clad bottom as she wiggled and cussed her way farther under the thorny bush.

He had heard Girl Scouts use stronger language, but he had to give the nymph extra points for creativity. He'd never heard that particular word used as an adjective before. Whatever the woman was after, it wasn't coming easily.

He reached down and lightly patted the head of his dog, Flipper. He could feel Flipper's large, muscular body quivering with excitement. The hundred and fifty-pound Newfoundland wanted to go play with the enchanting woodland creature. It had been Flipper who had alerted him to the presence of a stranger in his parents' backyard that they should go investigate.

Ned and his dog had stopped over to check on his parents' home because they were out of town. Their house was in total darkness behind him, but most of their backyard was lit up by the light pouring out of every window and glowing in every outdoor bulb that the new neighbor had lit. The Las Vegas strip used less wattage per square foot. It was ten o'clock at night, and he needed his sunglasses.

A high-pitched yelping sound coming from under the rose bush caused him to reach for Flipper's collar instinctively. He didn't think the rose fairy would appreciate competing for space with the Newfoundland under the thorny bush. She would surely be trampled into the mulch and weeds his mother never had time to pull. From the angle at which he was viewing the nymph, the dog outweighed her by a good forty pounds.

A string of inventive forms of torture caused him to chuckle and step out of the shadows. Whatever it was that was yelping needed to be gagged. The high-pitched barking was causing the hair on the back of his neck to stand up. Fingernails scratching a chalkboard would be less irritating. Flipper, who usually wouldn't move an inch without a direct command, was pulling against the hold he had on his collar.

Flipper either wanted to go play with the annoying creature, or he was looking for a late night snack.

"Need any help?" he asked as he took another step closer to the intriguing visitor.

He cringed as the nymph jerked her head up and her short hair got caught on a thorn or two. He hadn't meant to scare her. He wouldn't be surprised if the woodland sprite put a curse on him. Did nymphs cast curses, or was that a troll? To be on the safe side, he offered a hasty apology, "Sorry, I didn't mean to startle you."

Norah Stevens felt a thorn dig into her scalp and the painful yanking of her hair as it tangled with the bush. She bit her tongue to hold back a heated word and glared at her mother's Pomeranian, Zsa Zsa, who was covered in mulch and hiding behind weeds, deep in the shadows. The four-pound diva seemed to smirk back at her. "I have one more four-letter word for you to think about"—she hissed softly—"cage." She started to wiggle her way out from under the bush. Thorny branches tugged at her hair, and one particularly sharp thorn scratched her shoulder. "First thing tomorrow morning, I'm buying you a leash and the most uncomfortable cage I can find."

The miniature dog had been a royal pain in the tush since the day her mother had spotted her in the pet store's window. It had been love at first sight. Nothing else would do but to have the spoiled Pomeranian join their family. Her mother had even kept the ridiculous-sounding name some employee had bestowed upon the tiny dog. Zsa Zsa had made her mother smile. With that simple act, Norah had opened her wallet and bought her mother the dog as an early birthday present. Six months early.

Her mother deserved all the smiles she could get even if they came wrapped in some neurotic hairball that liked to get her nails painted and would only take a 'poo' if no one was watching. With her luck, Zsa Zsa had probably just fertilized the neighbor's rosebush.

It was a hell of a way to meet the neighbors. First impressions counted, and here she was crawling around on all fours, and without a pooper-scooper in sight.

She stood up and brushed her hands on the back of her jeans before running them through her short, spiky hair. She tried not to cringe when her fingertip rubbed against a particularly nasty scratch. She was dirty, tired, and in no mood to make nice with the neighbors. She had spent the past two days unpacking boxes; moving furniture; and putting up with Zsa Zsa, who had developed an irrational fear of seagulls. Norah wished she would have known that fact before moving to a small fishing village on the coast of Maine. She still would have moved to Misty Harbor, but Zsa Zsa might not have joined the family the week before the move. She wasn't looking forward to Zsa Zsa meeting her first lobster.

With a silent sigh and one last glare at the quivering spot beneath the bush, she forced herself to smile pleasantly and turned around. Her gaze collided with a solid wall of bulging chest muscles encased in a dark green T-shirt. She looked up. Way up.

The square-jawed man smiling back at her wasn't her neighbor. She distinctly remembered the real estate agent telling her and her mother that the neighbors were a nice married couple in their fifties. The man before her, doing a great job of imitating a modern day Hercules, wasn't quite thirty years old. Misty Harbor had just gotten a whole lot more interesting. She always was a sucker for a man with a crooked smile and laughing eyes. "Hi, I'm Norah Stevens, and I'm trespassing." She stuck out her hand in greeting and prayed she wasn't about to get a firsthand look at the inside of a jail cell.

"Ned Porter." Ned's smile seemed to slip a notch as he shook her hand. "No one trespasses in Misty Harbor. We're quite open to having rose fairies visit our gardens anytime, day or night."

Norah was startled not only by the electrified contact of Ned's touch but also by the sheer size of his hand. Ned Porter had huge, work-roughened hands. Hands like her father's. She quickly dropped his hand and then tried to cover up the insult by asking, "Do you get a lot of fairies around here?"

"Only during the summer months. Our winters tend to scare off even the hardiest of souls. Mythical or otherwise."

"Great, now I'm really looking forward to January." She tried not to roll her eyes.

Ned chuckled. "They're not that bad if you are prepared for them." Ned glanced at the rosebush. "I take it you're the new neighbor and not some rose fairy."

"How can you tell?" She looked at the sad rose bush. One lone yellow rose was in full wilt. It was the saddest looking bush she had ever seen. "Never mind, I think I've figured it out. If I was a card-carrying fairy and this was the best I could do, they would drum me out of the union."

Ned shook his head at the pitiful shrub. "My mother loves this bush. The more she tries, the worse it looks."

"This is your parents' house?" It was on the tip

of her tongue to tell him that her mother would gladly give gardening tips to his mother, but she wasn't even sure her mother's green thumb could save such a sorry-looking sight.

"Yes, they've been out of town for the past couple of days. Mom's sister is in the hospital down in Boston, so they are there visiting her." Ned's left hand maintained its hold on the dog. "Flipper and I just stopped by to check on things."

She glanced at the massive black dog. "Flipper?" Ned's chuckle was a deep rumble that sent a thrill skipping down her spine.

"He swims like a dolphin." Ned patted the top of the dog's head. "Can I ask what's under the bush? My first guess would be a dog, but I've never heard one bark quite like that before."

"Your first guess is right on the money." She glared at the bush and couldn't detect a glimpse of Zsa Zsa. The spoiled mutt had burrowed herself farther into the mulch, and she could only pray she hadn't christened it first. Her mother was going to be up half the night shampooing and blow-drying the pampered pooch. "At least the American Kennel Club calls it a dog."

"What do you call it?" Ned's glance was searching the shadows beneath the bush.

"In polite company, I call Zsa Zsa a spoiled rotten princess." Ned looked at her, and she could tell he was trying real hard not to laugh.

"You named a dog Zsa Zsa?" he asked.

"No, my mother named *her* dog Zsa Zsa. I have quite a few names that I call her, and if you were standing there for any length of time, you would have heard a couple of them." With any luck, he had just arrived and had missed her ranting and raving while crawling around in his parents' garden.

Ned's mouth twitched into that endearing crooked smile. "So it's your mother's dog that is under my mother's rose bush?"

Zsa Zsa gave a high-pitched yelp, causing Flipper to yank Ned another foot closer to the bush. "If my mother wasn't crazy for the mutt, I'd leave her out here to become snacks for the seagulls." Zsa Zsa's yelp turned into a pitiful cry.

Ned's smile turned into a look of concern. "Is she hurt?"

"No, she's terrified of"—she pointed upwards—"you know."

Ned stared at the beautiful woman before him and knew it had been too good to be true. Norah Stevens was packed into one enticing package, even if she was on the petite side for his usual taste in women. Worn jeans clung to a tiny waist and curvy hips. Her feet were bare, and the teeny tank top she wore showed a good two inches of smooth, pale skin between its hem and the waistband on her jeans. What the good Lord hadn't given her in height, he'd surely made up for in other attributes. His mother's new neighbor impressively filled out a tank top.

It was a real shame Norah's elevator didn't go all the way up to the top floor. The five earrings in her right ear and a few more in her left should have been his first clue. The second clue was what appeared to be eight rings on her delicate, little fingers and the two-inch spiked hair that might be more red than brown. High cheekbones and eyes that tilted upward at the corners gave her a fey look. Norah indeed had the look of the fairy he claimed her to be. An enchanting, bejeweled, slightly out of whack fairy.

When he'd first learned that a mother and her daughter had bought the house next to his parents' home, he had pictured an eight-year-old with long braids and skinned knees. Someone who would leave her bike out in the middle of the yard or require a swing set to be built in the backyard.

Ned's gaze followed Norah's finger, and he stared at the night sky, trying to figure out what she was pointing to. "I know what?" The only thing he could see besides the crescent moon was the stars. Somehow he didn't think Zsa Zsa was afraid of the stars or the moon.

Norah's generous mouth turned down into a frown. "She's terrified of s-e-a . . ." Norah started to spell the word.

"Seagulls?"

Zsa Zsa whimpered as Norah hushed him. "Shhh . . . don't say it."

He didn't know who was more certifiable, Norah or the dog who could spell. "You're kidding, right?"

"Afraid not." Norah glanced at the bush where the pitiful whimpering continued. In the hushed tone reserved for the breaking of bad news, Norah whispered, "We think it's a phobia."

Norah's elevator not only didn't reach the top floor, it was totally out of order. He now understood why a woman in her mid twenties was still living with her mother and crawling around under the neighbor's bushes in the middle of the night. If he hadn't heard the dog with his own ears, he would have suspected Norah of making up the entire story. "Maybe medication will help." To be honest with himself, he wasn't quite sure if he meant for the dog or the woman. It was a fifty-fifty split.

Norah cocked her head as if seriously considering the matter. "I don't know. She has an appointment next week with the local vet; maybe he can prescribe something. Do they make Prozac for dogs?"

"I know they make tranquilizers for animals. My parents once had a dog that had to take them every Fourth of July. He was terrified of the firecrackers. Who's the appointment with—Merle Sherman?" Merle had been the local vet longer than Ned's father had been alive. There wasn't a better vet around, as long as you didn't interrupt him while he was fishing at his pond. Then Merle tended to get a little cranky.

"That's the one." Norah reached her hand out and allowed Flipper to smell it. Flipper licked it instead.

"He likes you." His dog's tongue was almost as wide as Norah's palm.

"How can you tell?" Norah grinned as she scratched the dog behind his ears. Flipper rolled his eyes and moaned in ecstasy.

"He licks people he likes." He watched in envy as his dog plopped down in the grass and rolled onto his back. Flipper wanted Norah to rub his tummy. If only the male species of the human race had it so easy.

Norah laughed at the dog's antics and then knelt down and gave in to the silent command for a good scratching. "What does he do to people he doesn't like?"

Flipper's body vibrated with ecstasy, and his massive paws shook wildly.

"You don't want to know." Norah's laugh was light and totally carefree. The light, bubbly sound reminded him of water flowing over rocks in a shallow stream. Norah's voice hadn't been so gentle and soft when she had been cussing out her mother's dog. One thing was for certain—she wasn't a native Down Easterner. "Where are you from? I can't place the accent."

"Pennsylvania." Norah gave Flipper one last long scratch that sent the dog's legs into spasms of delight. "The Allentown area." She stood back up. "Even being named after a fish, Flipper is more a dog than my mother's will ever be."

"A dolphin is a mammal, not a fish." He pushed Flipper away from the rosebush. Now that Norah's fingers had stopped paying all that attention to his belly, Flipper wanted to go investigate the whimpering sound coming from under the bush. If Zsa Zsa was scared of seagulls, he didn't want to see her reaction to a hundred and fifty-pound Newfoundland. "Would you like me to get your dog out from under there?"

"I would love it." Norah bit at her lower lip. "But she nips when she's scared."

"Considering I can't even see her, her teeth can't be that big." He knelt down and looked under the bush. Way in the back, he spotted a tuft of brown fur sticking out of a pile of trembling mulch. The mound of ground wood chips was about the same size as one of his hands. He didn't want to offend Norah or her mother so he tried not to chuckle at the ridiculous sight. He'd had bigger critters crawl into his tent while camping.

With a quick movement, he gently snatched up

the little dog and hauled the squirming mound of mulch out from under the thorny bush.

Zsa Zsa started to bark and yelp like she was the Mini-Me of the hounds of hell. Mulch went flying in all directions. One well-timed nip and a scratch or two later, he placed the shaking furball into Norah's outstretched hands. If the dog weighed four pounds, it was due to the clinging mulch. He chuckled at the sight. "I've held bigger hamsters."

Zsa Zsa showed her tiny white teeth and growled at him before pressing herself up against Norah's chest, seeking the safety of someone she knew.

Flipper started to run around Norah, looking to play with the miniature dog. Zsa Zsa bared her teeth, snapped wildly, and generally acted like she wanted to rip Flipper apart.

Norah's gaze was on his now empty hands and not on the tiny Pomeranian. She wasn't paying any attention to Flipper, but there was fear in her eyes. Most people would fear for their safety when confronted with a massive dog the size of Flipper. Not Norah. The fear darkening those enchanting eyes had been directed at his hands as he'd passed Zsa Zsa to her.

His stomach dipped at the sight. He'd never had a woman fear him or his hands before. He quickly took a step back and grabbed hold of Flipper's collar. The fear faded, and Norah seemed to take a breath.

In the distance, a door opened, and more light flooded the yards. A voice called out into the night, "Norah?"

Norah pulled her gaze away from Ned's hands and the distant memories. She glanced over at her mother. "I'll be right there, Mom." Zsa Zsa started to squirm in her arms.

Ned looked over at the woman standing on the back porch of the other house. She was a petite woman wrapped in a cotton bathrobe and slippers.

"Where's Zsa Zsa?"

"I've got her, Mom." Norah's grip tightened on the small squirming dog. "She snuck out of the house when I opened the back door to take out some of the empty boxes."

"Who's with you?"

"Ned Porter, ma'am. My parents live here, but they are out of town for a couple of days. I just stopped by to check on things." Ned debated going over to introduce himself properly, but somehow, he didn't think Norah's mom would appreciate a guest while she was in her pajamas.

"Is everything all right?"

"It is now," he said. Ned chuckled at the mess Zsa Zsa was making of Norah's light green shirt. A lone mulch chip clung to the enticing swell of Norah's breast. *Lucky, lucky mulch chip.*

"Mr. Porter had to drag your dog out from underneath his mother's prize rosebush." Norah plucked another piece of mulch off the dog and brushed aside the piece that was clinging to her chest.

He glanced at Norah and whispered, "Mr. Porter's my father. I'm Ned."

"She wasn't any trouble, was she?" Norah's mom sounded anxious.

"No problem at all, ma'am." Ned reached over and plucked another piece of mulch off the dog. He chuckled when Zsa Zsa tried to nip him.

Norah tapped the dog on its pint-sized nose.

"Behave or I'll take you down to the docks." Norah's generous mouth turned up into a breathtaking smile. "Thank you for rescuing my mother's dog, Ned."

"Any time." He loved her smile, but he couldn't fail to notice she avoided looking at his hands. For some reason, he didn't want this strange and magical creature to leave. "Do you need any help unpacking boxes or moving furniture?" He couldn't picture either woman pushing around a sofa or hauling mattresses up the stairs. Didn't they have anyone to help them move in? No husbands? No family? No boyfriends?

"Thanks for the offer, but we are just about settled in now." Norah stepped between two bushes making up the small hedge that separated the properties. "It was nice meeting you, and I hope your aunt gets better."

"She's getting out of the hospital tomorrow, and the pleasure was all mine. Good night, Norah." Entranced, he watched as Norah made her way to the back porch and placed Zsa Zsa into her mother's waiting arms. He could hear Norah's mom coo and scold the dog all the way into the house. Norah gave him a wave and then followed her mother in.

He released Flipper to go scout out the new and interesting scents that now permeated his parents' backyard. He leaned against a wooden picnic table and felt the cool night breeze against his face as he studied the small cottage-style house next door. In the growing darkness, he watched as the exterior lights from Norah's house were extinguished one by one. Somehow, it seemed fitting that the rose fairy with the spiked red hair and more jewelry than a gypsy queen had taken the light with her.

* * *

Half an hour later, Norah was still putting away her grandmother's good china into the dining room's hutch. Her mother had unpacked, washed, and dried the good dishes before taking her shower. She had volunteered for the job of putting it all away since her mother was elbow deep in doggie shampoo and conditioner. Zsa Zsa was docilely standing in the kitchen sink, enjoying every stroke and rub of her mother's fingers. The Pomeranian acted like she was at a five-star spa and resort.

"You're spoiling her, Mom." Norah repositioned the soup tureen so it would be in the center of one of the four glass doors on the cabinet.

"By giving her a bath?" Joanna Stevens gently poured another cup of lukewarm water over the sudsy animal. "You'd rather she smelled like decomposing wood chips and Lord knows what else?"

"No." She placed one of the serving trays up behind the stack of dessert plates. The service for twelve, along with every companion dish known to mankind, barely fit in the antique cabinet. "I was referring to the amount of hygiene products you've bought her." She glanced at the huge basket overflowing with doggie care items sitting on the counter next to a pink, fluffy bath towel. Her own bath towels were yellow, and she had purchased them on sale at Wal-Mart. Zsa Zsa got 100 percent Egyptian cotton. Her mother had the nerve to say the dog wasn't spoiled. "She even has her own toothbrush and toothpaste."

"You don't want her to get tartar buildup, do you?" Joanna rinsed the dog one last time and then carefully placed her on the pink towel.

"Heaven forbid that she'd have to get her teeth scraped and cleaned like the rest of us." She wrinkled her nose at the soaking wet dog. Without her hair being all puffed out, Zsa Zsa looked like a drowned rat.

"What's with you tonight, Norah?" Her mother wrapped the dog up into a big ball of expensive cotton. Only Zsa Zsa's miniature face was sticking out of the cocoon. "You seem tired. Maybe we've been overdoing it lately. There's no need to get everything unpacked right away. We put a pretty big-sized dent in the boxes, and everything we absolutely need is away."

"I'm fine, Mom." She gave her mom what she hoped was a convincing smile. "Just a bit embarrassed at being caught underneath the neighbors' rosebush losing a battle of wills against a four-pound dog." This time her smile was the genuine thing. She could still see the look on Ned's face when she'd told him that Zsa Zsa had a fear of seagulls. Ned hadn't known if he should help her get the dog out from under the bush or have her committed.

"Ned Porter seemed like a nice young man." Her mother's gaze was probing.

"He was very helpful." She placed the bone china cups on their saucers and scattered them throughout the cabinet. "What color are you thinking about painting this room?" As a change of subject, it was guaranteed to work. It was the first thing her mother had said when she'd signed the settlement papers on this house. She was looking forward to painting every room in the place any color she wanted to. It had been a strange statement from a woman who'd never painted a room in her life. Every room in the house Norah had grown up in had been white. White ceilings, white walls, and light beige carpeting had dominated every room. Norah hadn't even been allowed to paint her bedroom walls when she was a teenager, let alone hang a poster or two in the sterile environment.

Had it been any wonder that she had fallen in love with the dorms at college and had rarely come home to visit?

Her mother took the bait as she studied the white dining room walls. "Blue." She softly rubbed the towel against the dog. "I'm thinking a deep, rich blue to match the pattern on the china."

Norah smiled as she put away the last plate. Joanna's prize possession was her mother's china. She watched as her mother fluffed out Zsa Zsa's hair and then plugged in the hair dryer.

As the hum of the dryer filled the kitchen and the dining room, Norah jammed all the crinkled newspapers into the empty boxes and carried them to the back porch to join the other stack. Her mother was right. She was exhausted, but it was a good tired. It was the tired feeling you got from physical labor and accomplishing something. The downstairs rooms were in pretty good shape, and her mother's bedroom looked a lot better than her own. She had been too busy helping her mother to worry about the upstairs where her two rooms and a bath were. Her mother would be appalled if she knew Norah was still digging through boxes to find clean underwear and her deodorant.

Norah leaned against the porch post and studied the house next door. Ned's parents' home was once again in total darkness. Not even a hall light was lit to warn away potential burglars. Ned and Flipper were long gone. She had heard them drive away about five minutes after she returned home.

She had lied to her mother. She wasn't fine. Tonight, she had discovered a horrible truth about herself. She had been afraid of Ned and his obvious physical strength. She had the heart of a coward, and she was darn grateful for the fact that Ned wasn't their neighbor. How would she have the strength to keep hiding that fear day after day?

It was one more thing to hate her father for. Vincent Stevens, the man who had given her life, had put that fear and cowardice into her heart.

How was it possible for her mother to look at six-feet, two-inch Ned and think he looked like a nice young man, when all Norah kept seeing were his hands? Big, work-roughened hands.

Hands like her father's.

Hands that hit, and hit hard.

Norah could close her eyes and still see the night over a year ago when those hands had shattered her trust, her respect, and the love she had always felt for the man who used to bounce her on his knee and give her horsey rides.

Chapter
Two

Norah stood beside Peggy Porter and tried not to let her anxiety show. Four angry lobster fishermen were standing in the middle of her front yard voicing their discontentment with her first weekly article. While the lobstermen weren't very eloquent in their speech, they were vocal.

Loud enough for her mother to head back inside the house to try and calm Zsa Zsa down. The four-pound Pomeranian had taken an instant dislike to the shouting men. Their voices had been loud enough for her new neighbor, Peggy Porter, to come storming over to find out what in the world was going on.

Peggy looked like she could armwrestle and beat every one of the angry men. Norah now knew where Ned got his height and his broad shoulders from—his dear old mom. Peggy Porter stood six feet, one inch tall and had the shoulders of an NFL linebacker. Her brown hair, which was cut short, was liberally sprinkled with gray. Peggy was wearing a pair of cutoff jeans, a Rolling Stones concert T-shirt from what had to be one of their first American tours, and construction boots. Her cheeks were sunburnt and her lips were chapped, but she had a mischievous look of laughter in her light blue eyes as she shouted right back into the faces of the men. Peggy looked like a woman who was enjoying herself immensely.

Norah loved the woman on sight.

"Leland and Lonny Higgins, you should be ashamed of yourselves." Peggy Porter crossed her arms against her ample chest and glared down her nose at the sweaty, stubble-jawed men. "You too, Oscar and Russ. I have half a mind to call your mothers and tell them how you big oafs are terrorizing a poor, defenseless woman."

Norah watched as Russ, a forty-something-year-old man, kicked a tuft of grass with the toe of his sneaker. Oscar, the baby of the group in his early thirties, winced as his windburnt cheeks reddened further. Leland and Lonny didn't seem frightened of the prospect. She wasn't sure which was Leland and which was Lonny, but they had to be brothers. The good Lord wouldn't have cursed two unrelated men with a nose like that.

"You don't know what she wrote, Peg," whined Oscar as he twirled his baseball cap between his fingers.

"Yeah, you don't make your living by hauling in lobsters all day," added one of the Higgins men.

"No," countered Peggy, "I make it by hauling in tuna." Peggy's stance grew more rigid and formidable. "I read her article this afternoon, and I couldn't find one untruth in it."

"She's siding with them!" shouted Russ.

Norah knew who *'them'* was—the Atlantic States Marine Fisheries Commission. Her first weekly article, which had pointed out the benefits of the mandatory dredging and counting of lobsters off the coast, was causing an uproar. Her boss had warned her that most of the local lobster fishermen held that practice in contempt. She had known she might not be making friends with the article, but she hadn't figured on some of the more vocal fishermen knocking on her front door and voicing their displeasure.

She should have known that life in Misty Harbor would be throwing her some barbs. Her new job at the weekly paper, the *Hancock Review,* had been going too smoothly. Her mother and she had finally settled into their new home, Maine's summer was absolutely gorgeous, and Zsa Zsa had stopped trying to escape every time they opened a door. Life had been great up 'til about five minutes ago.

"As I recall," Peggy said, "Norah didn't voice her opinion one way or the other. The article stated facts, not opinions."

"The facts were wrong," Oscar said.

"Just because you don't agree with them, doesn't make them wrong." Peggy's shoulders relaxed now that the shouting had died down to a low roar. "Didn't you guys read Thomas Belanger's introduction for Norah's articles? He told you why she was hired to write 'Views From The Other Side.' Norah doesn't have any family in Maine to sway her opinions. She also isn't from around here, and she has never lived on the coast before. She's the perfect candidate for writing these kinds of articles." Peggy wrapped a muscular arm over Norah's shoulders and gave a little squeeze of support. "It's her job to take the other side of the argument and try to get thick blockheads like you guys to open your minds a little."

Norah felt as if the bones in her shoulders were in a vise. Peggy Porter had the grip of a boa constrictor. A fiercely protective, but incredibly sweet, boa constrictor. Maybe it was time to speak up and try to defend herself once again. She hadn't been doing too badly before Peggy had stomped across the yard and taken control of the situation. With her new job of playing devil's advocate, she was bound to run into upset citizens from time to time. Just because there were four big, physically strong men yelling at her this time didn't mean she couldn't handle them. She had to learn how to deal with them because there was no guarantee that Peggy Porter would be around the next time the Higgins brothers got their lobster-hauling shorts in a twist.

"I did ask Tom Belanger," she said, "if I could do an article on the lobster fisherman's point of view. He informed me that the paper had already run two separate articles covering that in the past six months, plus countless editorial letters."

She tried to smile to soften her words, but her gaze kept straying to Oscar's huge work-roughened hands as he twisted and turned his baseball cap between them. Her gut got that queasy feeling she hated so much. "I'm sorry if I offended anyone; that wasn't my intention."

Peggy gave her another squeeze that nearly knocked her to her knees. "Don't you dare go apologizing to these bullies. You didn't offend anyone, especially this sorry lot." Peggy glared at each man to show her displeasure. "They'd have to have feelings to be offended, Norah. This bunch hasn't had an honest emotion since the day the town council took the beer vending machine out of the local fire hall."

"That wasn't right!" shouted Leland, who now appeared more upset about the loss of a beer machine than about the mandatory counting of lobsters off the coast.

Norah tried not to chuckle as her stomach settled back down now that the men's anger was directed away from her. The men of Misty Harbor obviously had their priorities, and grabbing a cold one after fighting a fire ranked pretty high up on that list.

"What's going on here, Mom?" demanded Ned Porter as he stepped next to his mother and frowned at the four fishermen.

Norah had been so involved in the argument that she hadn't noticed Ned's truck pulling up to his parents' home, let alone him stalking across her front yard to join the dispute. Ned looked furious to find four men yelling at his mother.

She didn't blame Ned. Protecting your mother is what a child should do. Especially if that child was a full-grown adult, and Ned was definitely full grown.

Peggy gave her another comforting squeeze before releasing her shoulders. "Some of the local boys didn't like Norah's article from this morning's paper. I heard the shouting from the back patio and came over to give the poor mite a hand." Peggy gave her a friendly wink. "Norah might have been outnumbered, but she was holding her own against this obnoxious crew."

Ned's expression hardened into disbelief as he

glared down at the men. "Let me get this straight," his voice rumbled across the neighborhood. "You idiots knocked on Norah's door and then started yelling at her because of what she wrote in the paper?"

She took a half step closer to Peggy. The Ned she'd met the other night seemed big yet friendly. This Ned seemed not only threatening but also dangerous. It didn't help matters that he had obviously just gotten off work; whatever he did for a living wasn't done in a suit and tie. Ned looked like he'd just chopped down half the trees in the state of Maine. Well-worn jeans were molded to his legs, and a few specks of sawdust and dirt were scattered across his blue T-shirt. A nasty-looking scratch marked the back of one of his hands. He looked sweaty, hot, and entirely too, *male* for her peace of mind.

The other night she had thought Ned was good looking. In the bright afternoon light, she had to admit she had been wrong. Ned Porter was gorgeous, if a woman liked her men big, physical, and looking like they had just stepped out of an L.L.Bean catalog.

Three of the fishermen took a step back, away from Ned. One of the Higgins brothers was the only one either brave or stupid enough to hold his ground. "It wasn't like that, Porter."

Ned raised a dark brow and crossed his arms against his chest in a perfect imitation of his mother's earlier stance. "You are practically standing on Ms. Stevens' doorstep, and my own mother heard all the shouting." His square jaw hardened, causing a slight tic beneath his right eye. "How was it like, Lonny?"

Leland quickly stepped between Ned and his brother. "Now, Ned, calm down. I'll be the first one to admit we might have stepped over the line of being hospitable to Ms. Stevens." Leland flashed a quick smile in her direction and hurriedly swiped off his baseball cap. "But it was our livelihood she was writing about. Tempers have a way of getting a little riled when it concerns the paychecks."

"I read the article, and in no way did she threaten your jobs or your livelihood. In fact, if you open your minds and really think about it, she might be showing you a way to save that way of life for future generations."

"By having the government impose more rules and regulations on us?" cried Leland.

"Those rules and regulations are already here, and there's more coming. It's the nature of that particular beast." Ned shook his head. "That's the truth, and there's nothing that you, I, or Norah's article can do about it. Either you can be bull-headed and keep fighting a battle you will eventually lose, or you can attempt to be somewhat reasonable about it and try compromising."

"We stopped their dredging off the point last month," boasted Leland.

"Yes, you did; congratulations," drawled Ned sarcastically. "Keep doing it, and they will be dredging off the coast of Massachusetts, taking the lobster count from there, and setting your regulations by that dismally low number."

"Dredging destroys our breeding stock," said Oscar.

"All the damage they do, and they still can't get an accurate number," added Russ.

"They are a bunch of stupid scientists who sit in front of computers all day," said Lonny. "What do they know about lobsters?"

"It ain't fair," snarled Leland in disgust.

Ned shook his head. "Who ever told you that life was going to be fair?" Ned relaxed his arms, and the dangerous look left his expression. "Instead of shouting at some poor innocent journalist who was only doing her job, maybe you all should be putting that energy into figuring out a way to get an accurate count without destroying breeding stock."

"We already told them how many *catchable* lobsters there are out there," said Russ.

"You have to prove it to them, Russ. They are scientists. They need data and facts, not a bunch of unshaved, ripe-smelling, fresh off the boat lobstermen shouting numbers and stories at them off the top of their sunburnt heads."

Norah tried to hide her smile, but she had a feeling that she had failed when Peggy gave her a quick smile and another wink. Peggy looked quite proud and pleased with her son. She didn't blame Peggy. Ned was not only gorgeous; he also had a brain. She was impressed.

"I think an apology is in order." Peggy frowned at the men and started to tap the toe of her boot on the walkway. Peggy looked mean, formidable, and ready to get down to business if the men didn't comply with her order.

"I also think Norah needs to be reassured that the next time you guys take exception to her column, you will take your complaints to the *Hancock Review* office and discuss it with Tom, her boss."

Ned positioned himself on her other side. "I'm sure Ms. Stevens didn't appreciate finding four angry men on her doorstep."

Norah wasn't sure whether to laugh or to feel insulted. One minute, she was being yelled at by four men, and the next, she had two overprotective bodyguards. Both of whom topped her own five-feet, one-inch height by at least a good twelve inches. She was beginning to feel as if she had moved into the land of giants.

Before she could think of what to say to regain control of the situation and exhibit some backbone of her own, the men started mumbling hasty apologies.

"We're sorry, Ms. Stevens," muttered Russ.

"We didn't mean to scare you or anything," Oscar added with a small smile that seemed genuine.

"That's okay," she said. "You didn't really scare me, just gave me a moment of pause, that's all." She returned Oscar's gesture with what she hoped looked like a sincere smile. She was lying through her pearly whites.

She had been afraid when the four big men had started their shouting, but at least she hadn't acted like a coward. She had calmly made her mother take Zsa Zsa into the house and close the door. Her first instinct had been to protect her mother, which she had done. Her second instinct had been to run like hell and follow her mother to safety behind a closed and locked door before calling the police. But she had held her ground and faced the men. Thankfully, she hadn't had to face them alone for long. Before the shouting had gotten out of hand, Peggy Porter had barged onto the scene and taken control of the situation.

Ned gave her a funny look, almost as if he didn't believe her. Leland offered his apology, "Sorry, Ms. Stevens."

"Please, call me Norah. Ms. Stevens sounds like my mother." She took a deep breath and finally relaxed. "I must say it is heartening to see my first column get such attention." She would have preferred to have gotten rave reviews instead of outraged lobstermen, but one simple fact remained—like it or not, people were reading her column. What more could she ask for? "I can't wait to see what everyone thinks of next week's column."

With only a slight hesitation, Lonny cautiously asked, "What's it on?"

"The need for reassessing property values throughout the entire county."

Ned looked at her as if she had lost her mind. All four fishermen gaped at her as if she was some ghastly ghoul that had just risen from a grave and needed to be staked through the heart. She was definitely not on the right road to win friends and influence people. Her column, "Views From The Other Side," was going to make her an outcast.

There went any hope of acquiring a social life in Maine. Saturday nights were going to be long; boring; and, come winter, exceedingly cold. Maybe she should have used an alias for her byline.

Peggy let loose with a boisterous laugh as all four fishermen beat a hasty retreat. An assortment of dented and rusty pickup trucks started up and headed down the street. Peggy was still chuckling when she said, "Norah, I think you are going to need some friends."

She watched as the last truck turned the corner

and disappeared from sight. "I'll add them to my Christmas wish list."

Peggy slapped her arm across Norah's shoulders and gave her a big squeeze. "That's the spirit. Men like a gal with a sense of humor, don't they, Ned?"

Ned gave his mother a peculiar look. "We like that almost as much as having our properties reassessed for higher taxes."

Norah bit her lip to keep from laughing. Ned had picked up that matchmaking gleam in his mother's eyes, and he didn't appreciate it. She almost felt sorry for him. Almost. Ned was big enough to handle his own mother. She had her own mother to contend with.

Peggy's smile grew as she stared at her son. "I left a message on your cell phone earlier."

"I got it," Ned said. "That's why I stopped by before heading home to get cleaned up. You need me to pick up anything on my way back?"

"Nope, I've got it covered." Peggy turned her attention back to Norah. "We're having a casual cookout tonight. Just family, but we would love for you and your mother to join us."

"I really don't . . ." She started to refuse the invitation, only to have Peggy interrupt.

"You both have to come. I won't accept a refusal," Peggy insisted. "My son Matthew will be there, and so will the rest of our family. Everyone is dying to meet you, especially my two daughters-in-law."

Norah saw the gleam of excitement and determination in Peggy's eyes and wondered if this was how a tuna felt as it was being reeled in by the feisty woman. It didn't really matter; Peggy had charged to her rescue earlier. There was no way she could refuse the invitation. Besides, her mother was looking forward to meeting some of the neighbors.

"We'll be delighted to come." She refused to look at Ned to see how he was reacting to the spur of the moment invitation. "What can we bring?"

An hour later, Norah found herself sitting on a wooden bench at a picnic table and holding a sleeping two-month-old baby girl. She wasn't real comfortable holding infants, but no one had asked her feelings on the subject. Amanda's mom, Jill, had placed the baby in her arms and then gone dashing off to rescue her three-year-old son, Hunter, from a tangle of sticker bushes that lined the back of John and Peggy's property.

Jill's husband, Paul, was supposed to be out front getting Amanda's stroller from the car. He had disappeared five minutes ago and still hadn't returned. A fire was blazing in the brick barbeque, but no one was tending to it. Ned's father, John, the obvious cook for this evening's meal, if the apron was any indication, had joined Paul in the stroller hunt.

Her mom and Peggy had instantly hit it off and had disappeared into the house to put some finishing touches on dinner. There had never been a more unlikely pair of mothers. The Mutt and Jeff of the culinary world had been discussing the best way to hard-boil an egg so that it peeled easily as they had entered the house.

"How many times do I have to tell you, to stay out of those bushes, Hunter? They have sharp thorns." Jill plopped her three-year-old son onto the wooden table and started to dig through a Winnie the Pooh diaper bag the size of a small canoe.

Hunter swung his feet and grinned. "There was a bunny under there, Mom. I almost got him." He held up his little hands until they were about a foot apart. "I was this close."

Norah couldn't help but smile back. Hunter looked so proud of himself. The nasty-looking scratch on his arm didn't seem to bother him, nor did the smaller one on his cheek. Hunter might have only been three, but he was obviously one of those rough and tumble kids. The boy looked just like his father, only a smaller version. A lot smaller.

She had thought Ned was a physically big man. His brother, Paul, was taller and, if she wasn't mistaken, broader in the shoulders. Even Jill looked like a woman who could take care of herself.

Maybe there were growth hormones in the Misty Harbor water supply.

Jill smeared some antibacterial cream over the scrapes and then gently placed an Elmo bandage over the longer red one on Hunter's arm. The Elmo bandage coordinated with the two Big Bird and Cookie Monster bandages already on his knees. "Try not to damage yourself any more today. I'm running out of bandages." Jill swung Hunter up, placed a loud kiss on his unscratched cheek, and then steadied him on his feet.

"Daddy, Daddy!" shouted Hunter as he dashed to his father, who was pushing the empty stroller into the backyard. "I saw a bunny!"

"You did?" Paul Porter swung his son up into his arms. "Was it a big bunny or a baby one?"

"A big one, but Mommy won't let me get him."

Paul glanced at the scratch on his son's cheek and chuckled. "That's because she's a girl, and she doesn't want you to get hurt." Paul tossed Hunter high into the air and safely caught him back into his arms. "Mommies don't understand the thrill of the hunt."

Hunter glanced between his father and his mother with a look of confusion on his face. Jill stood there, raising one brow and glaring at her husband with her hands on her hips. Norah wasn't sure what was going on, but whatever it was, it didn't bode well for Paul.

"But, Daddy," Hunter said in a loud whisper. "Mommy shot that twelve-point buck on top of our fireplace." Hunter placed his mouth closer to his daddy's ear. "You know, the one you always make faces at?"

Jill grinned. "That's right, Hunter." Jill plucked her son out of his father's arms. "Some mommies understand the thrill of the hunt just fine. They also understand daddies whose biggest buck was only a ten pointer."

Hunter laughed as his mother spun him in circles.

Norah wasn't sure if she should laugh at Paul's offended expression or be appalled that she was about to have dinner with a bunch of Bambi killers. Maybe she should stick with the salads to be on the safe side. There was no way she wanted to bite into a burger only to discover her meal had been frolicking merrily through the woods the week before.

"So this is where the party is?" A man bigger than Paul Porter stepped around the side of the house. A boy a couple of years older than Hunter was perched on his massive shoulders. The pair could have hung Christmas lights from the gutters without a stepladder.

Ned's father joined them. He had a small girl atop his shoulders. "Norah, I would like you to meet John Jr., my oldest boy, and his wife, Kay. This is Norah Stevens. She and her mother, Joanna, just moved in next door. Joanna's in the kitchen helping your mom get the rest of the stuff ready."

Kay, who was bringing up the rear of the group, looked like she was about thirty; she was carrying a massive bowl filled with what appeared to hold some kind of salad. The bowl probably weighed more than Hunter, but Kay wasn't breaking a sweat. "Hi, Norah; hope you like potato salad." Kay placed the bowl in the center of the table.

Norah wasn't positive, but she thought the table groaned. She eyed the bowl with interest. She had seen smaller blow-up pools for kids. "Who's coming to dinner—the entire state of Maine?"

Jill and Kay both laughed. "Nope, just the Porter men."

She looked at her and her mother's meager contribution to the cookout and tried not to groan. Here she had thought they had gone overboard on the veggie and cheese trays. With no time to run out to the store or to really make something, they had raided the refrigerator for every raw vegetable in sight. Her mother had made a killer veggie dip, while she had cubed cheeses and sliced up ring bologna and some pepperoni. She had thought the trays would easily serve twenty people. Now she wasn't too sure if they would suffice as appetizers.

The feeding of the Porter men could bankrupt a small, oil-enriched kingdom.

"This little monster is Tyler the Terrible," John

Jr. said as he swung his son off his shoulders and reached for his daughter. "And this little princess is Morgan the Magnificent."

Tyler, who was missing a front tooth, growled like a dinosaur. Morgan, who was dressed all in pink, said, "Uncle Matthew calls me Morgan the Menace." The three-year-old, adorable-looking girl seemed very proud of that assessment.

Kay rolled her eyes. "Matthew is the menace. That's the last time I'll ask your uncle to watch either one of you for a couple of hours." Kay looked at Jill for support. "Do you believe he was trying to teach Tyler to burp the ABCs?"

Paul laughed, even though Jill elbowed him in the side. "How far can you go up to?" asked Paul while rubbing his ribs.

John Jr. beamed with fatherly pride. "He's up to L, but the M, N, O, P combination is giving him a hard time."

Kay elbowed her husband in his side, and by his grunt, Norah had the feeling she had put some weight and muscle behind that sharp jab. Norah almost felt sorry for him. Kay looked like a woman who could win a lumberjack competition. There was nothing petite or delicate about either of Peggy Porter's daughters-in-law. Kay and Jill both reached the six-foot mark, and while they weren't model thin, they were definitely curved enough for their husbands to appreciate the fact they had been born men. Both women had long hair that was pulled back in ponytails and not a speck of makeup on. Kay wore a plain gold wedding band and a rugged-looking watch. Jill just had on a silver wedding band. They both seemed to favor denim shorts, T-shirts, and thick-soled sneakers.

She felt overdressed in a long, crinkly, red and white swirled skirt, a red tank top, and a pair of red leather sandals embellished with a dozen silver coins that jingled merrily when she walked. It was the same outfit she had worn to work all day.

She looked like a gypsy queen at a lumberjack conference.

Kay sat down next to her as Jill took the sleeping infant and placed her in the stroller. Morgan, Tyler, and Hunter headed for the sticker bushes to see if they could spot the bunny. "Kids, stay away from the bushes; I just cleaned you both up." Kay shook her head as the men went and joined the kids in the hunt. "I swear, sometimes the men are worse than the kids."

"Just sometimes?" Jill laughed. "I must have married the wrong Porter. Paul's worse than ten Hunters."

She tried not to laugh as both men and all three kids plopped down on the ground to peek underneath the biggest bush. Peggy's grass had the same terminal condition as her rosebush. The Porters' lawn was more brown than green, due to huge patches of dirt showing through little tufts of dried dead grass. Clouds of dust encased the great hunters and were probably scaring off any rabbit within two hundred yards.

"Where, Daddy? Where?" shouted Morgan as she wiggled her way closer to the bush. "I don't see him."

All four males groaned in unison. "Hush, Morgan, sweetie." John Jr. whispered in a choked voice. "You will scare him away."

Jill and Kay were chuckling softly at the scene. Norah joined them. She could see Paul's and John

Jr.'s shoulders shaking with laughter. "I take it that Morgan isn't the sportsman of the family."

"Morgan has one volume—full blast." Kay smiled softly at the picture the rest of her family was making.

"Sh-h-h . . . Morgan, he's right there," her father said. "See, he's all brown with big ears."

Morgan tried to wiggle closer, but her father had a hold on the back of her shirt. "Let go, Daddy." Morgan's legs started to kick at the dirt and grass. "I want to see him better."

"You can see him just fine from there, sweetie." John Jr.'s grip tightened as Morgan managed to wiggle herself a couple of inches farther under the bush.

All three women watched enthralled, wondering who was going to win this physically unmatched tug-of-war. Norah's money was on little Morgan with her blond pigtails and wide smile.

"What are we looking for?" asked a deep, rumbling whisper.

Norah jumped a good two inches off the bench, but thankfully, she controlled the scream that was lodged in her throat. Jill and Kay's only reaction was to turn their heads and smile. "Hi, Matt," Kay said.

"Shhh . . . We're hunting wabbits," Jill whispered back with a pretty good imitation of Elmer Fudd.

Matt grinned at the sight. John Jr. was holding Morgan back by the waistband on her shorts. If she wiggled any farther under the bush, Morgan would moon the entire neighborhood.

Morgan poked her head out from under the bush. "Uncle Matt!" she screamed in delight as she backpedaled. Thankfully, John Jr. released his daughter's shorts as she jumped to her feet and sprinted across the yard. Hunter and Tyler groaned as the rabbit ran out from under the bush and streaked across the neighbor's yard before disappearing from sight.

Matthew caught Morgan as she launched herself into his arms. "Hello, Menace. I see you haven't lost your touch."

Morgan's little arms encircled his neck. "Mom says you are the menace, not me."

"She did, did she?" Matthew's grin was pure wickedness. "I guess the next time I watch you little monsters, I need to teach you how to corral a skunk."

"Me too!" shouted Hunter as he latched onto Matthew's leg.

"Sure thing, squirt." Matthew's gaze captured hers. "Hi, I'm Matt Porter, since no one sees fit to introduce us."

"Norah Stevens." She smiled up into his light blue eyes. Matt had eyes the same color as his mother's. "My mother and I just moved in next door." She nodded her head in the direction of their home. "Your mother invited us over for a cookout."

Matt glanced around the yard. "Where's your mom?"

"She's inside helping your mom with dinner."

A boyish smile curved his mouth as he leaned in closer and confessed, "Good, because she usually needs all the help she can get."

She couldn't help but smile back with appreciation. Matthew Porter was gorgeous, and if she wasn't mistaken, there was a hint of flirtation in his blue eyes. "Mom's a great cook." She wasn't exaggerating; her mom was a fantastic cook. Joanna Stevens could make canned tuna taste like five-star restaurant cuisine, while she had trouble cubing cheese.

"Oh good, Matthew, you've met Norah." Peggy pushed her way out of the back door carrying a tray loaded down with what appeared to be ten pounds of hamburger patties and three packs of hot dogs.

John Porter took the tray from his wife and headed for the barbeque.

Norah prayed those hamburger patties were really beef. She had no idea what venison looked like, and she wasn't prepared to make a mortal enemy out of the Disney Corporation.

"We were just getting acquainted." Matthew maneuvered Morgan onto his shoulders. The little girl giggled with delight. Dirt from Morgan's sneakers streaked Matthew's shirt, but he didn't seem to notice or care.

"That's nice." Peggy beamed with parental pride. "Matthew's my next to youngest, and he does preservation work on old historic buildings."

Ned's deep voice interrupted his mother's sales pitch for her son. "He also loves children, is kind to animals, and flosses at least once a day." Ned carried a cooler into the backyard and bared his teeth at his brother in a remarkably false smile.

Flipper galloped into the yard and, with a cheerful bark, headed straight for Hunter and Tyler.

Matthew smiled back at his younger brother. "Oh, look who joined the party—the runt of the litter, Ned."

Chapter
Three

Ned tried not to think about what kind of fool he had just made out of himself. He had been rounding the corner of the house when he'd heard his mother practically throwing Matthew at Norah. His mother had no shame, and Matthew had seemed more than willing to be thrown.

Norah's reaction was a little harder to gauge. He couldn't tell if her laugh had been a response to his obvious distaste for his mother's matchmaking or the fact that Matthew had referred to him as the runt of the litter. At six feet, two inches, he was hardly a runt; however, not only was he the youngest at twenty-seven, but he was also the smallest male Porter. Thankfully, in his eighteenth year, he had experienced that desperately needed growth spurt, so he could now at least claim an inch in height over his own mother.

Being the baby of the family sucked.

He placed the cooler, packed with drinks and ice, on the ground near one of the picnic tables.

After his brothers had gotten married and the grandkids had started to make an appearance, his parents had bought a second table to fit everyone. Tonight, with the added company, it was going to be a tight fit.

Ned didn't even have to guess where Matthew would be sitting. He had seen that competitive gleam in his older brother's eye. With less than two years separating them, Matthew and he had been competing against each other most of their lives. With his uncharacteristic jealous remarks, he had unintentionally made Norah the prize.

It was the last thing he had planned on doing. Norah, or any other woman, deserved better than that. Besides, he had no intention of asking Norah out. At a very delicate height of five feet, one inch, she was the polar opposite of what he was looking for in a woman.

He had always pictured himself with a woman who was like his sisters-in-law. Kay and Jill were tall, sturdy women who could not only take care of themselves and their families but who also loved the outdoors as much as his brothers. They were the perfect match for his older brothers, John and Paul, and their contented marriages proved it. When it was time for him to settle down and start a family of his own, he wanted an independent, nature-loving woman. One who enjoyed hiking, kayaking, and camping under the stars as much as he did.

Norah looked like a good nor'easter would blow her off her feet, and she wouldn't be able to walk two feet into the woods without scaring off every animal within three hundred yards. Norah jingled when she moved. Bracelets clanged on her wrists, and the silver charms that circled one of her delicate ankles tinkled when she walked. Tonight, even her shoes gave off a chiming melody.

Norah Stevens was one noisy woman.

"Oh good, you brought beer," said Paul as he reached into the cooler and pulled out a cold one.

"There's soda, water, and juice for the kids too." Ned reached under the ice and pulled out three juice boxes as Hunter and Tyler came running.

He handed each of his nephews a drink and chucked an ice cube high into the air. Flipper caught the ice before it had a chance to hit the ground.

"Here you go, sweetie. I didn't forget you." He handed Morgan, who was still on his brother's shoulders, her box and tried not to smile as a sliver of ice slid off the box and fell into Matthew's hair.

"What can I get you, Norah?" Tonight, the green of her eyes seemed darker, more mysterious. Which made him question his own sanity. He'd never once thought a woman's eyes were mysterious. What was it about Norah Stevens that attracted him so?

The red of her blouse should have clashed horribly with her red, spiky hair. For some unknown reason, it didn't. The deep, dark red color of her hair had to be as fake as the dozen or so diamonds marching up the outer edge of her ears. No one with a lick of sense walked around with that much money stuck in her ears. Then again, no one in her right mind would poke that many holes in her ears.

"Water would be great, Ned," answered Norah.

Norah stood up and helped Morgan jam her straw through the slit in her juice box. "Here you go, sweetie."

Morgan smiled, remembered her manners, and

said, "Thank you." Her little hands gripped the box hard as she stuck the straw into her mouth and slurped. Liquid poured over the side of the box and into Matthew's hair.

Matthew cringed, and Norah's mouth twitched. "Maybe you should put her down to drink that." Norah's voice kept breaking on a laugh she fought not to release.

"It's a little too late for that." Matthew shuddered as a drop of apple juice slid over his jaw and down into the neckline of his T-shirt.

Ned almost felt sorry for his brother. Almost, but not quite. Sibling rivalry was far too ingrained into their personalities. Just because he wasn't about to ask Norah out didn't mean he liked the idea of Matthew dating his rose fairy. "Betcha that's cold." He eyed a second drop of juice as it rolled down his brother's jaw.

Matthew gave him a look that promised retaliation in the future for that comment. "I take it that you've already met Norah?"

He twisted the cap, breaking the seal on the water bottle, and handed it to Norah. He had no idea what compelled him to answer, "We stood in the moonlight discussing roses and fairies."

By the gleam of speculation and slack-jawed astonishment, it seemed every member of his family heard his reply. By the looks his brothers were giving him, one would think he had just admitted doing lap dances down at the One-Eyed Squid. He fought the flush of embarrassment threatening to sweep up his face. What was so unusual about him talking to a woman in the moonlight? "Now, if you would excuse me, I think I'll go help Dad with the burgers."

He'd started to beat a hasty retreat when Norah's soft voice stopped him in his tracks. "Ned?"

"Yes?"

Norah raised the bottle. "Thanks."

"You're welcome." He turned and walked over to the brick barbeque.

His father handed him the metal spatula and then continued placing the patties on the grill. "Glad to see you aren't going to let Matthew walk away with the girl without a fight."

"We aren't fighting, Dad." He eyed the barely cooked burgers, wishing they were burnt so he could flip them. "Matthew can have any girl he wants."

"Except that one, right?" John Porter put the last hamburger patty on the grill. His father kept his voice low so they wouldn't be overheard.

"Norah's free to date anyone she chooses." He pressed down on a couple of burgers. The sound of grease hitting the hot coals below had a nice, calming effect on his nerves. He was still trying to figure out what had possessed him to rush to the store on his way home for the drinks and a bag of ice. He had dumped everything into the cooler, hurried through his shower, and headed back to his parents in record time. Yet Matthew had arrived before him and had naturally taken an interest in Norah. It wasn't every day that a single, beautiful woman moved to Misty Harbor, and his brother wasn't a fool.

"I don't know, Ned. Moonlight, flowers, and magical creatures sound pretty serious to me." His father sliced open the packs of hot dogs while glancing over at the picnic tables where Norah and Matthew were talking.

"I found her under Mom's rosebush." He smashed a couple more burgers and took a hasty step back as flames and smoke erupted from the coals.

His father shook his head as he glanced at the bush in question. "What was she doing under there?"

"She was trying to retrieve her mother's dog." He flipped the first few burgers.

"Zsa Zsa?" His father chuckled as he started to place some hot dogs on the grill.

"I wouldn't laugh too hard. The rat has some sharp little teeth." Ned looked at his thumb where a small indent, the size of a Pomeranian tooth, was still visible. A little black and blue area had formed around it.

"Now I understand." His father took the spatula out of his hands and started to flip some burgers. "Norah does have the look of some fey woodland creature, doesn't she?" Grease sizzled, and smoke rose. "I think it's the slant of her eyes that does it."

"I called her a rose fairy." He picked up a fork and started to turn the hot dogs. With her high cheekbones and eyes that tilted slightly upward, Norah did have the "fey" look of some woodland nymph.

"You might be onto something there."

"There's no such thing as fairies, Dad. Rose ones or otherwise." His father had obviously helped himself to one too many beers if he thought otherwise. He neatly turned the next row of hot dogs, lining them up side by side.

"Have you taken a close look at your mother's rosebush lately?"

He glanced across the yard. The sickly bush appeared a little greener than normal. But it might have been a trick of the fading evening light. "What's wrong with it?"

"Nothing is wrong with it. In fact, just the opposite. There are three new buds on it. They aren't open yet, but they are buds. Wouldn't believe your mother until I came outside and saw them for myself."

"Three buds?" As far back as he could remember, his mother's rosebush had never had three buds at the same time on it. The bush barely survived from season to season. "Maybe Zsa Zsa fertilized it."

"Don't tell your mother that." His father groaned with that thought. "She'll have me pooper-scooping Joanna's backyard and feeding my collection to every shrub in the yard."

He chuckled at the thought of his father cleaning up after Zsa Zsa. "For your dignity's sake, my lips are sealed."

"Now, this I have to hear," Paul said as he joined them at the barbeque. "Spill the secret."

"What secret?" asked John Jr. as he handed his father a cold beer and joined them around the grill.

Ned muttered in disgust, "There is no such thing as secrets in this family." His brothers always had their noses in his business, claiming they were looking out for him. As a young boy, he had returned the favor as often as possible by spying on them and usually ratting them out, unless their bribe was too good to pass up.

"We were discussing your mother's rosebush." His father took a sip of beer and went back to flipping burgers. "It has three new, and very healthy-looking, buds on it ready to bloom."

Both of his brothers turned and stared at the bush in awe. "Really? Wow, how did that happen?" asked John Jr.

"What has she been feeding it?" asked Paul.

"Don't tell your mother, but we believe Zsa Zsa has been fertilizing it."

"Zsa Zsa isn't big enough to fertilize a dandelion," said Paul.

"Who's Zsa Zsa?" asked John Jr.

"It's a what, not a who." Ned glanced over his shoulder to make sure no one was eavesdropping on their conversation. "It's a four-pound Pomeranian that belongs to Norah's mother."

"Joanna seems mighty attached to her, so try not to laugh at it or step on it." John Porter flipped another row of burgers. "Darn little thing gets right under your feet, and you can't see it."

A horrifying thought occurred to Ned. "Dad, you didn't step on her, did you?" Zsa Zsa having a run-in with one of the Porter's notorious big feet spelled disaster.

"No, but it was a close call"—his father took another sip of beer before adding—"twice."

The back screen door slammed shut, and a high-pitched barking echoed through the yard. His father took another sip of beer before turning back to the burgers. "Speak of the devil. Boys, watch your feet."

Flipper's ears perked up as he made a beeline for the smaller dog. "Flipper," Ned raised his voice, "heel."

Flipper stopped in his tracks and sat. It would

have been an impressive show of command, but Zsa Zsa took Flipper's retreat as a show of weakness and charged the bigger dog. Thankfully, Norah scooped up the Pomeranian in mid charge.

"Oh no, you don't." Norah gently tapped Zsa Zsa on the nose. "Behave yourself, or you're going home."

Joanna, who had followed the dog out of the house, placed a bowl of fruit salad on the table and reached for her dog. "She's just excited by all the people." Zsa Zsa quieted down and glanced around like she understood what Joanna had said and knew she was now the center of attention.

Ned wasn't positive, but it appeared as if the darn dog was smiling.

All the kids came running to see the tiny dog with the pink bow in her hair. Zsa Zsa's toenails were painted to match the satin bow. More than likely, neither his nephews nor niece had ever seen such a ridiculous sight.

Joanna sat down and happily introduced the audience to pint-sized Zsa Zsa. The miniature dog lapped up all the attention while poor Flipper sat there wagging his tail and whining.

Ned's five-year-old nephew, Tyler, was the first to take pity on Flipper. The boy gave the Newfoundland a big hug. "Come on, Flipper; let's go find that rabbit."

Morgan and Hunter, not to be left out of the fun, dashed after Tyler and the dog.

John Jr. shook his head. "I better stick close to the great hunters. Tyler just got over a case of poison ivy." John Jr. headed after the barking dog and shouting kids.

"Three against one isn't fair." Paul finished his

beer and placed the empty bottle in the plastic re-cycle container by the back door. "I better go help him. Last time he was in charge of those three, they talked him into allowing them to go swimming out at Summer's Point. I thought Kay and Jill were going to kill him when they found out." Paul hurried after his brother.

John Porter chuckled. "Kids will keep you young, Ned. You should give some serious thought to settling down and making a couple of those rugrats of your own."

"Kids will keep you broke, Dad." Just because his father didn't look over at Norah didn't mean he didn't have a particular woman in mind to become the mother of those future grandchildren. His father was about as subtle as an elephant in a strawberry patch.

Ned eventually wanted a couple of kids, but at twenty-seven, he wasn't in a hurry to lose sleep, change diapers, and worry about college tuition. He was more interested in finding the right woman, falling in love, and going on a honeymoon—a very long honeymoon.

As for his father wanting him to settle down—if he settled down any further, they would be holding his wake and burying him next to his great grandfather, Captain Horatio Porter. His life was on the same excitement scale as watching a snail crawl. Misty Harbor wasn't geared toward an exciting nightlife or even a day life.

The small, close-knit town only came to life during the tourist season. Then, the tourists mostly consisted of families and the occasional honeymoon couple. The Maine coast didn't make the top ten list for singles looking for action, love, or a tan.

While bikini-clad women lined sandy island beaches drinking fruit-flavored drinks with tiny umbrellas stuck in them, Misty Harbor was serving up lobsters, clam chowder, and a cold mist spraying in your face as the waves crashed against the rocky shore.

If you didn't find the love of your life during your high school years, chances were you weren't going to find her in Misty Harbor. Most of the girls went away to college and stayed away. He couldn't blame the girls or the women they eventually became. A good portion of the men never returned home either after receiving their degrees. In some ways, Misty Harbor had been a slowly dying town.

Lately though, the town was experiencing a much needed population growth. Last year, he had attended more weddings than funerals, and in March, he'd had a blast buying little trucks for his boss's first child. Daniel and Gwen Creighton's son, Andrew, was born during a March blizzard that had made driving impossible. Thankfully, Gwen's sister, the town's doctor, had been a short snowmobile ride away, and she had arrived in plenty of time to deliver her nephew. Gwen had pulled through the at-home delivery like a champ. Daniel had barely survived the experience.

By the size of Doc Sydney, she was expecting her own bundle of joy any day now. Even Ethan Wycliffe's wife, Olivia, had either taken up smuggling watermelons, or she was about to make a contribution to Misty Harbor's growing population. The way things were going, in a couple of years, they would need to add on to the Misty Harbor Elementary School.

Everyone's taxes were about to go up.

"Ned," said his mother, "could you please go get the baked beans. The casserole dish is sitting on the counter." Peggy Porter placed the tray of condiments onto one of the picnic tables. "Be careful; it's hot."

He tried not to roll his eyes as he headed into his parents' house. His mother's beans would not only be hot, but they would also be burnt and covered in a thick, black crust that turned to ash in your mouth. No one would ever confuse his mother with Julia Child or Martha Stewart. Over the years, he and his brothers had learned to hide their distaste of their mother's beans. Their current trick was to feed them to Flipper, who seemed quite partial to his mother's cooking. Of course, Flipper would be hurt and confused as to why he was being shut out of the bedroom tonight after eating nearly a quart of baked beans.

Ned stepped into his mother's kitchen and wondered which of his sisters-in-law had been cleaning up. Usually, his mom created mountains of dirty dishes, pots, and pans when she cooked, and every surface in the room was splattered with whatever she had been fixing.

He and his brothers had gotten so good at guessing what was for dinner by the splattered surface of the stove or by what was dripping down the front of cabinet or two that, to this day, Peggy Porter still hadn't figured out how her sons had known it would be meatloaf, tuna casserole, or one of the other three meals she knew how to make. She had chalked it up to big appetites and love. None of her boys or her husband had the heart to tell her the truth—she cooked worse than she could garden.

Dinners might have tasted like charred roadkill and lay like lead bricks in your gut, but there had been plenty to go around . . . and around. Quantity was never the issue with his mother's cooking.

He picked up the two lobster-shaped potholders, reached for the baked beans, and froze. While the aged green casserole dish was the same one his mother had used to make her baked beans for his entire life, the contents weren't hers. There were no burnt or incinerated beans. No blackened ash coated the steaming and deliciously smelling beans. Even his sisters-in-law couldn't have performed such a miracle. That left one person—Norah's mother, Joanna.

Maybe the entire Stevens family was enchanted. Norah had caused the sickly rosebush to bloom, and Joanna had taught his mother the secret of pulling food out of the oven before it turned to ash.

He had no idea if there were culinary fairies, but he wasn't about to argue the point. He picked up the fragrant side dish and headed out back to enjoy the bounty.

Norah laughed at the joke Matthew had just told for her mother's benefit about a man who walked into a bar with a parrot on his head, a duck under his arm, and an alligator on a leash. Her mom, who had joined them a minute ago, seemed to appreciate the humor too. Matthew was handsome and extremely attentive, and if she had to guess, she would say he was flirting with her. She should have been flattered by all the attention; instead, her gaze and thoughts kept wandering to Ned. Something had put a smile onto Ned's face, and she couldn't figure out what.

Ned had entered the house; while he had not really been scowling, the look on his face had been close. No one was in the house, yet he came back out wearing matching lobster oven mitts on his hands, carrying a hot casserole dish, and looking like he was holding the winning lottery ticket. She was dying to know what had put that sexy, crooked smile on his face.

Curiosity was the curse of all journalists. As far as curses went, she had it bad.

"Here we go," said Ned's father, "hot off the grill." John Porter set a plate piled with grilled hamburgers in the center of the table.

"Kids," called Jill, "time to eat."

Three noisy kids and Flipper came running. The two dads came at a more leisurely pace but appeared just as excited by the prospect of food.

Kay rolled her eyes at the dirty group. "All of you kids go inside and wash up."

Jill looked at her husband, Paul, and sighed. "That order includes you two *older* boys. You should know better than to roll around in the dirt right before dinner."

"They started it." John Jr. tried to defend himself by pointing at the kids with one hand, while brushing off the dirt clinging to his jeans.

"Yeah, they double-dog dared us," added Paul while hastily swiping at his T-shirt.

The three kids snickered, and tried to look innocent at the same time. Tyler actually whistled, stared up at the sky, and toed a clump of dead grass. Morgan batted her eyelashes, while Hunter just stood there and grinned.

Norah almost lost it when Matthew started to choke, and her own mother was biting her lower lip while pretending to fuss with Zsa Zsa's bow. The kids were adorable. The men were charming, and the women were gracious. The Porter family was warm, friendly, and loving. They were everything a family should be and more. If she could learn to ignore the sheer size of them, she really would enjoy herself. But how did one ignore a backyard full of giants?

Her mother didn't seem to be bothered by their size. Why should it bother her so? Her mother had more cause to fear physically large men than she did. So why wasn't her mother jumping every time someone accidentally bumped into her? Why wasn't she anxious to get out of the shadows of the giants and head back home where it was safe? By the expression on her mother's face, one would think she had been the one to hit the lottery.

Joanna had been so excited to get invited to this little get-together, that she had changed her outfit three times. In a way, she couldn't blame her mother. While she was at work all day, her mother was home alone working in the gardens, cleaning, or painting some rooms. The Porter family was the first neighbors they were really getting to know.

The neighbors on their other side, the Harpers, were a young family. Karen Harper had stopped over the day after they had moved in with a plate of welcome brownies. With a part-time job and three school-age children, there had been just enough time for a quick exchange of names and hellos before Karen had to rush back home.

Tonight, her mother was enjoying herself immensely, and there was no way she would the ruin the evening for her by suggesting that they head back home as soon as they were done eating. They would be there to the end. Her mother deserved to have friends and neighbors who wouldn't look at her with that knowing look in their eyes. For years, everyone had known about the turbulent relationship between her parents. Everyone that is, but her. Over the years, her mother had become very skilled at hiding the fact that her father, when drunk, became abusive both verbally and physically.

For years, she had had the impression that her mother was a bit on the clumsy side, which explained the occasional black eye, black and blue marks, and even a broken wrist once.

She had been blind to the abuse that had been going on right under her nose for years. Her mother might have been a good actress, but it didn't excuse the fact that she hadn't noticed. Now, the guilt she was feeling was enough to consume an elephant.

Logic told her that she hadn't been responsible for her father's actions or the pain her mother had suffered at his hand. But logic didn't rule the heart, and her heart broke anew every time she thought of what her mother had endured. Tonight she would smile and be neighborly for her mother's sake. No matter how uncomfortable she became.

"What can I get you, Norah?" Paul stood next to her holding an empty plate.

Matthew quickly picked up another plate and looked at her mother. "Joanna, what would you like to start with—a hamburger or a hot dog?"

Jill and Kay both gave the men a funny look before turning back to help the kids with their plates.

"A hamburger would be great, but I can wait on

myself, Paul." She took the plate and smiled. "Thanks, but why don't you go help your wife? She looks like she's got her hands full."

Paul took one look at his wife and rushed to her side to help.

Jill was trying to balance two paper plates, while Hunter was not helping the situation by trying to scoop potato salad onto one of the plates. The plate was bending at a dangerous angle when Paul rescued the sliding food and saved Hunter's dinner. "Hey, watch out there, son. You're putting too much on the plate."

"I'm hungry, Dad." Hunter straightened his hot dog.

"Well, that's good, but you've got to take it easy on the plates." Paul ruffled his son's dark hair. "You can always come back for seconds."

Norah smiled as Hunter scooted up onto a bench next to his grandfather. The boy looked so tiny next to the large, burly man. Yet Hunter beamed with delight as his grandpop carefully squeezed ketchup onto his hot dog for him. "Thanks, Grandpop."

"You're more than welcome, Hunter."

John Porter gave his grandson such a tender, loving smile that Norah could feel the love from where she was sitting. John Porter was a gentle giant, and she and her mother had nothing to fear from him.

She turned to the dish of baked beans at the exact same instant as Matthew. Their arms bumped, and she reacted instinctively. She jumped back, putting a safe distance between them. Matthew handed her the serving spoon, saying, "Here you go." Matthew didn't seem to notice her sudden jolt.

"Thanks." She took the spoon as her gaze met Ned's across the width of the table. Matthew might not have seen her jump, but Ned had. She could see the questions in his eyes. Questions she didn't want asked because there was no way she would be answering them.

She quickly averted her gaze and looked at Peggy Porter. "This looks delicious, Peggy; did you make it?" She scooped up a big spoonful of beans.

"Sure did." Peggy looked so proud of herself. "It's an old family recipe. But I must say that I've never seen them turn out so fine looking. They sure can make one's mouth water."

Jill and Kay stared at the casserole dish in wonderment. Norah had to wonder how much influence her mother had had in doctoring up the beans. It was quite obvious by everyone's reaction that the beans she had just piled on her plate weren't Peggy's normal dish.

"Gee, Peg, when are you going to give me that recipe?" Kay watched as her husband, John Jr., wolfed down another forkful of his mother's beans.

"I already gave it to you, Kay." Peggy looked confused and just a little bit offended that her daughter-in-law hadn't remembered.

"You did? When?"

Jill looked like she wanted to ask for the recipe too, but wasn't about to risk it.

"About six years ago when you married my son." Peggy looked over at her oldest son, who was still eating the baked beans. "I figured you were now part of the family, so I gave you all the recipes that my mother-in-law had given me. The way my mother cooked, you wouldn't have wanted any of her recipes."

"That was for the other baked beans you usually make. I want the recipe for these." Kay swiped another forkful of the beans off Tyler's plate. "These are delicious."

"That's the same recipe, Kay."

Now it was Kay's turn to look confused. Norah gave a quick glance in her mother's direction and knew what had happened. Joanna had doctored up Peggy's recipe without the other woman knowing it. Her mother was looking guilty. A change of subject was definitely in order before Peggy's feelings got hurt. "Hey, what's the best cell phone company to go with up here? My boss wants me to get one since I'll be out of the office while working on some of my articles."

Two different answers came her way from five different people.

Chapter Four

Joanna Stevens was bored. She had been bored most of her life, so she should be used to it by now. She wasn't. She stood in the middle of her backyard watching Zsa Zsa chase some flying insect around in circles and had what some would call an epiphany. She looked at her cute little cottage and the beginnings of a garden and realized she wasn't really living.

She was doing exactly what she had done since the week she had graduated from high school and gotten married. She cooked, cleaned, and tended the flower beds. Instead of waiting for her husband to come home at night, she was now waiting for Norah. She no longer had to tiptoe around an abusive husband who was quick with his insults and who occasionally lost his temper and struck out with his superior strength. She had Zsa Zsa to keep her company during the day, but it still wasn't enough.

She wanted to accomplish something with her

life besides giving birth to Norah, knowing her way around a kitchen, and being able to tell the difference between a flower and a weed. She wanted to meet people, socialize, and become part of the community. Maybe even travel a bit. Get a passport and get it stamped at least once a decade. She needed something on her calendar besides the biannual dentist appointments and yearly mammogram. She not only wanted to live; she also wanted a life.

Since a life wasn't going to come knocking on the door and invite itself in, she would have to be the one to go out and find it. The first thing she needed to do was to get a job and to start practicing her smile for her passport photo. Traveling wasn't cheap, and it was a mighty big world out there.

While the divorce settlement and her share of the profits from the sale of her old house had been generous, she wasn't a wealthy woman. She had used the bulk of it to purchase the cottage. Norah was sharing the daily living expenses, but the home was in her name. Norah had insisted upon it. Norah had insisted on quite a few things during the past year and a half. It almost was like their roles had been reversed. Norah was the responsible adult, while she played the role of the obedient child.

Things were about to change.

She loved her daughter dearly, and the last thing she wanted was for Norah to put her life on hold because of her. For the last year and a half, Norah had stood beside her and helped her get through the divorce, the selling of their home, and even the court hearings regarding her father's abusive behavior. Norah had given up any form of a social life to be with her through the difficult months.

Now it was time for her daughter to get back into the swing of things. Norah was a beautiful young woman who deserved a chance at finding love and happiness.

If the amount of interest her daughter was stirring up with the single men in town was any indication, Norah was about to embark on a very busy social life. Two nights ago at the Porter's cookout, she had overheard Matthew Porter asking Norah out to a movie. Unbelievably, Norah had turned him down. She had a sinking feeling that she was the reason why. As long as she was home day and night, Norah would feel obliged to keep her company there. Slowly and surely, her daughter would become a bitter old maid living with her lonely old mother. All they would need would be a bunch of crazy old cats and doilies covering every square inch of overstuffed furniture to complete that dismal and depressing picture.

Enough was enough. Norah obviously wasn't going to do anything about the situation, so she guessed it was going to be up to her to get not only her own life but her daughter one also.

Joanna stripped off her gardening gloves, packed up her tools, and called Zsa Zsa. The gardens had been neglected for years; a couple more days weren't going to make a difference. It was a beautiful sunny morning, and the tourist season was just starting in Maine. Someone was surely hiring for the season, if nothing else. How hard could it be to operate a cash register or to serve up a bowl of chowder?

An hour later, Joanna headed downtown with

Zsa Zsa leading the way. The Pomeranian's yellow bow matched her own sundress and the snappy sandals she had bought herself last summer during a predominantly dark period in her life. The dress hadn't particularly cheered her up then, but seeing Zsa Zsa prancing on the end of her pink, glittery leash now brought a grin to her face and put a bounce in her step. Spring had always been her favorite season.

Today is the first day of the rest of my life, and what a life it is going to be! Visiting Paris in the springtime was going to be the first place she put on her "Must See" list.

The few people she passed on her walk all had stopped and praised the Pomeranian on how adorable she looked and on how well she behaved. Zsa Zsa was a people dog and the perfect instrument to use to make the acquaintance of some of the local residents and a few tourists. Everyone loved Zsa Zsa, who lapped up all the attention as if she was a movie starlet and it was her due.

The dog's only problem was that she was terrified of seagulls. The closer they got to the docks, the more anxious Zsa Zsa became. By the time they reached Main Street, which paralleled the water, Zsa Zsa was in her arms with her face pressed against Joanna's chest. The occasional child's laughter brought her head up, but there was no way the dog was leaving the safety of her arms while the gulls cried and swooped above them. There had to be some poultry blood running through Zsa Zsa's veins.

Joanna glanced up and down Main Street at the assorted shops. While she couldn't readily see any "Help Wanted" signs, she wasn't deterred. For Misty

Harbor being a small town, there were quite a few businesses she could try. Claire's Boutique showed promise, as did The Pen and Ink.

Books or clothes? She loved them both, but Claire's looked busy, and The Pen and Ink was closer. With that decision made, she set her straw tote on a bench, gently released Zsa Zsa from her leash, and placed her inside. The little Pomeranian loved to be carried around, and she seemed to feel safer within the depth of the tote than she did, out in the open where those vicious gulls could swoop down at any moment. Most of the time, people didn't even realize there was a miniature dog inside her bag, and Zsa Zsa was very fond of napping in the tote.

"Now, you be a good girl, and don't chew the lining." Joanna placed her wallet and keys safely in the pocket inside the tote. She zipped it closed and then playfully tapped the dog's nose. Just last week, Zsa Zsa had chewed her way into her change purse and almost choked on a dime. She wasn't taking any chances today.

The tote and two others just like it were brand new additions to her summer wardrobe. She had found them in the swimsuit department in J.C. Penney's over in Bangor and had known they would be perfect for Zsa Zsa; they also had a zip pocket large enough to hold all her items. Today's model was made out of natural straw and had yellow and purple silk flowers attached to the front. It probably would have looked better on the beaches of Waikiki, instead of on the rocky coast of Maine, but she liked it. In the large scheme of things, that was what really mattered. She wasn't out to impress anyone.

Okay, maybe she was at least out to make a good first impression on her potential boss. But somehow, she didn't think a little fashion faux pas would keep her from being hired. If she could just find anyone willing to hire a forty-five-year-old woman who had never held a paying job before in her life. With one last scratch behind Zsa Zsa's right ear, she picked up the tote and headed for The Pen and Ink.

The store was just as she had pictured it would be from the outside. It was all dark wood, masculine, and dusky, as if someone was afraid that sunlight would ruin the merchandise. A bell chimed above the door as she stepped inside, and a deep voice called from the depths of the shop, "Look around; I'll be there in a moment."

She shrugged her shoulders and looked around. The atmosphere reeked of old musty books and cigar smoke. She wrinkled her nose. The entire shop smelled like the bottom of an ashtray. Floor to ceiling bookcases were jammed with everything from hundred-year-old hardbacks to Spiderman comics. There was no rhyme or reason to the order that she could detect. She lightly ran her fingertips over the spines of some childhood favorite Nancy Drew originals that were scattered throughout old issues of *National Geographic* when it hit her. There was a system after all. Whoever stocked the shelves placed the books or magazines by color.

A quick glance at the other shelves confirmed her suspicions. Everything was indeed arranged by color. How in the world did anyone ever find anything? More importantly, how did anyone stand the stench of what had to be a century of cigar and pipe smoke that penetrated every square inch of the shop? Who would buy a book that reeked of her Uncle Fred's den, which she remembered from her childhood visits?

She didn't know what would be worse—working all day in such gloom or heading home at night smelling like one of Uncle Fred's stogies. Either way, there was no way she'd spend more time than necessary in this particular shop.

A glance into the back connecting room of the shop explained the smell. The back half of The Pen and Ink was a tobacco shop. Two ancient leather chairs sat on either side of a small, round table. A chess board, apparently in mid game, and two overflowing ashtrays filled the table. Whoever was moving the white pieces seemed to be winning. An old globe took up one corner, and an expensive area rug covered most of the dark wooden floor. The faded rug had a few burn marks. Someone should be counting his or her lucky stars that the whole place hadn't been burnt to the ground. Glass jars containing pipe tobacco filled half the shelves. Cartons of cigarettes and boxes of cigars were jammed everywhere else.

How was it possible that this room looked worse than the book section?

Deep within the tote, Zsa Zsa sneezed. The poor baby didn't like the smell any more than she did. The owner obviously had better things to do than wait on a customer. It was time for her to head over to Claire's Boutique and see if they were accepting applications.

She was halfway to the door when footsteps sounded behind her at the exact instant that Zsa Zsa sneezed again.

"God bless you." A deep voice broke the silence.

She turned and politely smiled. Since Zsa Zsa couldn't thank the man, she would. "Thank you."

"Can I help you with anything?"

"I just stopped in to have a look around." She felt a little guilty for leaving so quickly. "I just moved into town, and I was out for a walk. It's such a beautiful day."

"That it is." The gentleman held out his hand. "I'm Gordon Hanley, and this is my domain."

"Joanna Stevens." She shook his hand. Gordon Hanley was at least six feet, two inches tall, and he was in his mid fifties. Her first impression was that she should invite him home and give him a good meal with an extra slice or two of pie. The man was pale and entirely too thin. With an old book in one hand and a smoldering pipe in the other, he looked as if he should be wandering the hallowed halls of academia. There was something scholarly about Gordon Hanley.

"Welcome to Misty Harbor, Ms. Stevens."

"Thank you, and please call me Joanna. It's a wonderful town. Everyone is so nice and pleasant."

"To you, I can't imagine them not being nice."

She wasn't sure, but she got the feeling Gordon Hanley might be flirting with her. It was a new experience. She had noticed him glancing at her bare left hand. "You have a very"—she searched for the right word and came up with—"unique store, Mr. Hanley."

"All my friends call me Gordon." His hazel eyes seemed to brighten at her use of the word "unique." "If you're ever in the market for a book or a good cigar, you know where to come."

"That I do." She smiled and turned to go.

Zsa Zsa sneezed again before she could make it to the door.

"Oh, Joanna?"

"Yes, Gordon?" She slowly turned and faced him.

A smile was tugging at the corners of his mouth. "I do believe your pocketbook sneezed again."

"I know. She's allergic to smoke." With that, she turned and walked out of the door. There was no sense in explaining Zsa Zsa. Because if she did, she would have to haul the sneezing Pomeranian out of the tote and subject her to more smoke, which would make her reaction worse. Better to keep Gordon guessing as to what was in the bag.

Being a woman of mystery held a certain appeal to her this morning. If she was starting a new life in Misty Harbor, she might as well add some excitement to it. Even if the mystery was only a sneezing dog.

She slowed down as she passed Bailey's Ice Cream Parlor and Emporium. On the sidewalk directly in front of the shop, both white iron tables with matching chairs and pink umbrellas were empty. Inside the shop, she could see two teenagers scooping out ice cream to what had to be half a dozen more teenagers. The ice cream parlor was obviously the local teenage hangout.

The shop next to Bailey's wasn't open for the season yet. Fishing net, red plastic lobsters, and assorted seashells were in the display window. Through the window, she could see a woman and two teenagers unpacking boxes of what appeared to be T-shirts and other tourist merchandise. She bypassed those shops and headed for Claire's.

Claire's Boutique was the total opposite of The

Pen and Ink. Where Gordon's store was dark and gloomy, Claire's was white and bright. All the display racks and shelves were painted a crisp white. The walls were a pale yellow, and the floor was gleaming golden oak. Merchandise in an array of summer colors and fabrics was everywhere. Wide windows, each displaying a well-dressed mannequin, allowed in an abundant amount of sunlight. Two crystal chandeliers hung from the ceiling, and there were even a dozen yellow roses in a antique silver vase near the cash register. Elegant described the shop and the merchandise.

Joanna didn't know what she wanted to do first—ask if they were accepting applications, or try on the gorgeous silk skirt with matching sleeveless blouse the mannequin by the front door was wearing. The calf length skirt was a swirl of blues and greens, while the top was a solid blue with big silver buttons. She already had the perfect shoes and bracelet to match the outfit.

The temptation bore a designer label and was one hundred percent silk.

The fact that both dressing rooms seemed occupied curbed her temptation for the moment. Job first, shopping spree second. She walked over to the distressed white armoire filled with lightweight summer sweaters and wanted to drool. Thoughts of employee discounts started to dance through her head.

"May I help you with something?" A pleasant-looking, middle-aged woman wearing pearls and a classic linen suit stood beside her.

Joanna glanced around the shop and counted one other sales clerk and two other customers. Claire's was doing a nice, brisk business this morning. Hopefully, they would need some extra summer help. "I'm Joanna Stevens." She held out a hand. "My daughter and I just moved to town."

The woman shook her hand as her mouth turned up into a warm, friendly smile. "Claire Bonnet, and welcome to Misty Harbor."

"Claire Bonnet, as in Claire's Boutique?"

"The one and the same." Claire glanced around her store with pride. "Twenty years in business, and I still marvel in wonder every morning when I open up."

"It's a magnificent shop, and I'm already in love with three different outfits." The white capri pants matched with the red, white, and blue Americana sweater would be perfect for a cool summer day. And who could resist the lavender sundress displayed in the front window?

Claire beamed. "Well, what would you like to try on first?"

"Oh, I didn't come here today to shop. I stopped in to see if you were hiring." She watched the expression on Claire's face. She knew what the answer was before the boutique owner spoke.

"I'm sorry, Joanna; there aren't any openings. My sister, Emma, works here full time, and during the summer months, we both have daughters who help out when needed." Claire gave her an apologetic smile.

"That's okay, Claire. I was just walking around town, and your shop struck me as being a wonderful place to work." She glanced at the mannequin by the front door, the one wearing the stunning blue outfit. "I'll make you a deal. If you can give me any leads on who might be hiring, I'll stop back in to buy an outfit." The type of clothes she would be buying would depend on what kind of job she landed.

"Oh dear," Claire fingered the pearls at her throat. "I can't think of anyone who is hiring off the top of my head. Most of the places in town hire teenage help for the season. Have you checked the local paper?"

"Not yet." There were a dozen copies of last week's paper sitting at home on the coffee table. Norah's first byline in Maine was in that paper, and she wanted to make sure she had plenty of copies for posterity's sake. She should have pored over the "Help Wanted" ads while drinking her morning cup of coffee.

"You could check down at The Catch of the Day, the local restaurant. Gwen might be looking for some extra help. She had a baby a couple months ago, and her business is thriving."

"Great." She turned away from the temptation of the blue outfit. "Thanks for the tip, Claire."

"I hope to see you back."

"Oh, you'll see me back. As soon as I have a special occasion to dress up for, I'll be here."

Claire chuckled. "I'll be open."

She walked out onto the sidewalk. The temperature had gone from pleasantly warm to hot. What she needed was something cool to drink before heading over to the docks where the restaurant was located. Bailey's Ice Cream Parlor and Emporium seemed to be the logical choice, as well as being the closest.

Five minutes later, she found herself sitting outside at one of the white iron tables under its pink umbrella and drinking a root beer float. Zsa Zsa sat on the chair next to her daintily licking at a scoop of vanilla ice cream in a plastic bowl. As Zsa Zsa was in the shadow of the umbrella and the table, the sea gulls weren't visible to the dog, and the special treat was keeping her mind off their occasional cry.

"Joanna?"

She glanced up and smiled. "Karen, what are you doing in town without the boys?" Her neighbor Karen Harper was seldom seen without her three boys in tow.

Karen sat down in the empty chair. "They are fishing with their grandfather today while I'm at work."

"Taking a break?"

"More like taking an early lunch. I forgot to pull something out of the freezer for dinner tonight. So I'll grab a quick lunch, figure out dinner, and take the three loads of laundry off the back line and fold them, all before heading back to the gallery." Karen glanced at her watch and sighed. "I really need to be going. What brought you into town—just enjoying the day?" Karen reached over and scratched Zsa Zsa behind the ear. The dog never looked up from her frozen treat.

"Actually, I'm looking for a job." She toyed with the long-handled plastic spoon in her cup. "I tried Claire's, but she wasn't hiring."

"Really?"

"Really." She tried to sound upbeat. "Claire said she had enough help for the season."

"What I meant was, are you really looking for a job, and what kind?"

"Yes, and I'm open to any suggestions on what kind. I have no experience, but I'm willing to learn."

"Full-time, part-time, or seasonal?"

"Doesn't matter. Full-time would be great, but beggars can't be choosers. Do you know of anyone hiring?"

"The gallery."

"Wycliffe Gallery where you work? I'm afraid I don't know anything about art, Karen." Oh, she knew what she liked when she saw it, and she could tell a Rembrandt from a Picasso, but that was the extent of her knowledge.

"Neither did I when I first started working for Ethan. He prefers to handle all the special customers, and he does all the buying. I handle the average tourist and some of the locals. They know what they like when they see it, and I ring up the sale and wrap up the merchandise."

"I could do that." She was confident she could work a register. She hadn't had a chance to visit the gallery yet, but she was hoping it wasn't the kind that displayed all that modern art a lot of galleries were fond of. The modern kind of paintings that looked as if five-year-olds had thrown paint at a blank canvas or mixed concrete with bicycle tires and toilet seats and claimed it was the meaning of life.

"What kind of hours can you work?" Karen asked. "The job would require some evenings till eight and weekends."

"That's no problem. I'm free to work any and all hours necessary." Norah was big enough to get her own dinner, and if she wasn't there at night, maybe her daughter would accept an invitation or two from some of the local bachelors.

"Ethan's wife is due to have their first baby in August, and he really wants to spend more time helping her out right now and after the baby is born. With the three boys out of school for the summer, I can't commit to any extra hours. I barely have enough time as it is." Karen glanced at her watch again and got to her feet. "Listen, Joanna, I have to run. Go down to the gallery and talk to Ethan. He's there now; make sure you tell him I sent you." Karen gave a quick wave and then hurried away.

Joanna sat there staring at the glob of ice cream melting in her float. Working in an art gallery sounded a lot more exciting than asking people if they would like fries with that. The way Karen described the job, she wouldn't need a college degree in art to handle the customers, nor had she mentioned computers. It had taken Norah almost a year to get her comfortable enough to use her computer to e-mail distant family members. The one time she had tried surfing the net, she'd ended up at a porn site. She considered herself lucky that she hadn't had a heart attack when a certain picture had popped up on the screen.

Any job that didn't require computer skills was fine with her.

Joanna took one last sip of her float and tossed it and Zsa Zsa's vanilla ice cream into the trash can. She placed the dog back into the tote, touched up her lipstick, and headed for the gallery. It was her first hot lead of the day, and she wasn't about to waste the opportunity.

Three minutes later, she studied the exterior of the renovated building that was now Wycliffe Art Gallery. At one point in time, it must have been some sort of marine building. It was sitting right on the docks, and it was large enough to house a boat or two. Recently, someone had added huge windows and had painted the wooden structure a deep crimson red with glossy white trim. An intriguing wooden sculpture of a pelican stood by the front door, along with a couple miniature trees in massive concrete, seashell-encrusted containers. It was the perfect building in which to house an art gallery in a harbor town.

She peered into the tote, saw that Zsa Zsa was indeed napping after her morning snack, and walked into the light-filled gallery. Thankfully, no unrecognizable sculptures or dayglow-orange paint-splattered canvases greeted her. The sound of a mother trying to hush her child could be heard over the soft classical music that was being piped in through small speakers. The walls were a cool white, and the antique wide-plank flooring gleamed. An occasional area rug was scattered throughout. Wide windows overlooked the harbor, and what appeared to be some original wooden walls were being used as partitions and added wall space to display more paintings. Plank stairs with a rope railing and banisters led to a second floor.

Whoever had designed the place knew what they were doing. Her money was on Ethan Wycliffe.

She glanced around and counted two customers. One, an elderly gentleman who looked like he'd just stepped off a yacht, was studying a painting of the ocean. The other was the young mother with two undoubtedly bored children. She didn't know who she felt sorry for: the harried-looking mother or the two children who were being dragged through an art gallery. Ethan Wycliffe was nowhere in sight, but she could hear distant voices coming from the second floor.

"If you two don't stop it, we are going back to the hotel, and Grandmom Reid won't be getting a birthday present." The young mother looked ready to walk out.

She didn't know where Ethan was, but she knew the look of a woman at the end of her patience. Ethan was about to lose a customer. She reached into the tote, gently stroked the top of Zsa Zsa's head, and softly whispered, "Wake up, Princess; it's show time."

Joanna walked a couple of feet closer to the family. "Excuse me, ma'am, but do you think your children could help me entertain Zsa Zsa here?" She lifted the dog out of the bag and smiled as the eyes of both children grew wide with delight. The mother looked relieved yet cautious. "She's perfectly gentle," she reassured the woman, "and we'll stay right here in the middle of the gallery, so you can keep an eye on the children."

"Can we, Mommy?" cried the little girl, who looked to be about four.

The slightly older boy echoed his sister's wishes. "Please, Mommy. We'll be good."

The woman looked at her for a moment as if sizing her up, before turning back to the kids. "You will behave yourself, and listen to Ms. . . . ?"

"Stevens, Joanna Stevens," she answered. "And this is Zsa Zsa, and she knows two tricks."

Both kids came hurrying to the center of the gallery. Joanna didn't blame the mother for being cautious. In this day and age, one didn't leave her children with strangers. "If you both sit down, I'm sure Zsa Zsa will do them for you." Two little butts hit the wooden floor in an instant.

A moment later, she was squatting down, and

the Pomeranian was sitting prettily and rolling onto her back so the children could give her belly a rub. She kept the children entertained as their mother viewed the gallery while keeping a careful watch over them.

A man carrying an exquisite clay vase came down the stairs. He was followed by a middle-aged couple who were happily talking about the vase and how well it was going to look in their family room. The good-looking man, who was only a couple of years older than her own daughter, gave her and Zsa Zsa a grateful smile before setting the vase on the counter and ringing up the sale. Ethan Wycliffe had made his appearance, and she had to wonder if she had just blown her chance at the job by bringing her dog into the gallery.

"Excuse me, Ms. Stevens." The young mother joined her children. "Thank you ever so much for entertaining Brad and Sophie."

"My pleasure; they weren't any trouble at all." She scooped Zsa Zsa up and cradled her in her arms.

"Could I get your opinion on something?"

"Sure." She followed the woman over to the far side of the gallery and hoped she could be of some help. Oil paintings and watercolors dominated the area.

"I need a birthday present for my husband's mother." The woman pointed to a beautiful oil painting of a lighthouse with the morning sun rising behind it. "I like this one, but I also think she would like this one." The other painting had an Asian feel to it. It was done in soft watercolors and portrayed a garden in bloom.

She saw the beauty in both paintings. "They are

both wonderful." In her opinion, she liked the garden painting better, but that was her taste, not this woman's mother-in-law's. "What do you think she would like? Does she like to garden and have a lot of flowers in the house, or is she more inclined to walk along a beach or to sit for hours staring at the ocean?"

"Flowers." The woman studied the watercolor. "Definitely the flowers." The woman gave her a smile. "Thank you."

"I didn't do anything, but you're welcome." She wandered away as the woman went to speak to Ethan.

The gallery had some amazing paintings and sculptures. She studied each one carefully before moving on to the next display. Zsa Zsa, who was nestled in the crook of her arm, seemed to enjoy herself too. She heard Ethan waiting on the woman and a moment later, little Brad and Sophie came to say good-bye before they left the gallery. The woman gave a friendly wave, and then they were gone.

The captain of the yacht drifted up the stairs, leaving her and Ethan alone. "I would like to thank you for both helping my customer and entertaining her children so she had some time to look around." Ethan joined her by the window overlooking the harbor. There were more wooden sculptures between the gallery and the water. A patio door opened to the outdoor display area.

"You're welcome." She rubbed Zsa Zsa's back. "I hope you aren't too upset with me for bringing my dog into the building."

Ethan chuckled as he eyed Zsa Zsa. "Dog? Is that what it is? I've seen bigger hamsters."

"And how many hamsters have you had in your gallery?"

"None that wore a yellow bow." Ethan smiled at the dog. "Can I help you with anything, Ms. . . . ?"

"Stevens, Joanna Stevens." She held out her free hand. "My daughter and I just moved to Misty Harbor. In fact, Karen Harper is my neighbor."

"Oh, I'm sorry. If you came to see Karen, I'm afraid she had to take an early lunch."

"I know. I ran into her earlier, and she said you might be interested in hiring some more help around here." She tried not to appear too hopeful or desperate. "I was wondering if I could fill out an application."

Ethan's smile grew. "Can you work full-time?"

"Yes."

"What about nights and weekends?"

"I'm free."

"Joanna, you're hired." Ethan looked immensely pleased with himself.

"Oh, don't I need to fill out some paperwork and all?" She was momentarily stunned to find herself employed so quickly.

"Of course; the government loves paperwork. When can you start?"

"Any time." She gently placed Zsa Zsa back into the tote. She was free to start this afternoon, but she didn't want to appear too eager.

"Good. Karen can do most of your training." Ethan hurried to the back room. In a daze, she followed him. "Is your dog always so friendly to children?"

"Of course. Zsa Zsa loves kids. The only time she gets anxious is when she's around seagulls."

"Seagulls?" Ethan looked up from the file cabinet drawer he was digging through.

"Long story; don't ask."

"Okay." He went back to the search.

"Ah, Mr. Wycliffe?"

"Ethan, please." He pulled out a blank job application form. "What is it? Ah, I know—salary." He mentioned what she thought was a fair and reasonable amount.

"That's fine, but I think you should know I really don't know a whole lot about art." There, she had said it. Before she got her hopes up about heading back to Claire's to buy that blue outfit for her first day of work, she needed to be straight with Ethan. He seemed like such a nice man.

"I don't know a whole lot about becoming a daddy, but that's not going to stop my wife from delivering our first child in August." Ethan grinned. "Lack of knowledge is curable." He handed her four different sheets of paper. "Fill all of these out, and bring them with you tomorrow morning. You start your training at nine."

She took the papers. "I'll be here."

"One more thing, Joanna."

"What's that?" She was almost afraid to ask.

"Make sure you bring Zsa Zsa. The kids are going to love her."

Chapter
Five

Norah headed downstairs and wondered what was in the refrigerator that she could heat up for dinner. It was Friday night, and she had the house to herself. Her mom and the four-pound hairball were working till nine. Who would have guessed that her mother would go out and get herself a job? Not only was her mother pulling in a paycheck, but Zsa Zsa was also doing tricks for doggie treats. The whole world had gone insane, and someone had forgotten to tell her.

She glanced at the crystal vase filled with long stem red roses and suppressed a chuckle. The crimson roses that her mother had received from Gordon Hanley were the exact same color as blood. She had met Mr. Hanley last week when she had been in town searching for the latest *New York Times* bestseller. The Pen and Ink had been the logical choice of a place to start her search. The amazing thing was that Hanley had known exactly where it was placed in his hodge-podge shelving system. He had gone right to it and pulled the book out of the middle of a hundred or so other books with black spines. Hanley had been polite and talkative. They had enjoyed a lively discussion on politics and on the first article she had written for the *Hancock Review.* But the whole time they were chatting, she couldn't shake the feeling that he was hiding in the shadows of the shop or behind the steady stream of smoke his pipe produced. Hanley was a tall, thin, pale man with an angular face who had an aversion to sunlight. Norah had christened him the vampire.

It seemed fitting that the vampire of Misty Harbor sent bloodred roses. She only wished that it hadn't been her mother he had sent them to. Then again, she would have missed the sight of her mother blushing like a school girl when the delivery man handed them to her. She should be the one sending Gordon Hanley a thank-you note for putting that look of wonder back into her mother's eyes.

She headed into the kitchen and glanced at her own bouquet of flowers that was placed in the center of the dining room table. They weren't roses. They were a wonderful mix of irises, carnations, roses, and a couple birds-of-paradise to give the arrangement an exotic flair. She only wished the bearer of the bouquet had been half as intriguing. Gregory Patterson had shown up on her doorstep carrying the flowers and a dinner invitation two nights ago. He'd ended up staying for a cup of coffee and a couple of sweet rolls her mother had just pulled from the oven. Gregory had seemed nice, but she just wasn't interested in going out with him or any other man.

After Gregory had left that night, her mother had started in on her about her staying home all the time and her lack of a boyfriend. She had heard the lecture before, but this time, she had had ammunition with which to fire back. She had overheard her mother on the phone with Gordon Hanley as she was gently but firmly turning down his offer of dinner. Tit for tat. Both of the Stevens women weren't ready to dip their toes into the dating water.

Norah opened the refrigerator and stared at its contents. There was plenty to choose from. Her mother still hadn't gotten the feel of working a forty-hour week and running the home at the same time. Joanna Stevens was overcompensating in a huge way. Before noon today, her mother had cooked a meatloaf and a batch of brownies, washed and folded two loads of laundry, run Zsa Zsa to the vet, and vacuumed the entire downstairs. She didn't know what terrified her mother more: the thought of dust bunnies or fleas or of her twenty-four-year-old daughter not having something to snack on when she got home from work.

It was ridiculous the way her mother did everything, but the more she tried to help out or to talk to her, the more her mom protested. Her mother was either going to work herself into an early grave, learn that she wasn't superwoman, or work whatever it was that was bothering her right out of her system.

Her mother did have a lot to work out of her system, so she would give her another week or so of waxing and polishing before stepping in and laying down some rules. In the meanwhile, there were meatloaf and brownies for dinner, and hopefully, a decent movie would be on television. It was either that or finish unpacking upstairs.

Her clothes and most of the bathroom stuff had found their proper places. The bedroom was decent, and a person could even walk around the bed. It was the other room up there that was a disaster area. A person couldn't walk two feet into the room without stumbling over a box, a chair, or even a lamp or two. Somewhere in the fifty or so boxes of books scattered throughout the room were at least a dozen books she hadn't had a chance to read yet. By the time she got around to unpacking those boxes, the pages would be yellowed with age.

In her apartment back in Pennsylvania, she had had a lot of six-foot high bookcases. She had sold every one of them at a yard sale before they had moved to Maine. The room upstairs had slanted ceilings, and there wasn't any room for high bookcases. When she had some free time, she needed to find an office supply store and buy a bunch of three-foot high ones. Maybe then she would find the energy or the desire to start unpacking her small library's worth of books.

Meanwhile, she could sneak a brownie before dinner, and her mother would never know. Heck, she could even have two if she wanted. There was something good coming out of her mother having a job, besides the joy it was obviously bringing her. She couldn't remember the last time her mother had been this happy or excited about anything.

The sound of the doorbell prevented her from reaching for that first brownie, which her mother would have sworn would ruin her dinner.

She opened the door and had to jump back a couple of inches as a bouquet of yellow roses was nearly thrust into her face, startling her. "Hey!"

"Oh, sorry."

The flowers were lowered, giving her a clear view of the man holding them. "Can I help you?" She didn't think the man was a delivery person. For one thing, he was dressed like a banker about to attend a stockholders' meeting, and second, his thinning hair was slicked back over his bald spot with enough grease that, if it were instead applied to the right wheels in Washington, even they would turn.

"I'm Wendell Kirby, and you must be Norah Stevens." Wendell had the smile of a politician.

Her hopes that he had come to court her mother faded. "Yes, I'm Norah. Pleased to meet you, Mr. Kirby."

"Wendell, please." He thrust the flowers into her hands. "As the President of the local Chamber of Commerce and the owner of the only motel in town, I wish to welcome you to Misty Harbor."

Imagine that—a politician who owns his own motel. Business and pleasure all rolled up into one. "Do you greet every new resident personally?" She lifted the roses and breathed in their scent.

"Only the beautiful ones." Wendell's smile widened at his witty comment.

"Who welcomes the ones you don't consider beautiful?" She didn't think of herself as beautiful. Fair looking or passable, but not gorgeous. She would rather people remember her for her brains, not because little children hadn't screamed in horror at her face.

Wendell's smile slipped a notch, and he quickly

changed the subject. "I read your columns, and I must say that you are a breath of fresh air to the *Hancock Review.* You are just what the paper and this town needed."

"My boss will be glad to hear that." She leaned against the door jamb. There was no way she was inviting Wendell, Misty Harbor's equivalent to Casanova pond scum, into the house. "So you wouldn't mind if the county went through and reassessed your property value for tax purposes?"

This week's column had pushed more than one person's hot button. Tom Belanger, her boss, had said that if she kept this up, he would need to hire her own personal body guard. She had voted for a young Kevin Costner or Brad Pitt. Tom had voted for a nicer, less controversial assignment for next week's column. She was currently researching the medical advantages of eating blueberries. Everyone knew that blueberries tasted great and helped the local economy. It was her job to make readers realize how good they were for you.

"As a property owner, I mind greatly." Wendell's good-hearted chuckle was as fake as a wooden nickel. "But as President of the local Chamber of Commerce, I must tell you that the added tax revenue could bring in some much needed help to revitalize the town. Think of all the extra services we could offer to attract more tourists."

With a larger tax base, services across the board could be improved and added upon, just like she had stated in her article. "More tourists mean fewer empty motel rooms, right?"

"That's the name of the game."

She wondered how many older residents, the ones who were living on Social Security and meager pensions, wanted to play Wendell's game. Her guess was that not too many of them did. "Anything for commerce?"

"That's why I've been elected President six years in a row." Wendell's chest puffed out.

First thing Monday morning, she was asking her boss if she could write her next article on some people's idea of commerce. "Six years. My, that's a long time." Wendell had to be either blackmailing or bribing the voters for that kind of loyalty. She couldn't put her finger on it, but there was something sneaky or desperate in the middle-aged man's eyes.

"It's nothing compared to the reward I feel doing my civic duty." The look Wendell was going for, she thought, should have been congenial. Instead, he looked like he was suffering from constipation.

She was going to need a pair of boots soon. The level of BS was rising. Wendell wanted something from her, and she wished he would hurry up and get around to the reason behind his visit and the roses. "Civic duty is so important nowadays. Young people just don't seem to grasp the concept."

Wendell blinked, obviously unsure of whether she was serious or being sarcastic about his age. Wendell was old enough to be her father. In all honesty, she wasn't sure if she was serious or not. It depended on what Wendell wanted from her. Men who came bearing roses usually only wanted one thing, and it had nothing to do with the Chamber of Commerce. Unless your profession was the oldest one in the book.

"I feel it's my civic duty to give you a personal tour of our lovely town." Wendell waved his hand over his shoulder in the direction of Main Street. "We can start with a nice dinner at the best restaurant in town and then take an evening stroll. I can point out the highlights of our quaint little village and let you in on all the little secrets."

She'd rather French kiss a toad. "I'm real sorry, Wendell, but I can't." Behind Wendell's back, she saw Ned get out of his truck in front of his parents' house and look her way.

"Oh, I insist." Wendell started to get that desperate look in his eyes as he took a step closer.

She took a hesitant step backward, realizing that she didn't know this man at all. "I said I was sorry, but I can't have dinner with you or go on a tour of the town." She held the roses back out to him, hoping he would take them and leave.

"Why not?" Wendell didn't raise his voice, but there was a new, harder edge to it.

"Because she already has a dinner date"—Ned Porter stepped up behind Wendell—"with me." Ned never took his gaze off Wendell.

"Porter?"

"Kirby?" Ned's smile didn't reach his eyes. "I see you brought Norah some flowers."

She didn't have a date with Ned, but she wasn't about to bring that up now. She was too thankful to him, once again, for riding to her rescue. What was with this town and men showing up on her doorstep? "The flowers are from the Chamber of Commerce," she said, hoping to defuse whatever situation was brewing.

"I'm sure the Chamber would love to know they are paying for the flowers Wendell hands out to all the single women who move into town." Ned took a step closer to her. "Right, Kirby?"

"I bought those roses with my own money." Wendell looked offended and guilty at the same time.

"So why did you tell Norah they were from the Chamber of Commerce? Are you using your Presidency as a pickup line? Isn't that against the bylaws or something?"

Wendell nervously straightened his too tight tie and tugged at the hem of his suit jacket. The buttons were a little tight across his stomach. "I wasn't trying to *pick up* Ms. Stevens, as you so ineloquently put it. I was offering to take her for a nice dinner and then to give her a personal tour around town."

"I'm sure the Chamber values your devotion to your position." Ned's voice dripped with sarcasm. "As you can see, Ms. Stevens has other plans for this evening. But I'm sure she appreciates the roses. I happen to know she's quite partial to them."

Norah was getting tired of being treated like she wasn't even there. She thought about saying something to both men, but she noticed a slight flush on Wendell's face. She wasn't sure if he was embarrassed at being caught asking her out or if he was angry. She didn't want to push the subject either way, and she really didn't want Wendell Kirby showing back up on her doorstep tomorrow or any other night. Ned obviously didn't have a problem with people thinking they were dating. She took a step closer to him. "Thank you, Wendell, for the flowers. They're lovely, and"—she turned to Ned and gave him a smile that she hoped looked secretive and seductive—"this town has made me feel most welcome."

Wendell grumbled something under his breath. "Well, I see you two are busy. Again, welcome to

Misty Harbor, Ms. Stevens, and if I can be of service to you or your family, please don't hesitate to call." With a slight nod to Ned, Wendell turned and walked to his car.

She stood there and continued smiling at Ned. A moment later, a car door slammed, and an engine started.

"How long are you going to stand there smiling at me?" Ned's gaze was following Wendell's car down the street.

"Is he out of sight yet?"

"He is now." Ned turned his attention back to her. "You okay?"

"I'm fine." She frowned at the roses. "What's with the men in this town? Either I have them yelling at me, or they give me flowers. Didn't anyone ever hear of a nice happy medium, or is everyone bipolar?"

"I haven't yelled or given you flowers," Ned said.

"No, you just rescue me from the idiots who do." She laughed at the absurdity of it all. She'd never had this problem back in Pennsylvania. Maybe it was the long cold winters that made the men in Maine nuts.

"I didn't think you needed rescuing either time. For being such a little bitty thing, you were holding your own." Ned's smile held approval. "I just don't think it's right that you are forced to hold your own on your own doorstep."

"Hey, Porter, it's the twenty-first century. Women don't like to be referred to as *little bitty things*." The man was the size of Paul Bunyan. Every woman was little compared to him.

"Point taken." Ned chuckled and then hesitated for a moment before asking, "So would you like to go grab something to eat? Tony's over in Sullivan has the best pizza in the county."

It had to be the most uninspired invitation to dinner she had ever received. So why was she so tempted to go? Ned was good looking, and he was her neighbor's son and her appointed knight in shining armor. All of which were good reasons to take him up on his offer of pizza. But they weren't the reasons she was going to accept. Wendell Kirby, and every other man, was.

When Wendell had gotten that belligerent look on his face, she had realized she couldn't keep living in fear. She had never used to be afraid of men. That fear was slowly poisoning her against life. She wanted her old life back. She needed to get back the trust her father had shattered, and to do that, she needed to spend time with men. Preferably big men. Men like the Porters. If she couldn't trust Ned, who could she trust?

"I have to warn you; I love pizza." She gripped the cellophane wrapped around the roses with both hands so Ned wouldn't notice their trembling. "We might have to go dutch."

Ned's glance skimmed her from head to toe. Laughter was in his brown eyes, but he managed not to smirk. "I think I can afford to feed you, Rose Fairy."

Ned shook his head at Norah's outstretched hand, paid the vender for the two cherry snow cones, and handed one to Norah. "I told you, my treat."

Norah put the money away, took a small bite of the ice treat, and smiled. "You got that same look on your face as you did in Tony's when I finished my half of the pizza."

Ned plucked a couple of napkins out of the dispenser and then moved away from the vender's cart. A family with four kids, all of them shouting what flavor they wanted to the poor man, were crowding around the cart.

"I just have never seen someone so . . . " He glanced at her tiny waist and remembered her warning against calling her little. ". . . beautiful eat four slices of pizza before."

Norah snorted and took another bite. "I warned you that I love good pizza, and Tony's makes some of the best pizza I ever tasted."

Ned shook his head at her waist and her flowing skirt. What was with Norah and all the long, crinkly skirts and jewelry? Maybe she had gypsy blood running through those fairy veins. "I've seen you in jeans."

"What's that got to do with pizza and snow cones?" Norah moved around a mother pushing a stroller with a screaming toddler in it.

He cringed when the little girl hit a particularly high note. The town of Sullivan was pulling in a lot more tourists than Misty Harbor. Every shop on Ocean View Street was open, and they were attracting a lot of foot traffic. The arcade at the end of the docks with its fancy merry-go-round and assorted pinball machines and games was a surefire hit with all the kids. Even the fast food place at the edge of town was jam-packed.

He preferred the peace and quiet of Misty Harbor.

"I was just wondering where you pack it all." He steadied Norah as she stumbled on an uneven plank on the wooden dock. "Careful, the wood is warped in places."

"I noticed." Norah shook her head and side-stepped two teenagers holding hands and walking so close to each other that not an inch of the fading evening light could be seen between them.

What he'd noticed was that Norah hadn't flinched when he grabbed her elbow to steady her. He had to wonder if it was because it had happened so fast that she hadn't had time to think about it, or was it because she knew him better and felt safer? He led her to an empty bench out of the main traffic flow to finish their dessert.

"You don't get out much, do you?" Norah tried to look innocent, but she failed miserably.

"What's that supposed to mean?" He got out plenty.

"I know this isn't a real date or anything, but when you are out with a woman, you aren't supposed to refer to her eating habits as *packing it all away.*"

"Can't blame a guy for commenting, Norah. You matched me slice for slice." Ned chuckled at the memory of Norah biting into that first slice, rolling her eyes, and moaning in ecstasy. There was definitely something sensual about the way she ate pizza, not that he would tell her that. "I haven't seen a woman eat that much since my sisters-in-law were pregnant. Barley's Food Store had to have double shipments in for months, and Paul had to take on a part-time job when Jill carried Hunter."

Norah's laugh could have been declared as the eighth wonder of the world. "You're making that up. I've seen both your sisters-in-law, and neither one of them could be classed as fat."

"I didn't say they were fat." If Kay and Jill ever teamed up against him, they could wipe the floor with his sorry butt. He didn't want to think about what his brothers would do to him for even insinuating a thing such as their wives being an ounce overweight. Both of his brothers thought that their wives were the best thing to happen since the cordless drill. "And I definitely didn't say that you were either. In fact, I implied the opposite was true."

"You did? When?"

"When I said I've seen you in jeans." Ned chuckled at the look of disbelief on her face. "Under those enormous skirts you wear, a guy would have a hard time figuring out whether you have a hollow leg, thunder thighs, or elephant calves. In tight-fitting jeans all the mysteries are clearly revealed."

"It was dark in your parents' backyard that night." Norah seemed extremely interested in the boats in the harbor.

"I've got excellent night vision."

"So what mysteries were revealed?"

"Ah, if I didn't know better, Ms. Stevens, I would think you were fishing for a compliment." He spread his feet out before him and leaned back on the bench, enjoying himself immensely. The evening was turning out a lot better than he would have thought. There was no way he was telling Norah what her jeans had done to his imagination. His once dormant imagination had kicked into overdrive with visions of nicely packed denim dancing through his dreams. He didn't need a psychologist to tell him what that dream meant.

"Dream on, Porter." Norah snorted, spread her feet out in front of her, leaned back on the bench.

Oh, I intend to. He looked at her small, delicate feet and wondered if they were cold. The yellow sandals Norah had on offered no protection against the chill of a Maine evening, but they matched her sweater and the huge sunflowers on her skirt perfectly. The silver ankle bracelet and peach toenail polish looked sexy. It was the three silver toe rings that threw him. "Aren't they uncomfortable?" He had never seen a woman wear rings on her toes outside of a magazine picture before.

"Aren't what uncomfortable?" Norah's gaze followed his, and she wiggled her toes. "The sandals?"

"No, the rings on your toes. Don't they bother you when you walk?"

"You get used to them. It's not like getting your belly button pierced. I can take them off anytime I like."

"You don't, do you?" He remembered the enticing inch of skin showing between her tank top and the waistband of her jeans that night. But he couldn't remember if there had been a gleam of metal connected to her navel.

"Ah, not all my mysteries were revealed. We won't get into the tattoos." Norah chuckled and went back to eating her snow cone.

He thought about it for a moment. "You don't have any tattoos. As for the pierced belly button, I'm not too sure about that one. Any woman who has eight earrings in one ear and five in the other isn't too opposed to punching holes in her body." The difference in the number of earrings had driven him crazy all through dinner, but he wasn't about to ask. The less he knew about Norah, the better he might sleep.

They were complete opposites with nothing in

common, as their conversation during dinner had proven. His idea of fun was roughing it in the wilderness and sleeping under the stars. Norah's idea of roughing it consisted of hotels without room service and cars with broken air conditioners. She would never last an hour, let alone an entire weekend, in his beloved mountains.

"Why are you so positive about me not having any tattoos?" She stood up and tossed her empty paper cone into a nearby trash can.

He chucked his nearly empty cup and prayed that the cherry juice hadn't made his lips as red as Norah's. They started walking back to where he had parked his truck. "You don't have any on your ankles, arms, neck, or shoulder blades."

"Observant fellow, aren't you?" She laughed at a group of seagulls dive-bombing a bunch of rocks near the dock. A little boy and his father were tossing French fries to the birds. "What makes you think I don't have one or two somewhere in a lot less public spot?"

Now there was a thought that would haunt his dreams tonight. "Piercings and tattoos are for show. What's the sense in getting them if no one sees them?"

Norah's look told him exactly what she thought of that stupid comment.

He decided not to pursue the subject of Norah's private body parts. He needed his sleep.

Twenty minutes later, they pulled up in front of her house. His parents' house was dark, which was normal for them since they got up so early. Norah's house had a couple of lights lit inside, and the lights on either side of the front door were turned on. "Your mom must be home."

Norah glanced at the dashboard clock. "I can't believe it's after nine."

Friday night, and he was dropping off the girl before nine-thirty. He felt like he was sixteen instead of twenty-seven. "Come on. I'll walk you up to the door."

"You don't have to, Ned. I'm a big girl, and the door's right there." Norah opened the truck door and hopped down before he could help her.

Ned hurried around the side of the truck. "You don't understand. If my parents are peeking out their bedroom window and they don't see me walk you to your door and make sure you're safely inside before I leave, there will be hell to pay in the morning."

"Scare you, do they?" Norah teased as she walked up the path.

"Only my mom." He stopped at the doorstep and allowed Norah to dig through her purse for her keys. "She's got a mean right hook."

Norah chuckled. "Thank you for dinner and dessert. I really enjoyed myself tonight." Norah seemed to be taking an awfully long time to retrieve her keys.

He leaned in closer. His intent was to take her keys and unlock the door. Norah's flinch stopped him cold. So much for her being used to him. She either was still afraid of him, or she thought he was going to kiss her goodnight.

He slowly raised his hand and gently ran the tip of his finger down her cheek and across the corner of her mouth. Her cherry-stained lips trembled for a moment beneath his touch. "Good night, Rose Fairy." He turned and walked back to his truck before he did something incredibly stupid.

Chapter
Six

Joanna glanced around the gallery with the same sense of pride she had once held for her home alone. The two weeks she had worked for Ethan had not only been a learning experience, but they had also been rewarding. Working the cash register was easy, and dusting and displaying the merchandise to its advantage was second nature to her. Karen had taught her how to check in the pottery pieces Ethan ordered and how to keep track of inventory so that she could tell what they had in the back room in case a customer needed a certain piece. Ethan trusted her to handle the gallery on her own for short periods of time, and Karen was getting some much needed time with her family.

The aspect of the business that she found so amazing was that Ethan spent a lot of his time in the back room poring over Christmas merchandise and order forms. Here it was the last week of June, and Ethan wanted her opinion on crystal ornaments, hand-crafted elves that were selling for more than a thirty-two-inch flat screen television, and green and red hand-blown glass vases. Ethan was undecided on how many Christmas trees he would be putting up this year, let alone what color palette he would be aiming for. Ethan had other things on his mind besides the gallery. Namely, his very pregnant wife, Olivia.

Joanna had met Olivia quite a few times. Each and every encounter brought a new dimension to Olivia's growing stomach. Ethan feared his poor wife would either explode or fall forward and then never be able to make it back up onto her own feet before she delivered their child. Considering Olivia's size, she had to agree with Ethan, but she wasn't going to tell him that. Her boss had developed a few gray hairs over the past couple of weeks. She honestly didn't know how Ethan was going to make it through the next six weeks, let alone what he would do if the little one decided to arrive late.

It made her heart feel good to see two people so obviously in love and to observe the joy they were experiencing starting their family. It was what she wanted for her daughter, Norah. A man who loved her as much as Ethan loved his wife. She wasn't pushing for grandchildren, even though one day, she would love to become a grandmom. If and when they would have children would be Norah's and her husband's decision. She just wanted her daughter to find happiness. To find love.

Nothing had thrilled her more than when she had gotten home the other night and found Norah's note saying she had gone out with Ned Porter. Norah hadn't said much about the date, besides saying she'd had a good time. As far as she knew, Ned hadn't called Norah, and her daughter didn't seem to be hanging around the phone waiting for it to ring. It was a real shame their date hadn't turned out better.

She liked Ned and the entire Porter family. Peggy and John were wonderful neighbors who had a habit of sending over fresh fish occasionally. She, in return, had sent over some fresh baked goods. It seemed like a fair exchange to her, but John always seemed particularly thrilled to see a steaming pie or a plate of cookies.

There was one unattached Porter left—Matthew—but she didn't think that would work out, considering Norah had already turned down one date with him and had now dated his brother. Some things you would rather not keep in a family, and the same date would be one of them.

Joanna glanced behind the counter where she had placed a small doggie bed. Zsa Zsa was taking her before-lunch nap. The dog had more fun during the day than she did, and she was the one who loved her job. Zsa Zsa loved the children more. Ethan really appreciated having the dog there to entertain the children of browsing parents, leaving them more time to decide if they were interested in purchasing anything. Ethan swore that sales had risen since Zsa Zsa had begun coming to work and had even gone out and bought the Pomeranian her own bag of special treats.

Joanna left the dog to her nap and walked over to the piece of art that had been intriguing her since she first walked into the gallery two weeks ago. Every day, she studied the piece, only to discover something she had missed the day before. At first glance, the four-foot carving wasn't impressive. It appeared to be an old stump of a cut down tree with a new branch that had shot out of its side and was struggling for life. Only when a person got close enough to examine the piece did he or she notice the detailed carvings that were in the stump and lonely branch. So far, she had counted three tiny fairies hiding among the leaves and the root system. A miniature door was carved into the base of the stump, and what appeared to be a window or two was cleverly hidden within the bark. One of the roots was shaped like a rabbit, and there was a chipmunk peering out from under another section.

The enchanting sculpture was like one of those pictures where you had to find different hidden items. The problem with the carving was that there was no answer key. She had no idea how many items she was looking for, so she spent an inappropriate amount of time studying the piece.

"Have you found the Wise One yet?"

Joanna startled at the voice but didn't turn around. She hadn't heard anyone come into the gallery, but she knew who was standing behind her. The man who had carved not only the stump she was studying but also every other wood piece for sale in the gallery. Karl James had become an almost daily visitor to the gallery since she had started working there. Ethan and Karen both got a kick out of teasing her about her admirer. They both thought Karl was wonderful, and they were constantly singing his praises.

"Hello, Karl." She moved to the right but continued studying the carving. "What Wise One?" She didn't think he was referring to the cute little fairies or the animals.

"The old wizard." Karl stood still and watched her every move.

"There's a wizard carved into the stump?" She could feel Karl's gaze on her as she took another step to the right. There was something unsettling about Karl's gaze. She didn't get the feeling she was in any danger; in fact, she felt quite the opposite. Karl James looked at her as if she were the most beautiful woman in the world. No one had ever looked at her that way before, not even her ex-husband, Vince.

"Just his face and hat." She could hear the smile in his voice. "Keep going right, and I'll tell you when to stop."

She moved to the far side of the carving and finally looked over at Karl when he said, "Stop."

She couldn't stop her smile from forming. Today, he was dressed in a Hawaiian shirt with pink flamingoes all over it, dark green shorts, and sandals. His full beard was neatly trimmed, and his long gray hair was pulled back in a ponytail. Karl looked like an aging beach bum or one of those *Grateful Dead* musicians. The one that Ben and Jerry had named an ice cream flavor in honor of. To make matters worse, he had on a black ankle bracelet that appeared to be made out of rope and a diamond stud earring.

Karl James dressed totally inappropriately for his age.

So why did her knees get weak and her stomach feel like butterflies were fluttering about in it every time he walked into the gallery? The man was pushing fifty, and he dressed like he was an extra in a Gidget movie.

"Right there should do it." Karl rocked back on his heels and thrust his hands into his pockets.

"Do what?" She had no idea why he was grinning or what he was talking about.

"You should be able to see him from there." Karl seemed quite pleased about something.

It took her a moment to realize she was supposed to be looking for the wizard, not checking out Ethan's star artist. Karl James's carvings were becoming extremely sought after in the art world, and Wycliffe Art Gallery was the only one who sold them. Ethan was quite pleased with the arrangement, and Karl didn't seem to be looking for anywhere else to handle or show his work. In fact, Karl didn't seem to care if his carvings sold or not. Karl didn't take commissions, and Ethan had no idea when a new piece or two would be showing up at the gallery.

Karl was as laid back in his career as he was in his dress. What kind of man didn't care about his career? Where was his passion, his arrogance, his blinding self-confidence in his own greatness?

She studied the intricately carved piece of art, but she couldn't see a wizard or even the shape of a pointy hat. She squinted her eyes and concentrated on the leaves of the branch.

"Still can't see him?" Karl moved to stand beside her and followed her gaze. "He's not in the leaves. Only the fairies are in there."

"Three fairies, right?"

"Four." Karl's voice held a hint of laughter and pleasure.

There was a curse sitting on the end of her tongue, but she wouldn't utter the word. She glanced over at Karl and smiled. "You're enjoying yourself, aren't you?"

"I'd be enjoying myself more if you would have lunch with me."

"Every time you come in here, you ask me out to lunch. Why?" She was curious to know. She just couldn't picture herself as a woman Karl would usually date.

Karl cocked his head and studied her face. "Every time I ask you to lunch, you come up with another excuse as to why you can't go with me." He didn't seem insulted, only curious. "What's today's reason?"

She looked away from his kind and all-knowing brown eyes and stared unseeingly at the carving. She hadn't been on a date with any man other than her husband since she was seventeen. Eons ago. A lifetime ago. She wasn't even sure if she knew how to behave and act. It was the twenty-first century, the dating rules had changed dramatically, and someone had forgotten to mail her the updated and revised instruction sheets.

Months ago, when she had signed the agreement to buy the small cottage on Pepperell Street, she had told Norah she was ready to move on with her life. She was starting fresh. So far, she had made a promising start on a new life, but she hadn't taken the final step. The step that scared her the most. Forming a relationship with a man. Granted, a simple lunch down at Krup's General Store didn't constitute a relationship with Karl or any other man, but it would be a baby step in the right direction. Not only did she need to take that step for herself, but for Norah as well. Her daughter needed to see that not all men were like her father.

Vincent Alfred Stevens would not ruin the rest of her life. To fear other men because of what Vince had done would not dominate her or her daughter's life. She wouldn't allow Vince to win.

How much trouble could she get into during a one-hour lunch break sitting in a booth in the middle of town? Karl and she would have absolutely nothing in common besides his work. He carved the sculptures, and she loved them.

"I'll make you a deal." She didn't look at Karl. "Krup's makes the best BLTs, and I didn't pack myself a lunch today."

"You're agreeing to go to lunch with me?" Karl seemed pleasantly surprised.

"If you agree to tell me how many things I'm looking for in this sculpture and if you can wait until Ethan gets back from his lunch." Putting conditions on the date made it seem more like a business deal than a romantic interest on her part. She didn't want Karl to get the wrong idea about her or this one simple meal.

Karl rubbed his chin. He was trying to hide his smile, but he failed miserably. "You drive a hard bargain, Ms. Stevens."

"It's Joanna, please." There was something about Karl's smile that made her knees grow weaker. How could a man who had a full beard and dressed like he had attended Woodstock back in the sixties and smoked everything that was passed his way look so darn sexy? All the fresh sea air must have melted her brain.

Karl James was immensely pleased with himself. He had finally gotten Joanna to agree to have lunch with him. It had only taken him ten trips into the gallery. He would have sworn it would have taken over a dozen invitations; his police record; a credit report score; and possibly, a digital eye scan to get Joanna just to share a cup of coffee, let alone a whole sandwich and a vanilla shake. He'd never met a more stubborn or more fascinating woman.

"Want to tell me why you are so nervous?" He couldn't shake the feeling that Joanna was getting ready to bolt out of Krup's front door at any moment.

"Who says I'm nervous?" Joanna looked up from her plate.

"Your foot hasn't stopped moving the whole time we've been here, and your fingers have been fidgeting with the silverware." He glanced at her left hand that was toying with the spoon. "Do I make you nervous, or is it men in general?"

The secrets in her green eyes swirled, intriguing him further. "I'm not sure how to do this, Karl."

"Do what—eat lunch?" There was no way she should be uncomfortable in a social setting with a man. Joanna Stevens was a beautiful woman who surely had been in the company of many men before him. He knew she had just moved to Misty Harbor with her daughter, the new journalist for the *Hancock Review* who was pushing a lot of people's hot buttons. Joanna also was the owner of one very spoiled Pomeranian that went by the ridiculous name of Zsa Zsa. He wasn't sure if she was divorced or widowed, but he wasn't inclined to ask Ethan. He wanted to hear the story of her life from Joanna herself.

"I know how to eat lunch." Joanna gave him a look that spoke volumes. "I've been doing it every day of my life." Joanna took a sip of her shake. "It's just that this is the first date I've been on since my divorce."

"How long have you been divorced?" *One question answered, a thousand more to go.*

"It's been final a couple of months." Joanna nibbled on a chip. "Have you ever been married?"

"Many years ago. It lasted two years." He now understood her hesitancy to go out with him, but it didn't explain the vulnerability he sometimes glimpsed in her beautiful green eyes. Or the secrets. Secrets intrigued him, and this woman fascinated him more than most.

"What happened?" she asked.

"The marriage never should have happened in the first place. I wasn't husband material." He was always the first to admit that he was the reason behind his failed marriage. "My job took me away from home too often and for too long. Susan, my ex, deserved better than that. She wanted a family, and to be honest with you, I would have made a terrible parent."

Joanna seemed curious to know more. "Why? Don't you like children?"

"Love them, but back in my thirties, I was never around. It wouldn't have been fair to Susan or the children we might have had. Thankfully, we both realized our mistake, and moved on with our lives." He had been the one to realize it first while sitting in another bland hotel room a thousand miles away from Susan and the home fires she swore she kept burning for him. "Susan remarried, and she is now the mother of two teenage boys that are driving her nuts." He could smile about it now, but at the time, learning of Susan's impending motherhood had hurt. It had hammered home all the things in life he had given up for his career. He had vowed never to make that same mistake again. Life was too short.

"You keep in touch with her?"

"We've remained friends over the years." He had learned how unusual that was from other friends, associates, and family members who had gone through divorces. Most divorces ended with hatred, jealousy, and vengeance. He wondered how Joanna's divorce had ended.

"I didn't realize that being an artist took you away from home that much. Don't you have a studio or something?"

"Carving is my second career, and yes, I do have a studio next to my house. Bringing eight- or ten-foot sections of trees into my living room would ruin the floors." He was half tempted to tease her about coming out to his place one day so that he could show her his studio and she could look at his etchings. Somewhere beneath all of Joanna's wariness, he had a feeling there was a sense of humor. He was usually a pretty good judge of character.

Joanna softly smiled. "I imagine all that chipping and carving can cause quite a mess." Her left hand stopped toying with the spoon, and she finally seemed to relax. "What did you do before becoming an artist?"

This was the part where he usually jokingly said "a little of this and a little of that." He didn't want to hedge with Joanna. He had a feeling that she wouldn't appreciate it and that it would damage what little trust there was between them. "I really would rather my past not be broadcast all over town."

"Why not?" Joanna's gaze turned cautious.

He had been afraid of that. Joanna was attributing the worst possible scenario to his past, and her imagination was in overdrive. He could practically see the trust shattering in her eyes. "Because I have found that people see me for what I was, not for who I am."

"What were you?" Joanna's fingers went back to the spoon, and her one foot was shaking so much that he was amazed the vibrations didn't knock over their drinks.

What in the world did she think? That he'd just gotten out of prison, or that he had been a drug lord who had spent all his time flying in and out of Colombia? He lowered his voice so that the other people sitting at the counter or in the other booths couldn't overhear and tried to put her fears to rest. He whispered, "FBI."

Joanna went perfectly still and gave him a funny blank look. "What?"

He tried not to roll his eyes. Was it really so farfetched that he had worn a suit and tie for twenty-five years while working for the government? "I said"—his voice was just above a loud whisper—"I was an FBI agent." There wasn't a person in America who needed those initials spelled out.

Joanna blinked twice and then did something totally unexpected. She burst out laughing, causing everyone in the place to turn and stare at them.

He sat there, stunned. He'd known he was attracted to Joanna. Instant attraction and lust he understood. But sitting here, watching her eyes fill with tears of joy and hearing the wonderful sound of her laughter, he was overcome with another emotion. One that would have floored him flat on his backside if he weren't already sitting down. He was falling in love with the very prim and proper Joanna Stevens.

Norah pulled her old SUV into the driveway and gave thanks that the vehicle had made it back from Bangor. It was due for some major work, and she'd been putting it off so as not to drain her savings on a hopefully unnecessary expense. She was hoping to buy a new four-wheel drive vehicle before the first snowflake landed in Maine. So far that dream might turn into a reality if she continued nursing it along. But there were no more long hauls in the battered SUV's future. The trip up from Pennsylvania had been its last hurrah. An occasional trip into Bangor was about all it could handle.

This morning's trip to an office supply store had been necessary. Not only had her printer run out of ink, but she was also nearly out of paper, and she was tired of living with all the boxes in the spare room upstairs. Six brand new, three-foot high bookcases had been piled in the back of the SUV by some seventeen-year-old fullback on the local high school football team. The fun part now would be not only carrying them into the house and up a flight of stairs, but they also had to be put together.

It wasn't how she had been hoping to spend a gorgeous June Saturday, but she'd heard tomorrow was going to be just as nice. Since her mom worked today and had off tomorrow, she figured she'd stay at home today and tackle the room and then play tourist with her mom on Sunday. Maybe her mom would come clean about this Karl James guy. She didn't know what was going on between her mother and Misty Harbor's resident artist. All she knew was that they had gone out to lunch together nearly every day this week. Her mother had even gone in early yesterday to meet him before she had to start work at the gallery.

Working at the gallery was one thing. At first, she had been anxious about her mom working, but that had quickly faded when she saw how happy the job made her mother. Her mother had even stopped cooking dinner at eight in the morning. Joanna Stevens had entered the working world, one that was full of fast food, take out dinners, and frozen entrees. Nothing seemed to give her mother more pleasure than writing in all the spaces on the kitchen wall calendar. It seemed every detail of her mother's life was written on that calendar, from dental appointments, to her work schedule, to lunch dates with Karl.

She reached for the bag of merchandise and headed for the house. She should be thrilled that her mother was getting on with her life, but she couldn't shake the fear that her mother would be hurt again. She was waiting for the lunch dates to turn into dinner dates, and then she'd be the one up until all hours of the night waiting for her mother to come in. When in the heck had their roles in life become reversed? Her own mother was getting out more and having more fun than she was.

With that depressing thought, the bag almost slipped from her hand as she unlocked the front door and managed to stumble into the house. Not the best beginning, considering she had six bookcases to unload. She tossed the bag and her purse onto the couch and headed back to the car.

The hatchback swung up, and she frowned at the boxes. They looked bigger now than when the kid had loaded them. The printing across the top box claimed that they were the right measurements. She just prayed hernias didn't hurt too much. With a wiggle, a few jerks, and a couple of groans, she had the first box halfway out of the back when she stopped to catch a good breath before the hard part—picking that sucker up. Who would have thought particle board weighed so much?

"Give me that before you hurt yourself," was growled in her ear a second before a pair of strong hands lifted the box away from her and out of the car with ease.

Ned couldn't believe what he was seeing when he pulled up in front of his parents' house. Norah was attempting to lift a box that was nearly as tall as she and probably weighed a good sixty pounds out of her car. He'd had to sprint across her yard before the box tipped and ended up on her foot. "Where do you want them?"

He counted five other boxes in the back of her Bronco and tried not to roll his eyes. The woman had to be delusional if she thought she could get all of them into the house without major damage being done either to the boxes or to herself.

He didn't know what had caused his heart to leap into his throat—the thought of Norah being hurt, or the sight of her shorts riding up the backs of her slim thighs as she leaned into the SUV. Darn, how could such a little bitty thing have such a powerful effect on him.

"Thanks, Ned. They go in the house." Norah hurried ahead and held open the screen door.

Ned maneuvered through the doorway with only inches to spare. "Which room?" The house had a layout identical to his parents'.

"Upstairs and to the left." Norah led the way up the steps.

Ned watched the enticing sway of her hips as she climbed in front of him and nearly dropped the box. If Norah had any tattoos, they had to be tiny ones. Her off-white shorts barely covered the essentials, and the skimpy green top she had on left half her back bare. Norah had more skin showing today than she had the other night. Not a tattoo or imperfection in sight.

Norah stepped into the doorway on the right and gestured to the room on the left. The bracelets on her wrist jangled. "In there, wherever you can find room."

Ned looked into the room and chuckled. "Unless you are planning on putting this together on the couch, I would suggest we clear a space first." He wanted to ask what was in all the boxes, but he figured the answer was obvious—books. Why else would Norah buy six bookcases? He lowered the box and leaned it against the bathroom door.

"I don't think even Matthew and I had this much stuff in the room when we were growing up." He remembered the chaotic clutter of his youth, which had mostly consisted of sporting equipment, video games, and dirty laundry. Matthew had been the messier one, but they had both shared the groundings when their mother had tired of the mess.

"Oh, this room was your bedroom?"

"Yep, and I had to share with Matt." He had overheard his brother asking Norah out and had nearly laughed when she had told him no. "How about if I pile some of these boxes onto the couch to give us some room to work."

"I can do that if you're willing to carry up the other bookcases for me. When I bought them, I didn't think they would weigh as much as they do."

"Why don't you go hunt up whatever tools we are going to need to put these together while I stack the boxes onto the couch." He didn't have his tool box with him in his truck, but he was sure his father's garage would have whatever they might need if Norah didn't. It had been his experience that a lot of women tended to think that butter knives and a high-heeled shoe were the equivalent of a Craftsman screwdriver and hammer.

"I can't ask you to put them all together, Ned." Norah picked up the nearest box and piled it on top of an end table. "Just getting those shelves in the house and up the stairs will be a great help."

"I don't mind. I don't have anything else that needs to be done this afternoon." He reached for the biggest box and set it on the couch. It was either an entire set of encyclopedias or cannon balls. He continued to lift boxes as Norah stepped over and around furniture to open the two side windows. His gaze followed the sound of the charm bracelet that she had wrapped around one slim ankle. Norah had the right idea; it was getting awfully warm in the room.

"Where are you planning on putting the bookcases once I get them together?" With his luck, he would need to move the now buried under six tons of books couch.

"Against the length of the entire back wall." Norah waved her hand to where the sloped ceiling met the kneewall. "It's twenty-five feet wide. With the six bookcases, I've got twelve inches to spare."

Most of the space along that wall was already cleared, and there was just enough room for him to start to put the cases together. "Smart."

He liked the fact that Norah loved her books enough to have moved them from Pennsylvania with her and that she had eccentric taste in reading. Some of the titles he glimpsed had been textbooks; others poetry and a few nonfiction; but most had been fiction titles. He had a lot of the same titles on his shelves at home. "You go get the tools while I go get the bookcases." He headed for the steps.

Fifteen minutes later, he carried the last of the bookcases into the room and set it in the cleared spot. Norah had moved more of the stuff away from the wall. "Where's the tools?"

"In the case." Norah didn't bother to glance up from the box she was going through. She waved toward a pink, hard plastic case sitting on the floor.

He stared at the silly feminine-looking case for a moment before kneeling in front of it and opening it. He gingerly picked up the hammer and a screwdriver. He'd be laughed out of the state if Daniel or Quinn could see him at this moment. "Norah?"

"Yes?" Norah finally took her head out of the box.

"They're pink!" The handles to all the tools were pink. Even the razor knife was pink. He had never seen such a thing. Norm Abram would keel over in his Yankee Workshop with laughter.

Chapter Seven

"You have something against pink?" Norah looked at him as if she was expecting some smart remark.

My momma didn't raise no fool. "Nope, it's one of my favorite colors." He took out the razor knife and was impressed that the blade was still sharp and that all the little slots inside the case held the proper tools. He could tell that the tools had been used occasionally. He had seen grown women disregard a good tool as soon as the job was done, but Lord help the poor man who moved her curling iron or left up the toilet seat. "Can I ask where you found a *pink* set?" He was having a hard time swallowing the concept of a pink hammer.

"Under the Christmas tree two years ago." Norah helped him take all of the pieces out of the box. "Santa gave them to me."

He tried not to chuckle at the image of Norah, all sleepy eyed and fresh from a warm bed, sitting on the floor unwrapping presents Christmas morning. "You must have been a very good girl that year."

Norah's laughter filled the room as she opened the bag of screws and started to arrange them by size. "Let me tell you, Santa doesn't know everything."

He wasn't going to bite at that comment either. Norah thinking she was bad was one thing. Him picturing Norah being bad was another. If she startled when she was accidently touched, he'd be willing to bet she'd run from the room screaming when she saw his version of her being bad.

He forced his mind away from such tempting thoughts and glanced at the instruction sheet, the pile of wood, and then the neat rows of screws Norah was lining up. It could have been worse. He remembered the day he had helped his brother John set up a swing set for Tyler. It had taken the four Porter men seven hours and almost a case of beer to get the stupid thing together. And then, because they had followed the directions to the letter, the sliding board had been put on upside down. Kay and Jill hadn't let them forget that one yet, and it had been two and a half years. From that day forward, none of the Porters would use instruction sheets. They only made the simple more complex. They had also sworn never to allow a female near them when they were putting something together.

Ned glanced at Norah, who was trying to be helpful. "Why don't you find the books that will go on this shelf while I put it together." Her scent was driving him crazy. Norah smelled like she had just walked through a field of lavender. His mind was busy categorizing all of the body parts to which she would have applied the perfume.

"You don't need my help?"

"I can handle it." He smiled to soften his words. It wasn't Norah's fault he couldn't control his thoughts. He started putting the pieces together.

Norah shrugged her shoulders and started digging through the boxes of books.

He almost had the second bookshelf done when Norah asked, "Did you have lunch yet?"

"Not yet." It was almost one, and he had been planning on grabbing something at his parents'. He also had planned on cutting their grass for them. Between being out on the tuna boat all day and running back and forth to Boston to check on his aunt, his parents hadn't had a whole lot of time at home. He had convinced himself that he had a few extra hours to help them out and that coming by their place had nothing to do with their sexy new neighbor.

Norah got to her feet. The first case was in place and full. "Anything in particular that you don't like?" Norah stacked a couple of empty boxes in one another.

"Anchovies, brussels sprouts, and fifty-year-old Scotch mixed with a game of frisbee where you aren't allowed to use your hands."

Norah arched a brow, but her lips were twitching. "Dare I ask?"

"An old college dare that the fifty-year-old Scotch warped my judgement on."

Norah grinned. "Ah, but did you win?"

"Only second place. The very well-endowed Stephanie Zelinski won first because she had a more inventive way to toss a frisbee without using her hands." He shook his head at the memory. "It wasn't a fair competition to begin with. All the judges were guys."

Norah's laughter followed her out of the room and down the steps.

He had the second bookcase in place and was emptying the box containing bookcase number three when Norah came back up the steps carrying a tray loaded with sandwiches, drinks, and a plate of brownies. "It's time for a break, Ned. The least I can do is feed you." She set the tray on the end of a coffee table. "I already cleared us a spot to sit. Bathroom's in there"—she nodded her head in the direction of the small bath at the top of the stairs—"if you want to clean up."

Ned stepped into the cramped little bathroom and smiled at the memories. He and his three older brothers had shared a bathroom that looked amazingly like this one. How they had not killed each other was beyond him. There was barely enough room to turn around.

Norah's soap was yellow, and it smelled of sunshine. The entire bathroom, the shower curtain, rug, and matching towels, was done in rubber duckies. There was even a white basket filled with assorted rubber duckies sitting on the back of the john. He didn't know if he should be appalled at her decorating taste or laugh at her sense of humor.

He dried his hands and joined Norah. "Who's your decorator? Ernie?"

"Bert. I have this thing for the strong silent types who collect paper clips." Norah was sitting on the couch, where there was only a small space, leaving him the recliner. On the coffee table between them was lunch. "I hope you like chicken salad and root beer."

"Love them." He sat and dug into lunch. "Where's your mom? I haven't seen her lately."

"She and Zsa Zsa got a job down at Wycliffe's Gallery." Norah nibbled on her sandwich.

"Ethan lets Zsa Zsa into his gallery?" Ethan was a good friend when they weren't trying to kill each other on the ice. During hockey season, all bets were off. His friend was very particular about his gallery, and he couldn't imagine Ethan allowing a dog in there.

"He insisted," Norah tucked her feet up under her. "Zsa Zsa gets paid in treats when she entertains the kids of browsing customers. It's a win-win situation. Kids are happy, parents are happy, Ethan's happy because most of the browsers turn into customers, and Zsa Zsa just soaks up all the glory."

He chuckled at the thought. "Like Zsa Zsa wasn't spoiled enough."

"She's getting worse, and my mother encourages it. The only drawback is that her potty breaks are taken out back of the gallery, which is right at the docks."

"Seagulls." He gallantly tried to hold in his laughter.

Norah's laughter was contagious. They both cracked up thinking about the Pomeranian and all those birds. Norah wiped at the tears in her eyes. "Mom says she's getting better."

"How can she tell?"

"Because she doesn't have to use the umbrella anymore. Zsa Zsa actually goes outside to do her business without its protection. Mom just stands beside her and waves her hands in the air to shoo away any gulls that might be curious about what's going on." Norah bit her lower lip, but her green eyes sparkled with laughter.

"I think I would pay to see that." He couldn't imagine Ethan allowing such a thing. Either Zsa Zsa had caused a tremendous spike in sales, or Ethan's wife, Olivia, was finally taking some of the starch out of his collar. Ethan had always been a prim and proper gentleman, and as sophisticated as they came, unless he was suited up and out on the ice. Maybe it was impending fatherhood that was mellowing out his friend.

"You would have to hide."

"Why?"

"Zsa Zsa doesn't like anyone looking at her while she is attending to her business." Norah's tone indicated she was serious, but her expression was priceless.

"She's a dog." He'd never heard of such a thing.

"Tell her that. She thinks she's human." Norah reached for the second half of her sandwich. "It's my mom's fault. She created the monster; now she gets to live with her."

He'd readily admit to spoiling Flipper on certain things, like riding in the cab of the truck during below freezing winter days and taking him swimming in the cove on hotter summer days. But there was no way Flipper thought he was human.

Norah's smile slowly faded, and she got a serious look about her. "Can I ask you a question?"

"Sure."

"You know a guy in town named Karl James?"

"The artist?"

"That's the one."

"I know of him, but I can't say I know him. He doesn't come into town much, and when he does, he usually keeps to himself. Why?" Ned assured himself it wasn't jealousy he was feeling. Karl James was old enough to be Norah's father.

"My mom and he seem to be getting close." Norah popped a chip into her mouth.

"As in dating close?" He relaxed. Karl wasn't bothering Norah.

"They have lunch nearly every day at Krup's General Store, but my mom says they are just friends and that it isn't a date."

He could tell from Norah's expression that she didn't believe her mom. "If Karl's in town nearly every day, it must be serious." As much as he wanted to, he couldn't put her mind at ease. "Have you met him yet?" He couldn't picture the classy and elegant Joanna Stevens and the aged hippy, Karl James, together in a romantic way. Talk about opposites attracting.

"Not yet." Norah toyed with the remainder of her sandwich. "Think I should insist on her bringing him home one night for dinner?"

"I have no idea, Norah. She is your mother. I guess she can date anyone she wants to." Gee, it's a screwed up world if you have to worry about who your mother is dating. "Has she brought home other dates?"

"No, this is the first man she has shown any interest in since the divorce."

That could explain it. Karl was probably the first man to ask the lovely Joanna out, and she had readily accepted. Joanna had probably been married to some stuffy banker type, and she was ready to taste the wild side of life. He had to wonder if Norah knew about Karl's Harley. "What is your father like?"

Norah froze. "Why?"

"I was thinking that maybe she wanted a man who is his total opposite." He didn't like the way all the color drained from Norah's face.

"She divorced him; that says it all." Norah got up and started to gather up a few more empty boxes and other trash. "Take your time finishing your lunch. I'll take these down."

Ned sat there and stared at the empty doorway. Norah had practically run down the steps to get away. What in the world was all that about? If Norah didn't want to talk about her father, all she had to do was say so. He would have dropped the subject, but now his curiosity was skyrocketing off the charts.

Did her father have something to do with the fear he'd glimpsed in Norah's eyes at different times? Was he the reason she startled so easily or jumped when she was accidently touched by a male?

His stomach turned at the very thought.

He liked Norah in a way that had nothing to do with her being his parents' new neighbor. She had a sense of humor, and was intelligent, two traits he found very appealing in a woman. She was openly honest and refreshingly candid. Norah hadn't been out to impress him, and that simple fact affected him the most. Now, if she would only grow another ten inches and build up enough muscle mass to actually chop firewood, he would feel more comfortable around her. As it was, he usually felt as if he were posing in a Jolly Green Giant commercial with Norah as a little sprout. Give them a couple of cans of fresh-picked vegetables, and they would be all set.

He finished his lunch and went back to putting the bookcases together, more determined than ever to find out who had put that fear in Norah's eyes. Then he wanted ten minutes alone with the guy.

Two hours later, there was enough space in the room for him to help Norah move the furniture around. "Are you sure you want the couch there?" He'd never heard of anyone putting a sofa directly in front of bookcases.

"Yes, but leave about two feet between it and the shelves." Norah, who could now actually sit at her desk, was busy putting away office supplies and folders.

"What good is two feet going to do you?" He shoved the couch into the right position and frowned at the small space behind it. He had banged his head on the sloping ceiling at least fifty times so far today. He didn't remember the ceiling in his old bedroom being so low.

Norah went over to the sofa and walked the entire length behind it. Her hips never touched the back of the couch or a book. Her head never touched the ceiling. "See, there's plenty enough room."

"For you, yeah, but what about the rest of the world?" Five-year-old Tyler would barely fit back there, and there was no way he could stand in front of the bookcases without bending over and probably pulling something in his back.

"Ned, it's my private office, den, sitting room, whatever you want to call it. I'm not going to be entertaining up here, so the only person that has to fit back there is me. If I need a certain book, I can reach it without having to shove the couch out of the way."

He had to agree; for Norah, the room was perfect. A little cramped, but considering her size, Norah could fit another couch in here, and she would still be able to waltz around the furniture. The twenty-five by twelve room with its sloping ceilings felt like a walk-in closet to him. "I guess fairies don't need a lot of room."

"Listen, Porter, I don't make fun of your size." Norah put her hands on her hips and glared up at him.

"What's wrong with my size?" Lord, she was cute when she was mad.

"You're too big."

"You're too small," he countered right back. The heart of their problem was in the open now. Norah didn't like big men for some reason he was almost afraid to know about, and he was uncomfortable around little, petite women. He felt awkward and clumsy, which he knew he wasn't, but it didn't change how he felt.

He knew exactly when the awkward feeling had developed—in his senior year, when he'd finally had the famed Porter growth spurt. His girlfriend that year had been a cheerleader who was five foot, five inches tall. In September, he'd had a good two inches on her. By the time May rolled around and they went to the prom, he had towered over her, making them both feel awkward trying to dance. Kissing gave him a crimp in his neck, and he was always watching his feet.

Over the years, he'd learned to fit smoothly into

his body, but Norah's lack of height brought back all his old insecurities. "You got something against big men?"

Norah hesitated for a moment too long. He saw the spark of fear in her eyes before steely determination won out over it. "In general, no." Norah's chin rose a fraction of an inch. "You got something against short women?"

"In general, no." He couldn't resist teasing her back. He wanted to see her smile.

The corners of Norah's mouth kicked up. "Fine."

He nodded. "Fine. Now that we have that settled . . ."

"Yes?"

The caution in her eyes tore at his heart. Norah had lied. She was still leery of big men, even though she was putting on a very brave front. He wanted to ask her out for dinner, something better than pizza this time, but he held his tongue. He didn't think Norah would accept, and then the rest of the afternoon would be spent with an awkwardness between them. That was the last thing he wanted. Norah needed more time to get used to him. To his size. "Where do you want the recliner? Over there?" He nodded to the only logical space facing the portable television in the room.

"Please." Norah picked up a lamp and set it on the end table next to the couch. "I can't thank you enough, Ned. Without you, I'd still be struggling to get the bookcases into the house and up the stairs."

"No problem." He walked over to her desk and wrote down his cell number. "Next time you or your mom buy something big, heavy, or just awkward, call me. I'll stop by on the way home from work and bring it in for you." He knew his father or even Matthew would be more than glad to help Norah or her mom, but he wasn't going to leave their numbers. He wanted Norah to call him.

Norah glanced at the sticky note he stuck to the center of her desk. "Thanks."

Ned could tell by the way she wouldn't look at him that she was the one now feeling uncomfortable. "The room cleans up pretty well." Of course, if he had to spend any more time in it, he'd suffer from claustrophobia. He much preferred his office or even his living room with its large screen television and roaring fire in the winter.

Norah glanced around the room. "I guess you can say it's cozy."

Now that all of the furniture was in place, there wasn't anything left for him to do. "Well, I better get going. The grass isn't going to cut itself."

"Have I been keeping you from cutting it?"

"Nope. Did mine this morning." He gathered up the last two empty boxes. "Figured I come over and do my parents' yard since they are away this weekend."

"Anybody ever tell you you're sweet?"

He tried not to cringe. "Sweet, huh?" The kiss of death to any romantic relationship. He didn't want to be sweet. Nice would have been better. Sexy, the ultimate. "I think my Aunt Beatrice called me that when she pinched my checks when I was about five." He carried the empty boxes downstairs and stacked them on the back porch where Norah had piled all the other trash.

Norah followed him out onto the porch. "Thanks again, Ned."

"You're welcome." He really wanted to stay, but he couldn't think of an excuse. Norah's grass had been recently cut, and the flower gardens were shaping up nicely. "See you around." He stepped off the porch and headed for his parents' garage.

"Ned?"

He turned around. "Yeah?"

"Your Aunt Bea is a pretty good judge of character."

He chuckled all the way to the garage. Aunt Bea had married a con artist who had taken her for just about everything she owned. The story had a happy ending though. Aunt Bea had fallen in love with the prosecuting attorney, and they had been married for over twenty-five years now.

"So you really don't mind taking care of Zsa Zsa for the day?" Joanna looked at Norah, who was lying across Joanna's bed flipping through a garden magazine. The Pomeranian in question was weaving her way in and out of Joanna's feet, getting all excited thinking she was going somewhere. Today, the dog was staying home.

"I already told you, Mom, that I didn't." Norah tossed the magazine aside. "You and Karl have a great time in Bangor checking out all the competition."

"We aren't checking out the competition." Joanna frowned at herself in the full-length mirror. "I just mentioned to Karl that I wanted to see other galleries to see how they are set up, and he offered to take me into Bangor where there are a couple." Did the off-white slacks make her butt look big? Maybe she should change back into the navy.

"Karl sounds like a very nice man." Norah reached over the side of the bed and picked up Zsa Zsa.

"Would you like to come with us? Karl wouldn't mind." She slipped on her shoes and studied the whole effect in the mirror. Not bad for a middle-aged woman.

"No way am I playing third wheel on my mother's date." Norah snorted. "Besides, who will watch Princess here?" She flicked a finger at Zsa Zsa's blue bow.

"It's not a date."

"Keep telling yourself that." Norah laughed and indulged the dog by rubbing her belly. "Believe me, Karl thinks it's a date."

"How would you know? You've never met the man." Joanna picked up a lightweight cardigan and her purse. She was ready to go with five minutes to spare.

"Am I going to meet him this morning?" Norah seemed curious.

"Of course you are. What did you think? That he would sit out front and blow the horn till I came out?" Joanna wondered what her daughter was going to think of Karl. His first impression was somewhat disarming. With his loud shirts, long hair and beard, and sandals, one definitely got the wrong impression of him. "You know he's an artist, right?" Norah was going to flip when she saw the diamond stud earring in his ear.

"Yep, the one who does the wood sculptures down at the gallery." Norah noticed her hesitancy. "Why?"

"He just looks like an artist, that's all." Maybe this wasn't such a good idea after all. "Can I ask you a question and get an honest answer?"

"I'm not sixteen, Mom. You can't ground me if you don't like the answer, so shoot."

"What do you think of me dating?" There, she'd said it. She was dating Karl James. In no way could anyone construe this just as friends having lunch in the back booth at Krup's. She wanted her daughter's approval, but more importantly, she wanted Norah to see that she was fine. She was moving on with her life. That it was okay to move on.

"I think it's sweet." Norah grinned. "Now, don't get me wrong. I haven't met him yet, but if you like him, that's all I need to know. I trust your judgment."

"You do?" That was something she'd been hoping to hear.

"Of course I do." Norah sat up on the bed and plopped Zsa Zsa in her lap.

"Do you believe me?" She sat down on the comfortable reading chair she had placed in her bedroom and stared at her daughter. Norah was a beautiful woman, and it wasn't just a mother's prejudiced opinion. She just wished her daughter wouldn't dye her hair that bright a color of red. Norah had gorgeous naturally brown hair.

"When haven't I?"

"The day I told you I'd stayed with your father all those years because I loved him." She knew her daughter hadn't believed those words then, and she doubted she would believe them now. "Your father was a very good man ninety-nine percent of the time."

"Yeah, he's great. He only smacked his wife around one percent of the time."

Joanna cringed at the truth. "Yes, he did." They had gone over this before and probably would go over it again. "Your father only got that way when he drank." Of course, during the last years of their marriage, Vince had been drinking more than normal. It had been a terrible time in her life.

"Why didn't you leave him the first time he hit you?" Norah looked at her, and tears filled her eyes. "It was because of me, right?"

"Never." She needed to make her daughter see the truth. "I love you, Norah. Make no mistake about it, I would have walked and have taken you with me if he had ever raised a hand to you. You weren't the reason I stayed. I stayed with your father because I loved him."

"Until the night I happened by and caught him smacking you." Norah blinked back the tears. "The night he turned around and hit me because I was trying to protect you."

"With that one blow, Vince killed whatever love I still felt for him. He knew never to touch you." The nightmares about that night had finally stopped plaguing her. Vince had hit his own daughter. He had done the unforgivable. There had been no going back after that.

"But did you really have to attack him like that, Mom?" Norah managed a small smile. Time was finally healing that wound.

"He smacked you so hard you fell down." She gazed at her daughter's cheek and could still picture the black and blue mark his hand had left. "It was well worth the broken collarbone just to clobber him over the head with that lamp." She wasn't a violent person by nature, but something had snapped inside of her when Norah had hit the ground. No one, and she meant no one, laid a hand on her child. It didn't matter that Norah had been twenty-two years old at the time; she was still her baby.

Even today, she had a hard time believing she had smashed one of her good table lamps over her husband's head, but it had been the closest thing she could grab. Vince hadn't appreciated the headache and had given her a shove. She had ended up hitting the wall and cracking her collarbone. By the time she had shaken the stars out of her eyes, Norah had been on the phone to the police.

The neighbors had had a great show that night. She hoped they had enjoyed it because she never spent another night in that house. After a trip to the emergency room, Norah had taken her back to her apartment. Life, the selling of the house, and the divorce had all happened from there.

"Norah"—she leaned in closer and cradled her daughter's hands in between her own—"not all men hit women."

"Some do."

"Most don't." She squeezed Norah's hands and felt the rings her daughter liked to wear. "I need for you to stop feeling guilty. There is nothing for you to feel guilty about. I willingly and freely stayed with your father. It was my decision, and I was an adult at the time." She didn't know how else to express herself to Norah. Her daughter was carrying around a heavy burden of guilt. For some reason, Norah thought she should have been protecting her mother all those years.

"What will you do if a man ever hits you again?"

Was Norah afraid she would go right back into an abusive relationship? She knew that some women did, but she wasn't some woman. "Pray that the first object I pick up is heavy enough to do some

damage, and then call the police and press charges."
If she could find the courage to press charges
against her husband of twenty-five years, she could
do it to anyone. "You don't have to worry about
that, sweetie."

Norah gazed into her eyes for a long moment.
She wasn't sure what her daughter saw there, but
whatever it was, it seemed to satisfy her. "Okay."
Norah smiled. "So you like this Karl guy?"

The sound of the doorbell ringing caused them
both to jump. Joanna stood up; reached for her
sweater and purse, which she had placed on the
end of the bed; and chuckled. "Let's just say he's
different."

Norah followed her out of the bedroom. "How?"

"You'll see." She tugged at her blouse and
glanced in the mirror by the front door. This was
as good as she got. She opened the door and
smiled at Karl. "Come on in, and meet Norah."

Karl James stepped into the living room.

She could tell that he not only had dressed up
for the occasion, but that he was also nervous. Karl
had on a nice pair of khakis and another Hawaiian
shirt that had only tans and green palm trees, and
he was actually wearing shoes. "Karl, this is my
daughter, Norah."

"Hi, Norah, your mom is always talking about
you." Karl reached out a hand.

Norah shook his work-roughened hand and
grinned. Her mother was dating a Jerry Garcia
look-alike! No wonder Ned had wanted to know if
she had met Karl yet. "Nice to finally meet you,
Karl."

She glanced over at her mother who seemed

anxious and winked. Her mom relaxed and smiled back. "You two behave yourself up in Bangor today."

Karl glanced between mother and daughter. "You could come with us if you like. There's plenty of room."

"Thanks, but Zsa Zsa and I are planning on spending a relaxing Saturday at home." The dog wiggled and squirmed in her arms until Karl reached out and lightly scratched her behind an ear.

"If you're sure." Karl glanced over at Joanna. "Are you ready?"

"As I ever can be." Joanna seemed hesitant. "Are you sure you'll be okay?"

"Mom"—she rolled her eyes and shook her head—"how old am I?" She didn't know if her mother was that concerned for her or if she was that nervous to be going out with Karl. "You two go enjoy yourselves. Make a whole day of it. Heck, stay and have dinner there. I heard they have some great restaurants. Zsa Zsa and I will be fine."

Her mom and Karl left. Zsa Zsa whined as if her heart was breaking.

She stood in the living room and watched as Karl opened the passenger door to his pickup and helped her mother in. The gray ponytail had thrown her there for a moment, but at least, he was a gentleman. Her mother was dating a man who had longer hair than she did. How weird was that?

As the truck pulled away from the curb, the phone rang. She put Zsa Zsa down and headed for the kitchen.

"Hello?" She frowned down at the dog who had followed her into the kitchen and was now sitting by her feet looking up pitifully. Zsa Zsa probably wanted to be held all day. Great.

"Norah?"

"Yes?" She thought it was Ned, but she could hear a baby crying in the background.

"Hi, it's Ned, and I really, really need a favor."

"Okay, I'll bite." She owed Ned for all the work he had done last weekend.

"I need your help. My brothers and their wives went backpacking for the weekend. My parents were supposed to have the kids, but Aunt Sue took a turn for the worse, so they rushed to Boston late last night. Instead of seeing everyone disappointed, I volunteered to keep the kids for the weekend."

By the sound of it, the kids were having a blast. She grinned. "I see; so what do you need help with?" As if she didn't know already.

"Tyler is no problem. I can even handle Hunter and Morgan. But every time I put Amanda down, she cries. She wants to be held all the time, and I can't get her to fall asleep."

She could still hear baby Amanda in the background. Obviously, she wasn't being held. "I don't know much about kids, Ned." As she was an only child, she hadn't been exposed to a lot of children.

"You can hold Amanda. I saw you holding her at my mom's the other week. She likes you." Ned sounded desperate. "I'll bring you an entire load of firewood if you'll come over and help me out for a while."

Ned was more than desperate. A load of firewood wasn't cheap. "Can I bring Zsa Zsa with me? I got stuck babysitting her for the day."

"You can bring an entire circus complete with clowns and elephants if you'll just come."

"Okay. I'll leave in a couple of minutes." She needed a quick change of clothes. "Where do you live?"

Chapter Eight

Norah pulled in front of Ned's house and couldn't believe it what she saw. It wasn't a house; it was a log cabin, a huge log cabin out in the middle of the woods. She knew he worked in construction and built log homes; she just hadn't realized that he lived in one.

She picked up her purse and Zsa Zsa and got out of the car. Flipper came dashing around from the back of the house barking. The Pomeranian started barking back. She raised the fidgeting Zsa Zsa above her head and stood perfectly still as Flipper smelled her legs.

"Flipper, stop that!" yelled Ned as he stepped out onto the front porch. "Leave Norah and Zsa Zsa alone."

Tyler had beaten Ned out of the door and was hurrying down the steps to greet her. Three-year-old Hunter and Morgan followed Ned through the open screen door and raced after Tyler. For some reason, Hunter only had one sneaker on, and

Morgan was wearing only a pair of Care Bear underwear. A frazzled Ned stood on the porch holding a wide awake Amanda. She tried not to laugh at the sight, but it was hard.

"How's it going?" She shut the car door and petted Flipper, who whined contentedly under her hand. "Hi, Tyler," she greeted the five-year-old boy as he skidded to a halt in front of her, kicking up a spray of gravel.

"Hi, Norah. Uncle Ned said you were coming to rescue him."

"Did he now?" She glanced at Ned, who tried to appear innocent. Amanda was cradled securely in his one arm. Her little arms and feet were waving in every direction, but she wasn't crying. For some reason, she was wearing only a diaper, a T-shirt with duckies printed all over it, and one yellow sock.

Hunter and Morgan had finally joined Tyler as the greeting committee. "Hi, guys." Morgan's blond ponytails were crooked and messy, and she didn't seem to care that she was nearly naked or that she was calmly walking across sharp, little pieces of gravel. Hunter was the one hopping on one foot and acting as if they were hot coals.

"Can we play with Zsa Zsa?" asked Tyler.

"Sure, but let's wait until we are in the house. Flipper seems to upset her." The Pomeranian loved children and hated other dogs. She wasn't sure if Flipper's monstrous size bothered Zsa Zsa or if she was just jealous there was another dog on the scene trying to steal all the glory.

The kids all hurried toward the house. She walked at a more leisurely pace trying not to laugh at Ned. It looked like there were raw eggs on his shirt, and something brown and gooey was on his shorts. He hadn't shaved yet this morning, and he looked all rough and sexy, like he had just rolled out of bed. She really didn't want to think about Ned being in his or anyone else's bed. "What time did they drop them off to you?"

"Four-thirty." Ned held the screen door open for her. "They wanted to get an early start."

It was barely ten o'clock. Five and a half hours and Ned looked like he had already gone through hell and back once. She glanced at the baby in his arms and smiled. Little Amanda was merrily blowing bubbles with her lips. "Has she been up the whole time?" Amanda looked wide awake to her.

"I got her to sleep once for about ten minutes. As soon as I laid her down, she woke back up." Ned glanced around his house and grimaced. "Excuse the mess. It usually doesn't look like this."

"No problem." She could see that most of the clutter was kid related. One Dora the Explorer and two Spiderman sleeping bags were spread out on the living room's area rug, along with assorted pillows, stuffed animals, and overflowing suitcases. Someone didn't believe in packing light. By the looks of things, maybe John, Paul, and their wives weren't planning on coming back for the kids. "Do kids really need that many changes of clothes for one weekend?"

"If you think this looks bad, you should see the family room where all of Amanda's stuff was dumped." Ned led the way down the short hall and into the back of the house.

The entire back of the house was one huge open space. One end of the room was a big, roomy kitchen while the middle of the room had a nice size table and chairs. The other end of the room was the family room, which had a huge stone fireplace and multiple patio doors leading out to a screened-in porch. It would have been gorgeous if someone hadn't dumped what looked like an entire Babies"R"Us store in the middle of room. "How can one little baby need all of this?"

"Got me." Ned looked around the crowded room and shook his head. "I was still half asleep when they set this all up, carried in the three sleeping kids, and handed me a wide awake Amanda. Before I could even start a pot of coffee, they were gone like the wind. They couldn't get out of here fast enough." His expression softened as he glanced down at his niece in his arms. "She hasn't let me put her down since."

"Have any of that coffee left?" She had a feeling that she was going to need all the caffeine she could get. A portable playpen that was doubling as a crib was over by the unlit fireplace. A yellow and white swing was in position by one of the patio doors. An empty infant seat was sitting on the coffee table vibrating softly. A row of car seats of assorted sizes were lined up by the door leading into what might be an office or a den. Two diaper bags were on the couch, along with what appeared to be a dozen of baby blankets of different sizes and textures. A plastic baby bathtub stacked with towels, a half a dozen bottles, and a green plastic frog were on the kitchen table.

"I never got around to making it." Ned stepped over a scattered bucket of Legos that Zsa Zsa just sniffed. "I could put a pot on now if you like."

He looked like he could use the jolt more than she. The three older children were rolling around on the floor, trying to teach Zsa Zsa a new trick. The Pomeranian thought it was a game and was chasing the kids. "How about if I hold Amanda while you do that?" She reached out and took the happy infant. If Amanda started to cry, she was handing her right back to Ned.

"She was just changed and fed." Ned hurried over to the coffee pot. "I just can't get her to sleep."

She smiled down at the sweet baby. Amanda stared up at her in wide-eyed wonder. Amanda smelled like baby powder. "You change diapers?" She knew fathers pulled diaper duty nowadays, but Ned wasn't Amanda's father.

"Did you expect her to stay in the same one till her parents got home Sunday night?" Ned seemed amused about that possibility as he measured out the coffee grounds.

"I told you I wasn't very good with kids." Of course she knew the diaper had to be changed. It just seemed strange that a man would willingly volunteer for the job. Ned either loved his brothers and their families, or he was a super uncle.

"You're doing great with her." Ned pulled down two cups. "She's even starting to look sleepy. Keep doing whatever you're doing."

She wasn't doing anything but holding Amanda. She was standing by the table, keeping an eye on the other kids and Zsa Zsa, and slowly swaying back and forth on her feet. Amanda was looking a little dreary eyed now. "I think she might be going to sleep."

Ned seemed pleased with that possibility. "Did you have breakfast? I fixed the kids eggs a couple of hours ago. I could whip you up some."

Norah looked at the mess in the kitchen and tried not to laugh. Breakfast was still everywhere, and she meant everywhere—from the dirty dishes and plastic cups with cartoon characters on them to the two frying pans still sitting on the stove. "I ate already, but thanks."

Ned opened the dishwasher and started to load it while the coffee dripped.

"Can I ask why Morgan is only in her underwear?" It was driving her nuts. The little girl was now sitting in front of the television watching Sponge Bob.

"It's a bathroom thing." Ned scraped off the plates and stacked them in. "She's a big girl now, and she's begun using the potty all on her own. Problem is that she insists she can't go unless all her clothes are off."

"I see." She tried not to chuckle. She didn't want to bounce Amanda, whose eyes were finally closed.

"Kay says she will outgrow it soon." Ned piled in the cups and started to wipe down the counters.

"One would hope so. It might be a little awkward once she hits her teen years." She glanced over at Morgan, who was now clapping her hands and singing along with the television. Tyler was still playing with Zsa Zsa, and Hunter was building something with the Legos. Amanda's playpen was right in the middle of all the commotion.

"My brother is already getting gray hair just thinking about raising a teenage daughter." Ned poured the coffee. "What do you take in it?"

"Cream and sugar." Amanda gave a little sigh but never opened her eyes. She was finally asleep. "Is that a den or something?" She nodded in the direction of a doorway leading to another room.

"My office. Why?"

"Maybe if you move Amanda's playpen in there and partly close the door, it will keep the noise down. She might sleep longer for you."

Ned took one look at the sleeping Amanda and didn't hesitate. "Good call." He grabbed a lightweight pink blanket off the top of the pile and the playpen and carried them into the office.

She carefully followed, trying hard not to jostle the baby. She had no idea how to maneuver the sleeping infant out of her arms and into the bottom of the playpen without waking her. "Ned, I think I might need some help here," she whispered.

Ned fixed the nice soft pad in the bottom of the playpen and then gently lifted Amanda out of her arms. Amanda's little lips pouted for a moment and then seemed to search for the nipple of a bottle before relaxing into a sweet smile. She never woke up as he slowly laid her down and covered her up. "I am forever in your debt." Ned slowly backed out of the room.

She glanced around the room with appreciation. Both because it was the only room of the house the kids hadn't overtaken and because of the space. Now this was what an office was supposed to look like. The massive wooden desk had a new laptop sitting on it, and custom-made floor-to-ceiling bookshelves took up an entire wall, while a stone fireplace took up the other wall. Oh yeah, she could hunker down here over the winter months and write the great American novel. It was a real shame she had no idea of what the great American novel would consist of, but this would be the room to write it in.

She closed the door, leaving it open an inch or two, and followed Ned back to the kitchen. She gratefully took the cup he was holding out. "Thanks. I thought you built log homes?" It was an awfully impressive office for someone who played with oversized Lincoln Logs all day.

"During the good weather months." Ned took a sip of his coffee. "You can't do that kind of work during the harsher winter season, so I indulge in my other passion to pay the bills and keep Flipper in puppy chow."

"Which is?"

"I'm a freelance writer. Mostly for outdoor magazines. Hiking, backpacking, save the environment, articles like that."

"You're a journalist?" She didn't know why it shocked her to learn they had so much in common. Ned didn't look like any reporter she had ever met.

"No, I consider myself a freelance writer." Ned moved the diaper bags to the floor and sat on the couch. "I was an English Lit major in college; they didn't have any course called Log Construction 101."

She'd known he had gone to college. "Why not work in the field full time?" She sat down on the other end of the plush brown sofa and sank into its softness. All the children were now glued to the television watching the sponge who lived in a pineapple under the sea. Zsa Zsa was curled up in Tyler's lap.

"Doing what?"

"I'm sure the *Hancock Review* could use another good writer." Why hadn't he applied for her job when it had been open months ago? She glanced around his house and knew the answer. The salary, while decent, wasn't great. She would never be able to afford this house. Either log construction paid well, or she was writing for the wrong media.

"I figured out a long time ago, as my professors drummed it into my head, that I don't take directions very well." Ned reached over and shut the vibrating infant seat off. "I hate being told what I have to write and then having to do it on someone else's time schedule."

"Then you certainly don't want my job." It was one of the drawbacks to her job. Some of her assignments were just plain boring no matter how interesting she tried to make them. There was only so much anyone could say or do on the impending vote next month about putting parking meters on Main Street or about the fact that Sullivan's water authority wanted to raise their rates. "So you don't have deadlines?"

"Occasionally. Mostly, I write the article first, and send it to the magazine I think it fits. If they buy it, great; if not, I send it out to a different magazine. Sometimes, the editors of the magazines contact me for a certain article they have in mind for one of their issues. If the subject interests me and I have the time, I write it."

"Money's not a factor?" She'd never met anyone so independently wealthy that money didn't matter.

"Money always matters." Ned chuckled. "For the right amount, I can be persuaded to be very interested in a certain subject."

She chuckled along with him. Now she understood. Principles are nice, but they don't pay the bills. "Have you ever written about something you didn't want to or that you totally disagreed with?" She was thinking about the piece her editor wanted her to write next. Ned wasn't going to be too happy when she expressed the views opposing the logging industry. Flipper would go without his puppy chow if Ned didn't have those logs.

"In the beginning, yeah." Ned finished his coffee and set the empty cup on the table. "I was an unknown, so I had to take any article they threw my way. Over the years, I've not only made a name for myself, but I've also developed a pretty good feel for the market. I know what the readers of those magazines want to read. I don't write to please the editors any longer; I've learned to write for the reader. A really good editor will see that and appreciate my work."

"And if your job was to tick off everyone, what would you do?" When she'd first started the job at the paper, she had been thrilled to have a column of her own. She was now having second and third thoughts. The heart of the matter was that she had discovered she wasn't a confrontational person. She didn't like pushing people's hot buttons. She would rather make a friend than an enemy. As it was, she hadn't made too many friends since moving to Maine. Ned was probably her only one, and come two weeks, he wasn't going to be too happy with her.

"Someone giving you a hard time?" Ned's voice lowered, and a look of understanding softened his face.

"Ah, not yet." She didn't want to feel guilty. It was her job to write that article.

"Worried about an upcoming column?"

"Tom seems to know what buttons to push

around the county. He wants to open people's eyes and get them talking. Get them thinking outside of their safe, little boxes, as he so delicately puts it." As soon as Tom had mentioned the logging issues, she had voiced her objections against the piece. Her arguments had fallen on deaf ears.

"Tom's right, you know."

"Is he?" She wondered if Ned would remember this conversation in the coming weeks.

"Are you writing the facts and telling the truth as you see it in your column?"

"One man's fact is another man's fiction."

"Don't let the naysayers get to you, Norah. Write the facts; they will speak for themselves. Sometimes people need to see the other side of the story."

"Uncle Ned"—Hunter came running over to the couch and jumped on it—"I'm hungry."

Norah saved her coffee from being spilt all over the place and chuckled. "Easy there, Hunter."

Morgan came running over now that a commercial was on and climbed up on Ned's lap. "Me too, Uncle Ned."

Tyler, still holding the dog, bounced down between her and Hunter. "Me three."

"What do you guys want?" Ned seemed resigned to the fact that he was at their beck and call all weekend. He didn't seem too upset by it.

"What do you have?" asked Tyler.

"How about we do bananas?" Ned placed Morgan on her feet and headed for the kitchen. "Fruit won't ruin your lunch, and it will keep your parents happy."

She smiled at Morgan, who was spinning in circles. "Hey, ballerina girl, why don't we go find your clothes while Uncle Ned is peeling those bananas."

"Okay, but they're all wet. There was an accident in the sink," Morgan said as she dashed across the room heading for the powder room under the stairs.

Her feet faltered. What did Morgan mean by an accident in the sink?

Ned flashed her a crooked smile over his shoulder as he and the boys went in search of the bananas. "Thanks."

She felt the heat of that smile melting her knees and speeding up her heart rate. His smile wasn't the kind a man gave a friend. Ned was looking at her differently today. If she wasn't mistaken, there was now a subtle hint of desire in his gaze. Ned might have invited her over because he needed the help with the kids, but there was something more to the invitation.

The question now was what was she going to do about it?

By nine-thirty that night, Norah didn't know if she had the energy to get up off the couch and head home. She was exhausted. She watched as Ned slowly backed out of the den, partially closing the door behind him. Amanda was finally asleep for the third time that day and hopefully, for the night. The three other kids were crashed in the living room in their assorted sleeping bags, surrounded by a menagerie of stuffed animals.

"How do mothers do this every day?" She had new respect for the mothers of the world. Kay and

Jill in particular. The Porter children had been
nonstop all day. They had only slowed down long
enough to shovel food into their mouths before
moving on to the next activity. The boys had been
worse than Morgan, and the little girl had been
only semi-still while sitting in front of the television or when she had gotten her hair washed and
combed earlier. Ned had handled the boys' bath-
time, while she had done Morgan's with Amanda
looking on from her vibrating infant seat.

Ned plopped down on the sofa beside her. "Got
me how they do it. Working twelve-hour days placing logs is a vacation compared to this torture."
Ned leaned his head back, gave a hearty sigh, and
closed his eyes. A smile curved his mouth.

"You enjoyed yourself; I know you did." After
lunch, Ned had taken all three kids out back to
play ball while she sat in the shade cradling Amanda
and enjoying the view and the day. She had spent
hours watching Ned with the children and had realized how sweet, caring, and loving he had been
during every moment. Even when Hunter had
given Flipper his cupcake to eat or when Tyler had
accidently squirted him with the hose while filling
Flipper's water dish. Whenever Ned touched a
child, his voice had been soft and his hands gentle.

She glanced at his big work-roughened hands.
Hands that had cradled tiny Morgan's hands to
show her how to catch a ball. Hands that had
flipped the burgers on the grill and helped with
the boys' baths. Tender hands that had securely
held a squirming, slippery Amanda in her tub, all
the while making sure shampoo didn't drip into
her eyes.

Hands, she was positive, that would never strike

warming the cool evening air. Ned was built for
Maine's weather, while she, on the other hand,
wasn't looking forward to this coming winter.

"We're back to size, are we?" The corners of his
mouth kicked up into a small smile as he inched
closer. His chest was nearly touching her chin.

All it would take to put more room between
them was for her to lean back and press her back
into the side of the SUV. She held her ground.
"You started it."

Ned slowly put his hands on the roof of the
SUV. One on either side of her body. "So I did."
He studied her face as he blocked her in. "Can I
kiss you now?"

His tempting mouth seemed a long distance
away. "Can I stand on my tippy toes?" She didn't
want him to get a kink in his neck and then have to
stop short. She had a feeling that this kiss was
going to knock her socks off.

A low chuckle vibrated his chest. "You can do
anything you want as long as you kiss me back."
Ned slowly lowered his mouth and kissed her.

She stretched up and pressed herself into the
kiss. Into his heat.

Ned groaned deep in his throat but didn't take
his hands off the roof of the car. He didn't wrap
her in his arms and pull her closer. The only part
of her he was touching was her mouth.

She wanted more. Needed more. Ned was holding back, cheating them both out of their first kiss.
She wasn't going to allow him to do it. She
wrapped her arms around his neck and lightly bit
his lower lip.

Ned's hands left the roof and pulled her close as
his tongue swept over her lips.

One of them moaned, or maybe it was both of them. She didn't know or care. She was too busy sinking into his kiss to care if the world had stopped turning. Either she didn't remember what being kissed felt like, or Ned's kisses were in a class unto themselves.

Her fingers wove their way into his hair as she pulled him closer. Her tongue danced against his, and liquid heat pooled in her stomach.

The world shifted beneath her feet, and the next thing she felt was cool metal beneath her thighs as Ned sat her on the hood of her car.

Ned broke the intense kiss first. His mouth trailed away and nibbled down her neck to nuzzle a spot below her ear. "I knew it."

She tilted her head and gave him free access to anywhere he might want to trail that wickedly wonderful mouth of his. "Knew what?" Maybe the earth had stopped turning. She felt weightless and giddy.

Ned pulled back a couple of inches. His fingertip traced her lower lip with slow deliberation. "You taste like trouble."

She smiled and playfully nipped at his finger. "Is that good or bad?" By the way Ned was breathing heavily and by the slight tremble in his hand, she had the idea it might be good. Very good.

"Depends." Ned leaned forward and quickly kissed her again.

"On what?" She tried to pull his mouth back to hers, but he wasn't budging. There was no physical way to move him, so she pouted. There was no way she was done kissing Ned. She was dying of thirst, and she had just discovered the taste of water.

Ned grinned at her playful sulking, but he didn't

give her what she wanted. What she needed. "Definitely trouble."

"I'm not sure if I should be insulted or not." Ned seemed happy about something, but for the life of her, she couldn't figure out what. You didn't kiss a person senseless, tell her she was trouble, and then grin like a baboon about it.

"It's a compliment." Ned lifted her off the hood of her SUV and gently lowered her to her feet. He took particular care not to have her body slide down the length of his. "Are you going to come back tomorrow?"

"Are you asking?"

"Begging would be unmanly, wouldn't it?" Ned gave a low chuckle aimed at himself.

"The kids weren't that bad." She walked around the car door and dug the keys out of her purse. Her heart was still pumping a thousand liters of blood per second, and her voice still sounded low and husky. Ned Porter was the one who was trouble. A delicious, melt your socks kind of trouble. Where had the man learned to kiss like that?

"I'm not asking because of the kids." Ned held the door while she climbed inside.

"Who are you asking for?" She wanted to hear him say it. Say that she wasn't the only one feeling these feelings and missing that kiss. Suddenly, she was uncertain. Afraid that she had misread the entire situation and Ned. Could a man kiss a woman like that and have it not mean a thing to him?

Ned squatted down next to her and gently cupped her cheek. "Me, Norah." Ned's voice was a husky growl. "I want you to come for me."

She tried not to release the breath she had been holding in one big burst. A smile of wonderment pulled at her mouth. She hadn't misread the situation or Ned. "Would it be okay if I bring donuts for the kids?"

"They would love it." Ned trailed his thumb over her lower lip. "I wish I could drive you home, so I'd know you got there safely."

"I'm a big girl, Ned. I know how to drive at night." She wasn't insulted, even though she ought to be. In a way, it was kind of cute that Ned was worried about her. True gentlemen were getting few and far between in this everyone-was-an-equal world.

Ned's amused gaze roamed the length of her body, but he didn't comment on her size. "Promise to drive safely."

"Promise, and good night, Ned."

"Good night, Rose Fairy," Ned whispered as he closed her door and backed away from the car.

She started the SUV, gave him a quick wave and a smile, and pulled away. Thick trees were on either side of his driveway, but her headlights cut through the darkness and into the night.

The Jeep bounced over a couple of rough spots. Ancient shock absorbers screeched from the abuse. She glanced in the rearview mirror and saw Ned standing on the steps to the porch watching her leave.

She turned the bend in the drive and finally felt the blacktop of the road under the wheels. It would be smooth sailing all the way into town.

It was a real shame her relationship with Ned was going to be anything but smooth sailing after her column on the lumber industry hit the mailboxes.

Chapter Nine

Ned watched Norah as she pushed Tyler on the tire swing he had hung in the backyard this spring. Amanda was drooling on his shoulder, and Morgan and Hunter were trying to do somersaults while waiting for their turns again. Norah had been pushing for about half an hour, but she was still laughing with the kids and having a fun time. For what Norah lacked in height and weight, she made up for in sheer endurance. Norah could match any one of his sisters-in-law in the child care department.

He lightly patted Amanda's back. "Come on, young lady; you owe me a burp." She also owed him about three hours of sleep. He now understood why Paul and Jill had seemed so excited to get away for only one night. Being a parent to an infant wasn't conducive to a good night's sleep. At least Morgan, Hunter, and Tyler all slept through the night. He had actually gotten a shower and shaved this morning at six o'clock while all four kids were still sleeping. He wanted to be at least clean and presentable before Norah and that delectable mouth showed up on his front porch bearing donuts.

Those delicious sweets, which she had driven all the way into Sullivan for, had made her friends for life with the kids. Flipper had particularly enjoyed the frosted one with sprinkles that Tyler had slipped him under the table. The dog had probably gained five pounds this weekend.

Amanda bobbed her head and then let out a good, hearty burp that made him smile. She was definitely her father's daughter. Paul would be so proud. He used the spit-up cloth and wiped the drool of formula from her tiny rosebud lips before it got on his shirt. Today, he was trying to stay clean.

Eventually his brothers would show up and collect not only their children but also all the paraphernalia that was cluttering his home and overflowing his refrigerator. How one tiny baby required so many bottles of formula was still a mystery to him. The amazing part was that there were barely any full ones left. Amanda was also running out of diapers. Her parents better get their butts here before either one of those essentials ran out.

They had said they would be back before dinner, and it was almost that time now. Once they had all cleared out, he and Norah would be left alone for the remainder of the evening in peace and blissful quiet. He had a couple of steaks in the freezer that he could throw on the grill. Slide a few potatoes into the oven; toss a salad; open a bottle of wine; and presto, a romantic dinner for two. He could almost taste that steak and picture them enjoying the meal out in the screened porch with a few candles flickering nearby.

Standing in the screened porch, he watched as Norah brought the swing to a stop and Tyler jumped off and ran for the house. Norah, Hunter, and Morgan followed him at a more leisurely pace, with Flipper right on their heels. Tyler barreled onto the screened porch like he was on fire. He didn't see any tears or blood, which was always a good sign. "What's wrong?" The screen door slammed, causing Amanda to jump and begin fussing.

Tyler sped by him and into the house without a word.

He absently rubbed the baby's back and looked at Norah, who was smiling. "What's wrong with Tyler?" It couldn't be anything serious if she was smiling.

"He had to go potty." Norah and the kids came into the screened porch and plopped down on the chairs.

"We're hungry," Hunter said.

"Me too," Morgan added. Today, her hair looked much neater since Norah had been the one to comb it and put it up in pigtails this morning. Morgan also had on all her clothes and pink sneakers. Potty trips still required a complete strip down, but his niece was at least listening to Norah and putting her clothes back on.

Tyler, looking relieved, came back out of the house. "What's for dinner, Uncle Ned?"

Visions of that nice romantic dinner with Norah started to blur around the edges. Where were his brothers?

The ringing of the phone saved him from answering the kids. "I'll be right back." He headed into the house and picked up the kitchen phone. "Hello."

The kids and Norah followed him in. Norah reached for and carefully took Amanda from him as Paul's voice boomed in his ear. "Ned, that you?"

"Of course it's me; who did you think you were calling?"

"How come I'm not hearing any kids in the background?"

"Because I tied and gagged them all." He rolled his eyes and shook his head at Norah, who was giving him a funny look.

"That's good," said Paul cheerfully. "Hey, we're stopping in Franklin on the way back. We voted on picking up a bucket or two of chicken."

"Who voted? No one asked our opinions." His older brothers were always making decisions for everyone else. "We didn't get to vote, and we've been doing all the work."

"Who's we?"

"Norah Stevens and I." He flashed Norah a quick smile when she turned and looked at him. He prayed his brother wasn't going to make mountains out of molehills.

"The cute redhead?"

"Yes, Mom's neighbor." He knew Norah couldn't hear what his brother was saying, but she knew they were talking about her. "Make sure you bring enough for Norah. I'm sure she'll appreciate it." He wanted to end the conversation fast. He could hear both Kay and Jill in the background asking questions. "See you in about forty minutes," he said and then pressed the disconnect button.

"Looks like chicken for dinner, kids." He swung

Morgan up into the air. "That was your parents, sweetie. They are on their way, and they're picking up dinner. Think you can last that long?"

"Yes!" Morgan squealed with delight.

What was with girls and their high-pitched squeals? Hunter and Tyler both shouted, but they didn't squeal. He looked over at Norah and shrugged apologetically. "Hope you like chicken." He set Morgan back down on her feet and rubbed his ear.

"Chicken's fine." Norah looked apprehensive for a moment as she watched the three kids race into the living room to stare out the front windows. "I'm not causing any problems by being here, am I?"

"No." He stepped closer to Norah but didn't touch her. Today, she smelled like lavender. He watched her eyes, but not a trace of fear showed. The fear that he sometimes glimpsed in her beautiful green eyes bothered him. He relaxed and gently played with Amanda's hand, which was resting against Norah's bare shoulder. His niece's tiny fingers grasped one of his fingers and held on tight. "You do realize that there is going to be a lot of speculation as to why you are here."

"We'll tell them the truth." Norah's eyes sparkled with mischief.

"And that is?" He liked seeing her so relaxed and teasing around him. He definitely was going to have to kiss her more often.

"That you called me up begging for help with the kids. You couldn't handle them."

He laughed. "Do you think my brothers are going to believe that?" His brothers were smart enough to take one look at Norah and know exactly why he had called her yesterday morning. Norah had looked beautiful and comfortable yesterday dressed in a pair of shorts and a tank top. Today, she looked hot. Sexy hot.

Norah had traded in her shorts for a denim skirt that was short on material and long on temptation. Her plain green tank top from yesterday was gone, replaced with a skimpier, lacier white top. There was nothing indecent or out of the ordinary about her clothes. Hundreds, if not thousands, of women were probably wearing the same type of outfit today. However, on Norah's slim, compact body, the clothes should have come with a warning. A heat warning.

"Maybe not"—Norah's mischievous eyes sparkled brightly—"but your sisters-in-law will."

"Ouch." He bent forward and quickly kissed her surprised mouth while the kids weren't watching. "That's dirty pool. Kay and Jill won't let me watch them again if they think I can't handle them."

He had purposely kept his distance from Norah all day long. The need to taste her kisses had followed him into his dreams last night. Every time he had gotten to an interesting part in his dream, Amanda's cries had pulled him from Norah's arms. His frustration was running high, and he didn't need the kids running to their parents with tales about Uncle Ned kissing Norah.

"You like watching them, don't you?" Norah cradled Amanda.

"I'm only going to have so many nieces and nephews, so I like to get to know them. What about you—any nieces and nephews?" He didn't know too much about Norah or her family. Her parents were recently divorced, and she and her mother had moved to Maine, but that was about it. That and the fact that she didn't like to talk about her father. There was something to that, but as of yet, he couldn't quite put his finger on what had gone wrong in that relationship.

"I'm an only child." Norah sounded like that fact didn't bother her, but he had the feeling it meant something.

"I don't know if I should envy you or feel sorry for you. Growing up with three older brothers wasn't the easiest thing, but I wouldn't have it any other way." He took Amanda from her and started to change her diaper. "We're all pretty close."

"So why didn't Matthew help out this weekend?"

Ned looked up from what he was doing and grinned. "Because I didn't call him." He knew his brother would have dropped whatever he was doing this weekend to come help with the kids if he had been asked. Ned hadn't asked because he would have rather spent the time with Norah. He had counted on the kids acting as chaperons and making Norah feel a lot more comfortable with him. His plan had worked. She no longer jumped when he accidently touched her, and the fear was gone from her eyes.

"You called me instead." Norah's lips twitched with a smile she was trying to suppress.

He gave her a playful wink. "You're cuter," he said before turning all his attention back to a half dressed Amanda.

An hour later, he decided there were some merits to being an only child. His house was overrun with relatives. Paul had also called Matthew, who had shown up for dinner ten minutes before the food. The kids were running around like crazy, and his brothers were nudging each other like they had never seen a woman in his company before. To make matters worse, his sisters-in-law, who he used to like, were grilling Norah.

Norah looked a little shell-shocked. He couldn't blame her. The Porters en masse did tend to overpower people, both in their physical appearance and sheer numbers.

"Where did you say the playpen was?" asked Paul, glancing around the family room.

"In my office." Ned got up from the table and what remained of the Porter family dinner—one lone extra crispy chicken leg and two spoonfuls of cold mashed potatoes. "I'll get it for you."

He glanced at Norah, who was holding Amanda while Jill was loading all of the bottles into a bag. Kay was in the living room rolling up sleeping bags and passing them to John to carry out to the cars. Tyler was wrestling Flipper in the middle of the hall, and Hunter was bouncing on the couch. He didn't see Morgan, but she probably was outside loading the car with her dad.

He was trying to figure out how to get the playpen to close when Matthew joined him. "I think you have to remove the pad first, then unclamp the sides."

Matthew hadn't seemed surprised to find Norah at Ned's. Which meant Paul had told him on the phone. Ned wasn't quite sure what to say to his brother. Even with the dismally low ratio of women to men in the town, they had never competed for the same woman before. He didn't want to start now, but he distinctly remembered overhearing

Matthew ask Norah out. He also remembered Norah's very polite negative response.

He handed his brother the pad from the playpen, unclamped the sides, and gave the nylon loop at the bottom a tug upward. The playpen folded up nicely. "Thanks."

"You're welcome." Matthew started to shove the playpen into the nylon tote it had come in. "Norah seems right at home here."

His brother was being extremely nice. Too nice. He knew no one had missed the way Norah had set the table and how she seemed to know where everything was in the kitchen. He had seen Jill raise her eyebrows and give Kay a knowing look. Speculation on what other rooms of his house Norah might know her way around was flying fast and furiously through the Porter family. He'd be lucky if Norah ever talked to him again. "She's been helping with the kids all weekend."

"She seems nice." Matthew was waiting for him to fold up the cushioned pad.

"She is." He met his brother's gaze.

Matthew busted out laughing. "You still don't get it, do you?"

"Get what?"

"At Mom's cookout a few weeks ago, who do you think Norah was staring at the entire time?"

"I have no idea." He handed his brother the rolled up playpen pad. He refused to admit that the tightening in his gut had anything to do with jealousy.

"You, little brother." Matthew chuckled as he tucked the pad into the tote bag. "She couldn't take her eyes off you."

He stared at his brother as if he were insane. He

hadn't noticed Norah looking at him. "So that's why you asked her out—because she was watching me?"

"Nope, I asked her out so you would overhear and get jealous enough to ask her out yourself." Matthew zipped the tote closed.

"How did you know I'd overhear?" He had been in his parents' living room while they had been in the kitchen putting away leftovers. "You couldn't have seen me."

"Didn't need to actually see you to know you were there." Matthew picked up the bag and headed for the door. "Flipper was sitting in the doorway where I could see him. Your dog was staring right at the spot where you were standing." Matthew chuckled and gave him a wink. "You've got my blessings on this one, runt."

He stood alone in his office and watched his brother walk away. He didn't need his brother's blessing, and he still hated to be called runt, but a smile was tugging at his mouth anyway. Norah had been looking at him, and he had been looking back. It was nice to know the attraction had not only been instantaneous, but also mutual. It was also nice to know that he hadn't caused a rift between himself and Matthew.

Family was very important to him, but so was whatever was developing between him and Norah. There was something very special happening, and it wasn't only when he kissed her. Just spending time with her was wonderful and different. He was even getting used to all the noises she made whenever she moved. The gentle jangling of silver and copper bracelets, the tinkling of charms on her ankle bracelet, and even the sounds all her rings made when her fingers connected with something were becoming music to his heart.

Was it possible that this was the first step to falling in love, this waxing poetically about Celtic-designed jewelry on a certain little redhead? If it was, his brothers were going to be very amused in the coming weeks watching him fall.

Joanna glanced around her, feeling eighteen again. It wasn't a very comfortable feeling for a forty-five-year-old woman to be experiencing. Karl had picked her up after work, and instead of their usual BLTs or tuna melts at Krups, he had made reservations at the fanciest restaurant in town, Catch of the Day. It was Sunday evening, and the gallery had closed at six instead of the usual nine PM.

They had first stopped by her house to drop off Zsa Zsa. She'd had to leave the dog alone in the house since Norah was still at Ned's. She just hoped Zsa Zsa behaved herself tonight. The last time she had been left alone, she had gotten into a snit and chewed up one of the throw pillows on the couch.

She glanced around the crowded restaurant and realized she recognized a couple of the faces. Some of the people had stopped in the gallery; some were regulars at Krup's. Others, she could tell, were tourists. Misty Harbor was becoming home to her. She liked that. She liked that very much.

The last time she had been in a nice restaurant was when Norah had taken her out to celebrate her divorce. If her memory served her right, she had cried through the whole main entree for things that had never been and were never going to be. In a strange twist of fate, that sad little celebration had been a cleansing ritual. She had felt stronger than she had ever been when she left that restaurant, and she had been ready to start a new, different life.

Looking across the table at Karl, who was dressed in a retro Hawaiian shirt with his hair pulled neatly back in a ponytail, she had to marvel at fate and some of the strange twists it had been throwing at her lately. Who would have ever thought she would be dating an ex-FBI man who looked like he had dropped out of a rock and roll band back in the sixties. A man who wore an earring and drove a motorcycle. Her mother, if she were still alive, would have had heart failure.

"What did Ethan say when you told him about Howell's Gallery selling the same pottery for almost double his asking price?" Karl gave their waitress a smile as she placed their salads before them. "Thank you."

She gave the young woman a small smile of appreciation. "He asked if I saw anyone buying any of it." She had enjoyed browsing other galleries up in Bangor yesterday with Karl as her tour guide. In truth, Karl had been more interesting than the stuffy, highbrow galleries. She much preferred Ethan's style of sophistication and the relaxing, no pressure atmosphere. "I told him no. People were looking, appreciating its beauty, but I didn't see anyone buying."

"What did he say to that?" Karl placed the linen napkin across his lap, but he seemed more interested in what she had to say than in eating.

"He didn't say anything really. Just chuckled and went back to the pile of paperwork sitting on his desk." Ethan had been curious about some of her impressions both on the layout of the galleries and the merchandise. She had felt a little funny about voicing her opinion until she had realized that Ethan was really interested in what she thought. Then the poor man couldn't shut her up.

It was heady stuff having men not only ask for her opinion now but also seem to welcome it. The only opinion her ex-husband had ever asked her for was about what tie looked better with his suit on the rare occasions he accompanied her and Norah to church. Half the time, Vince had worn the one she hadn't picked just to irritate her.

"Ethan particularly liked my impressions of Christine's World of Art."

Karl almost choked on his cherry tomato. "You told Ethan I took you to Christine's?"

"Of course; it was one of the highlights of the day." The main highlight had been Karl's kiss goodnight. She had never kissed a man with a beard before, and she'd discovered she quite liked it. She wasn't sure if it was because of the beard or if a certain artist had a lot to do with her pleasure.

"Did you tell him about the mannequins?"

"How do you explain Christine's without them? I mean, they were throughout the entire place." Christine, as Karl had explained, was the wife of a very wealthy man, and for some reason unexplained throughout high society of Bangor, she thought it was her duty to be a patron of the arts. Christine's contribution was opening a gallery on her husband's dime and exhibiting the works of the starving artists of Bangor and the surrounding area.

There was a very good reason those artists were starving.

Joanna had never seen such a bizarre collection of paintings and sculptures in all her life. There was one entire section dedicated to paint by number pictures. Half of them weren't even done properly. Rusty farm equipment had been welded to empty missile shells and hailed as art. Horrible, frightening clay masks, all in the shape of animal heads and snapping and snarling, with saliva dripping from their mouths, lined an entire wall. For some strange reason, a stuffed grizzly bear greeted the clientele in the main foyer with its marble floors and crystal chandelier.

But the mannequins were what had caught her eye and imagination. Throughout all three levels of the gallery were scattered at least a hundred mannequins, all of which were dressed in outfits ranging from shorts and T-shirts, like tourists, to sequined gowns and tuxes for the opera goers. The mannequins were the customers, positioned so that they were staring at the displays with big painted on mouths wide open in wonder. No eyes. No noses. Not even hair; just wide open mouths gaping.

It had been strange seeing the plastic people wearing everything from well-accessorized Armani gowns to snow boots and parkas, but the weirdest part was that they were for sale. For a mere eighteen hundred dollars she could have owned her very own life-sized doll dressed in a Donna Karan suit and Jimmy Choo shoes.

Of course, Karl had whispered that that particular model looked, with her wide, obscene mouth, like a blow-up doll from a porn shop he'd once raided. She had been laughing so hard that they'd had to leave the gallery, and she never had gotten to see the paper clip structure displays. Karl had been nice enough to promise to take her back some other time, once the snobby clerk had forgotten what they looked like.

"What was Ethan's opinion of Christine's latest protégée?"

"He sprayed his coffee all over an invoice when I told him about the mannequin dressed like Roy Rogers and sitting on a stuffed horse." She chuckled at the memory and thought about all the fun she was having since she'd started working. "He made me promise to warn him before I talked about Christine and her latest *Save The Starving Artist* exhibit again." The amazing part was that Ethan gave her a paycheck at the end of the week for doing something she was finding so much enjoyment in.

"You and Ethan get along pretty well, don't you?" Karl dug into his salad.

"Yes, we do. Why?"

"Just curious." Karl gave her a smile that warmed her. "It's nice seeing someone happy in their job."

Karl knew the gallery was the first place she had ever worked. "Weren't you happy at the Bureau?" She found it fascinating that he had been a Federal agent.

"The day I had my twenty-five years in was the day I retired." Karl shrugged. "By the time I realized I was just butting my head against a concrete wall, I had too many years in to just walk away. I should have, but I didn't."

"What made you join in the first place?"

"I always wanted to be a cop like my dad and his dad before him." Karl wiped his mouth with his napkin. "During my training, I was approached and asked if I wanted to join the Bureau. I'll admit now that I was too flattered to say no. Next thing I knew, I was in Virginia learning the world was full of sick, twisted people that didn't follow the rules. Our hands, however, were tied with chains of red tape, rules, and regulations."

"Let me guess. You felt obliged to go after them anyway." She could see now how they had used Karl's youth and naivete to recruit him. There was a lot of good in Karl.

"Someone had to, but now I leave it up to the younger, more ambitious generation to go and get them." Karl smiled. "I don't regret it, Joanna. It was an experience of a lifetime, and on more than a few occasions, we actually got our man or woman, as the case may be."

"But it cost you so much."

"What did it cost me?"

"Your wife." She had seen the sadness in Karl's eyes when he talked about Susan and her kids. "A family of your own." Karl, even with being a sought-after artist and having a very busy career, was lonely. She knew the signs. She lived the signs.

"There are too many divorces nowadays to blame the Bureau. It didn't help our marriage, but there are many agents who are happily married and have children. They make it work."

"They aren't you." Joanna smiled as the waitress removed their empty salad plates.

"Are you saying I'm the type of guy who can't have a wife or a family?"

"Not at all." She gave him a teasing smile. "But if you're thinking about starting that family, you are definitely dating the wrong women."

Karl laughed along with her. "I'm too old to be starting one, but most of the women in my age group have children already." He shook his head and chuckled. "I've already dated a grandmother or two."

"Like me."

"You're too young to be a grandmother." Karl reached across the table and held her hand. "You look too young to have a daughter Norah's age."

"But I do. Norah's twenty-four."

"I know. I met her yesterday morning, remember?"

"Of course I remember. I'm not that old that senility has set in." Norah and she had talked when she had finally come in from her date with Karl last night. It had been nearing eleven o'clock, and Norah had been curled up on the sofa reading. She had a sneaking suspension her daughter had been waiting up for her, even though Norah had hotly denied that accusation.

"I didn't cause you any trouble by keeping you out too late, did I?"

Joanna snorted, then sheepishly said, "Almost. My daughter wants me to get a cell phone, so she can find me or I can call if I'm going to be late." She tried not to blush at the reversal of their mother-daughter roles.

"Excellent idea. I should have given Norah my cell phone number in case she needed you yesterday."

"Oh, she didn't need me." She smiled at the thought of her daughter being with Ned. "She was busy all day with Ned Porter and had just gotten home a little before me."

"I didn't know they were seeing each other." Karl could tell Joanna was pleased her daughter was getting out and about.

"Norah claims they aren't. Ned just needed help watching his nephews and nieces while their parents were away for the weekend."

"I see." So why was Joanna so pleased with herself? The flush in her cheeks brought a sparkle to her green eyes. Joanna had stopped fidgeting with the silverware by their third lunch date. She was more relaxed and open in his company.

"No, you don't." Joanna chuckled. "She went back over to Ned's house first thing this morning and told me not to make or hold dinner for her tonight."

"Didn't you tell her we already had plans for dinner?" It had taken him exactly one lunch date with Joanna to know he had to win her daughter over if there was going to be any chance of a relationship between them. Norah had been Joanna's whole world, but her world was growing. Zsa Zsa now played a very important part in it, along with Ethan's gallery. He'd never met a woman who loved to go to work as much as Joanna. He hoped he was becoming as important to Joanna as she was to him.

"Oh, I told her." Joanna's smile was slightly wicked. "After she told me about going to Ned's again."

He wanted to see that same smile curving her mouth while she was lying in his bed. Joanna Stevens was driving him nuts. Here he was pushing fifty, and he was totally, as his mother would have said, smitten with her. He could think of a couple other ways to phrase it, but Joanna didn't deserve those words. She had class, while he had seen the darker side of life, love, and lust.

"You're enjoying yourself, aren't you?" Joanna looked like a woman totally enjoying her life. "I take it you like Ned." He knew Ned and a couple of his brothers. The Porter boys came from good stock.

"Ned seems very nice, but I'm enjoying the fact that Norah is finally dating again."

"May I asked why she stopped?" Norah was a gorgeous young woman. Normally, he would have guessed a terrible heartbreak had put the tiny red-head off dating, but this was Joanna's daughter. There were secrets there.

Joanna's smile faded. "It was my fault." The secrets were back in her eyes.

"I can't imagine that." Joanna would never hurt her daughter in any way. "What happened?"

"I'd rather not talk about it, Karl." Joanna relaxed as the waitress carrying their dinner approached the table. "Oh look, the food's here."

He allowed Joanna to change the subject for now. With his connections, he could do a background check and find out every one of Joanna's secrets. But he couldn't bring himself to do that. He wanted Joanna to trust him enough to tell him those secrets herself.

"Oh good, I'm starved." He relaxed his posture and concentrated on putting Joanna at ease through the rest of the meal. She was a skittish little thing who sometimes acted as if she had been living in a cage or a prison for the last twenty-five years. Everything they did together or talked about seemed new and exciting to Joanna.

She had never ridden on a motorcycle, and she

wasn't sure if she wanted to try it on his. She even claimed that the last time she had been fishing was when she was ten; her father had taken her to some lake where they hadn't caught anything besides a waterlogged branch. Tuesday was her next day off, and he was taking her fishing out on Sunset Cove for the day.

He wanted to be the one to teach Joanna everything, from the feel of the wind in her hair to the joy of rowing a boat out into the middle of the cove to fish the day away. He also wanted to show her what was going to happen if she kept on kissing him the way she had last night when he walked her to the door. If they hadn't both known that Norah was inside the house waiting up for her mother, there was no telling how the night would have ended.

Joanna Stevens kissed like an angel with the devil on her mind, and he couldn't wait to kiss her again.

"I guess Norah's not home yet." Joanna walked up the walkway with Karl. Evening had fallen, and there weren't any lights lit inside the house. "Would you like to come in for some coffee?"

"That would be nice."

She glanced at the closed front door with its cheerful wreath made out of silk sunflowers. "I've got to warn you; Zsa Zsa doesn't like to be left alone."

Karl took the keys out of her hands and unlocked the door. "This means?"

"She might have destroyed the entire house while we ate dinner. I just can't bring myself to lock her in her cage while I'm gone." Joanna took a deep breath and opened the door.

"How much damage could she do? She's barely six inches high."

Karl was the first to laugh when she flipped the light switch. She didn't know if she should be mortified at the mess, furious at Zsa Zsa, or laugh along with him. "I must have left my closet door open."

Zsa Zsa had dragged every shoe and purse she could reach in the closet out to the middle of the living room floor. Thankfully, most of them didn't appear to be damaged by her little teeth. Only one victim, a wonderful little pink and green sequined clutch bag, lay torn to shreds on the rug. Sequins were everywhere, and Zsa Zsa was curled up on top of one of the couch pillows, apparently exhausted from her efforts.

"Bad doggie!"

The Pomeranian opened one eye and looked at her with total boredom. Her expression was so comical that Karl went into a fit of laughter.

Joanna bit her lip and tried not to join him. "Don't encourage her." She stared down at what had once been a stylish evening bag. "I liked that purse."

Karl stood beside her and stared solemnly down at the torn shreds of green satin, a gold clasp, and thousands of glittering sequins. "Is that what it was, a purse?"

She nodded. "It matched the gown I wore to my niece's wedding." Norah and she had flown to Colorado four years ago for the occasion. Vince had stayed home, claiming he needed to work to pay for the airline tickets.

Karl bent down and picked up the tattered piece

of damp, chewed up silk. "I'm sure with some super glue and thread, we can have it looking like new in no time." Karl's lips were still twitching with laughter.

She playfully whacked him on his arm. "You're incorrigible."

He caught her hand and pulled her to him. "And you are delectable." His mouth lowered to hers.

She went up on her toes and kissed him back. Mouth to mouth. Breath to breath. She had gone to sleep last night with his kiss on her mind. By this morning, she had blown it all out of proportion. No man could kiss that well, and she had been dying to kiss Karl again just to see how far off her memory had been.

Her memory hadn't done it justice.

The kiss was dangerously soft and sweet. It was seductive without being overpowering. She could feel the desire Karl was holding in check by the way his fingers trembled against her back. Desire she matched but wasn't ready to act upon. She wasn't ready for their relationship to take the next step. Trust wasn't built in a matter of weeks. She didn't know if she would ever be capable of wholeheartedly trusting a man again.

But she wanted to. She wanted to feel love and to give love freely.

Karl broke the kiss and slowly lowered his hands. "You're a dangerous woman, Joanna." He took a step back.

She laughed at the absurdity of that statement. The last thing she was was dangerous. "What makes you say that?" She had a hard time controlling her voice and her breathing.

"Because for the first time in life, I have this sudden need to vacuum." Karl glanced down at the scattered sequins. "Why don't you put the shoes and the purses away while I run the Hoover?" He bent down and handed her a navy pump. "Then we'll have our coffee."

Chapter
Ten

Norah couldn't believe she was having lunch with Kay and Jill. They had pulled her aside last weekend at Ned's and invited her for a girls' afternoon together. She couldn't refuse their invitation. Truth be told, she didn't want to. Kay and Jill were both nice and friendly, but she didn't think they had a lot in common. She was willing to give it a try though. Besides, what else did she have to do today? Her mom was either working all the time or with Karl. She had a feeling things were getting serious there, and she hadn't decided yet how she felt about that.

Jill was driving, and they were heading into Bangor. "You're going to love this place, Norah." Jill passed a truck that was doing about sixty as if it was standing still. Jill's SUV was in the same class as the military Hummer, but she hadn't heard her ask the F.A.A. tower for clearance for takeoff.

Kay acted as if having her ears pop from the decompression didn't bother her. Kay should have been an astronaut. "It's a tea room—like setting, but there are a lot of tables set outside in a garden."

"Sounds lovely." She couldn't imagine a more un-Kay and un-Jill place to eat. Tea parties in a garden just didn't seem like their type of place. "Do you eat there often?"

"No, neither one of us can drag our husbands past the bubbling cherub fountain or the doily welcome mat." Jill drummed her fingers on the steering wheel, looking for another semi to pass. "John and Paul won't go into any place in which the main color is pink."

She tried to control her mirth as she pictured two grown men being afraid of a color. "I see. So how did you find this place?"

"My mother told me about it," said Kay. "Her garden club meets there a couple of times a year."

It sounded like a place her mother would enjoy. She hung onto the "Oh shit" handle above the passenger door as Jill barreled down the exit ramp. Three blocks later, they turned into a small parking lot. Norah wanted to kiss the ground. Who in the world had taught Jill to drive, and why hadn't Ned warned her to make out her last will and testament before getting in the car with her?

"We're here," announced Jill.

"About time," muttered Kay as she opened up the back door and got out.

Norah slowly opened her door and climbed out. She was pretty sure her stomach and her nerves were back in Ellsworth somewhere. She made a mental note never to drive with Kay if Kay thought Jill was a slow driver. The little house next to them looked cute, but it was the gardens behind the brick cottage that were enchanting and overflowing with customers. "It looks lovely."

Jill and Kay grinned at each other. "Told you so." Kay looked so proud of herself.

Ten minutes later, they were sitting under a shady tree at a wonderful little table. A flowery tablecloth and matching napkins added to the garden effect. Tall glasses of iced tea with sprigs of mint were sitting in front of them.

Kay and Jill looked uneasy both at the surroundings and with her. Jill took the sprig of mint out of her tea and placed it on the paper doily that was acting as a coaster.

Norah took a sip of her unsweetened tea and thought it was delicious. "Okay, I can't stand it any longer. What's this all about?" She didn't know if she wanted to hear whatever was on their minds, but she couldn't stand the suspense anymore. There was a reason behind this friendly little outing. Her money was on Ned. He was the only common denominator. Somehow, however, she couldn't picture Kay and Jill driving all the way into Bangor with her to tell her she wasn't right for their brother-in-law.

She already knew she wasn't the perfect match for Ned, but the man could kiss. Oh, how that man could kiss.

"What do you mean?" asked Jill.

"Is this about Ned? Do you have a problem with us seeing each other?" She and Ned had gone out to dinner a couple of times this past week. Tonight she was going over to his place for steaks on the grill. So far their relationship hadn't progressed past hot kisses that ended up frustrating them both. But she wasn't ready to take the next step in their relationship.

"No, no, no," Kay uttered in disbelief. "Is that what you thought this was about?"

"Well, yes." She could see the look of distress on both of their faces. "So it's not about me seeing Ned?"

"No," Kay said. "We think you're great for Ned." Kay played with her napkin nervously. "It's more about us."

Jill nodded in agreement.

"What about you?" Maybe they needed a babysitter or something.

"We don't know how to explain this very well, but we're Porters now, so we are going to be blunt." Jill sat up straighter, mustered her courage, and asked. "How do you do it?"

"Do what?"

"Get the men to, you know, wait on you," Kay said.

"Wait on me?" She hadn't noticed anyone waiting on her. Wasn't she the one who had set the tables for their takeout chicken dinner the other night?

"Not really wait on you." Jill looked helplessly at Kay. "We're explaining this all wrong."

"John loves a strong, independent woman. One who he doesn't have to fuss over. One who loves what he loves. You know, camping, hiking, fishing, things like that," Kay explained.

"I would say he married the right woman then." As far as she could see, John and Kay were a perfect match.

"Paul's the same way. He likes knowing that if he

isn't home and I run out of firewood, I'll go out back, split a couple of logs, and keep everyone warm." Jill stirred another teaspoon of sugar into her tea.

"Being able to split firewood would, I think, be a bonus living in Maine." Norah had no doubt that Kay and Jill could cut down entire trees to keep their families warm. "I'm afraid I've never swung an ax in my entire life."

Kay and Jill looked at each other and smiled. "We kind of figured that one out for ourselves." Kay smiled at her to soften her words. "That's just it. I bet you that if you stood by a log with an ax in your hand, one of the Porters would come dashing over, take the ax away, and split the wood for you."

She wondered if she should mention that Ned had promised her an entire truckload of split wood for helping with the kids. "That would be bad?"

"No," clarified Kay. "The point is, none of the men would think twice if they saw Kay or me with an ax. And none of them would come rushing to do the job for us."

"We're not jealous, Norah." A becoming blush stained Jill's cheeks. "We just want some tips on being more girly like you."

"Our husbands, sad to say, treat us like buddies," added Kay. "We've watched them with you twice now. Once at the barbeque and once at Ned's. John actually waited on you, and Paul helped you clear the table. It was like we were invisible, and yet they stopped everything because there was a lady in the room."

"Well I'm glad they think I'm a lady, but so are

you two. I think they are just being polite, that's all." She relaxed now that they had that worked out. "I think Peggy just drilled good manners into their heads."

"Oh, they have manners all right," Jill grumbled. "Do you know what Paul bought me for my last birthday? Four brand new, top of the line tires for the SUV."

"John got me a vacuum for Christmas." Kay stirred the ice in her tea.

"Paul got me a new backpack and sleeping bag, and there were battery-operated boot warmers in my stocking."

"What did you want?" She was curious. If she had a husband and he bought her tires for her birthday, she was afraid she would have to divorce him or run him over with them.

"Something a little more personal." Jill pondered it for a moment. "Perfume maybe."

"Listen, Norah, we really appreciated you and Ned watching the kids last weekend." Kay grew silent as the waitress brought their fancy little sandwiches.

"The backpacking trip in the mountains was our husbands' idea of a getaway weekend." Jill looked at the crustless, triangle-cut cucumber sandwich before her and frowned. "You would think that for the price they charged, they would at least give you some meat in there."

Norah bit her lip. Kay and Jill looked like the quarter pounder with the works type of eaters to her. "Didn't you enjoy the trip?"

"Yes, but sweating all day and having nothing better than a mountain stream to splash off in isn't what we would call conducive to romance." Jill picked up her dainty little triangle and popped it into her mouth.

"I'm tired of being John's buddy." Kay looked at Jill, shrugged her shoulders, and blurted out, "We need your help, Norah."

"Sure, with what?"

"We see the way Ned's looking at you." Jill pushed her plate away.

"It's been a long time since Paul or John looked at either one of us like that." Kay didn't bother touching her lunch.

Norah tried not to blush. She had seen some of the heated looks Ned had given her, but she had hoped no one else had. "Let me get this straight. You want me to help you seduce your own husbands?"

"Yep." Jill met her gaze and didn't flinch.

"Why me?" What in the hell did she know about seduction? Or men, for that matter? "Can't you just go to Victoria's Secret and pick up something? Light a few candles, spray on some perfume, and open a bottle of wine?"

"We've never stepped foot into a Victoria's Secret, and John wouldn't drink wine if someone paid him. He's a beer kind of guy."

"We wouldn't know what to buy if we did go into the store," Jill said. "Neither one of us are up for a snobby sales clerk laughing at us."

"Never?" Norah looked at both women in wonder. She couldn't believe there was a woman under fifty who hadn't at least browsed through the lingerie section once or twice.

Kay and Jill shook their heads.

"Do you know where the nearest one is?" She

signaled to their waitress and asked for the check. Kay and Jill weren't eating their finger sandwiches.

"The mall." Kay reached for her purse and stood.

Jill joined her and jiggled her keys.

"Let's go." Norah grabbed her purse, pulled out a couple of bills, and handed them to the startled waitress. "Now, this is what an afternoon out with the girls should be about." They all walked briskly through the tearoom and out the front door. "John and Paul are going to be mighty surprised husbands tonight."

"Oh yeah," agreed Kay.

"Yeah, we have their credit cards," added Jill as she got in behind the wheel.

Norah looked at her mother, who was fussing over the roast, and then at the dining room table. It was set with fine white linens and her grandmom's best china. Her mother was pulling out all the stops on tonight's meal. There were even fresh flowers on both the table and the coffee table in the living room.

"You told Ned six, right?" Joanna slid the roast back into the oven.

"Yes, Mom." Norah couldn't believe how nervous her mother was at having both Karl and Ned over for dinner. "You told Karl six, right?"

"Of course I did." Her mother looked at her and then chuckled. "You were teasing me, weren't you?"

"Afraid so." Norah snatched one of the fancy little crackers her mother had arranged on a silver serving tray. The cream cheese and chives were a delicious touch. "Why so nervous? It's not like you haven't seen Karl nearly every night for weeks."

"I've never cooked for him before." Her mother smacked Norah's hand lightly when she reached for another cracker. "I forgot to ask him if he liked roast beef. I just assumed he did, and now it's too late. They will be here any minute, and the roast is done." Joanna looked at her in dawning horror. "Does Ned like roast? He's not allergic to beef or anything, is he?"

She chuckled and shook her head. "Mom, relax. Ned eats anything." Considering the size of the steak he had put away last night, her mother would be better off worrying about whether the roast was big enough. Karl was slimmer and less muscular than Ned, but they were nearly the same height. "I have never seen you put a bad meal on the table yet, and I'm twenty-four."

Her mother was a fantastic cook. It was a real shame she hadn't inherited that particular talent. Her idea of cooking dinner was poking holes in the film top and sliding the frozen meal into the microwave. But as Ned had pointed out last night, she chopped a mean salad.

"There's always a first time for something to go wrong." Joanna lifted the lid of the pot on the back burner and tested the potatoes. "Statistics show it usually happens at the most important meal too."

The sound of a motorcycle pulling into the driveway made her mother drop the lid back on the pot. "That's Karl."

"Has he gotten you on the bike yet?" She couldn't believe her mother was dating a man who not only wore an earring but also rode a Harley. A badass Hog that was the envy of every male in town. Then again, she was having a hard time believing she was having this double dinner date with her mother.

She felt as if she had stepped into the twilight zone of dating.

"Of course not." Her mother wiped her hands on her apron and then took it off. "Could you picture me riding the thing? I wouldn't even know how."

"You just sit there and hold on; that's it." She looked her mother up and down. "You would need a new outfit though. Taupe linen and silk clash with Harley black."

Her mother ran her fingers through her hair and checked her lipstick in the shine of the toaster. "What kind of outfit would be appropriate?"

She didn't know if her mother was really interested in going for a ride or if the thought of shopping for a new outfit was putting that flush in her cheeks. "Jeans, black boots, definitely a black leather jacket, and a cool pair of shades."

"Shades?"

"Sunglasses, Mom." The doorbell rang before she could tell her mom about the tattoos and the no bra rule.

Joanna hurried to the door as if it were prom night and her date was ten minutes late. Norah shook her head, popped another cracker into her mouth, and followed. The theme from the *Twilight Zone* was playing in her head.

Karl was standing on the doorstep. He was dressed in a lime green and pink Hawaiian shirt that could have blinded someone, and he was holding up two bottles. "I brought the wine. Flowers don't travel well on the bike."

"Two bottles?" Her mother stepped aside, and Karl entered the house.

"You didn't tell me what we were having, so I bought a bottle of red and a bottle of white."

She saw Ned's truck pull up in front of the house. "I'll go meet Ned." She left her mother and Karl alone and hurried down the walk.

Ned got out of the truck, opened his arms, and grinned. "Anxious to see me, are you?"

She wanted to throw herself into his arms and beg him to take her away for the evening. Watching her mother get all flustered and fluttery around Karl was just plain weird. She stopped short of his embrace. With her luck, her mother or his would be looking out the window. Exhibitionism wasn't her style. "You like roast beef, right?"

"Sure." Ned lowered his arms, leaned down, and gave her a quick kiss anyway. "If you cooked it, I'll eat it."

"My mother cooked, and you will enjoy every mouthful." She loved the way Ned smelled all fresh from the shower. "She's a nervous wreck over this meal."

Ned grinned. "Yes, ma'am. I will compliment her endlessly not only on her cooking abilities but also for having the foresight to bring you into this world."

"Just don't overdo it." She rolled her eyes. Her mother hadn't been born yesterday.

Ned glanced over at Karl's motorcycle, which was sitting in the driveway, and gave a low whistle. "Boy, I wish my mom was dating a guy who rode a Harley."

"I'm sure your father would have something to say about that." She couldn't believe boys and their toys.

"Not if he let my father take the Hog on a spin

up the coast for a couple of days." Ned reached for her hand and pulled her closer. "Only kidding."

"You better be." She liked the fact that for all his teasing, Ned had taken this meal with her mom seriously. He was dressed in a nice pair of Dockers and a plaid button-down shirt. There was not a wood chip or speck of sawdust in sight. He had even shaved.

"My mom would be the one riding it up the coast." He quickly kissed her again before she could comment. "Did I tell you that you look beautiful tonight?"

"No." She stood by the front door and playfully posed. "Feel free." She had picked up the gold and copper dress yesterday while shopping with Kay and Jill. Tonight, she had paired it up with her gypsy sandals and just about every copper and gold bangle bracelet in her jewelry box. She felt pretty and feminine.

Ned crowded her against the door. "How upset would your mother be if we missed dinner?"

She could feel the heat of Ned's gaze. This was the look Kay and Jill had been talking about yesterday. This was the look she was beginning to love. "Very."

Ned's mouth was playing with her ear. "You smell different tonight." His lips teased the soft spot below her ear.

Her knees started to melt, and she leaned in closer to his warmth. Ned knew exactly where to taste to make her want more. "It's a new perfume; do you like?"

"What's it called?" His mouth was doing incredible things to the side of her neck.

Maybe her mother wouldn't miss them during

dinner. She had Karl to keep her company. "Seductive Embrace." She had been envious of Kay's and Jill's plans for seducing their husbands, so she had bought a little weapon or two of her own. Thong underwear, garter belts, and the see-through black negligée Jill was eyeing were out, but a new fragrance and a Wonderbra seemed reasonable. Ned obviously appreciated her little shopping spree.

Ned groaned and took a step back. The heat in his gaze was raging brightly. "You like playing with fire, don't you?"

The old, naive Norah would have teased him and said yes. Then she would have lit the match herself. Experience had taught her differently. "People who play with fire usually get burnt eventually."

The heat in Ned's gaze cooled. He reached out and tenderly trailed a finger down the line of her jaw. "When do I learn who burnt you, Rose Fairy?"

She couldn't tell him. How do you explain to the man you are falling in love with that you are afraid he will turn around one day and become a monster? How could she tell Ned that without killing all that was wonderful and growing between them? She couldn't. Whatever was happening between Ned and herself was too new. Too fragile. She slowly shook her head and silently begged him to understand.

Ned frowned but didn't push the issue. "One day, you are going to have to tell me."

She gave a sad little smile. It was nice to know Ned was thinking about a future with her. If there was any chance of a future together, she would have to tell him. "One day." She reached up on her tippy toes and brushed his mouth with a kiss. "Are you ready for dinner?"

"With you, anytime." Ned opened the door, and the delicious smells of dinner cooking and the sound of Joanna giggling in the kitchen greeted them both.

Forty minutes later, she knew why her mother was so smitten with Karl James. The man had a wonderful sense of humor, and he obviously adored her mother. Joanna Stevens hung on his every word, which wasn't very hard to do considering the stories he told. The man had a way with words.

"You didn't," she gasped as she laughed along with everyone else at the table.

"Of course I tackled him. The man was running through the Dallas–Fort Worth airport in a chicken suit screaming about the sky falling." Karl chuckled along with them. "He was scaring the kids and the flight attendants."

"Then what happened?" Joanna was so engrossed in the tale that she actually had an elbow on the table.

"I straddled his back while spitting feathers out of my mouth until airport security finally caught up with us. They hauled him away on one of those golf carts they ride around in."

"In handcuffs?" Joanna asked.

"Nah, they couldn't fit them around his wrists with the costume on." Karl popped the last piece of his roll into his mouth. "What I didn't realize at the time was that some local television station had gotten ahold of the airport security tape and had aired it on the six o'clock news."

Karl shook his head. "It must have been a slow news day because stations across America picked it up by the eleven o'clock news. The footage was impressive as I had to make a leaping tackle dive over a row of seats to get him and then feathers began flying everywhere."

"You didn't get hurt, did you?" asked Joanna.

"Naw. But the next morning I showed up at work, and some clown had that chicken dance song playing at full volume throughout the place."

"Ah man. Did they bust on you bad?" Ned had polished off two servings of her mother's roast beef and lavished her with praise the whole time while doing it. Joanna had basked in the glory.

"Every chance they got." Karl smiled. "For about a month straight, someone kept hiding eggs in my desk. Never could figure out who the culprit was."

Norah stood up and started to clear the table. Dinner had been great, but the company had been better. She wholeheartedly approved of Karl James dating her mother. She had spent the entire meal checking out Karl, while her mother had not so subtly grilled Ned on everything from his job to his dog. She wouldn't be surprised if her mother insisted on a DNA sample.

"Here, I'll do that." Her mother tried to take the empty plate from her.

"I'll do the dishes, Mom. You cooked."

"Nonsense." Joanna started to clear the other end of the table. "Why don't you and Ned go take a walk or something. It's a beautiful evening."

"Why don't you and Karl go for a walk then?" she countered right back. Her mother could be very stubborn about how certain things were done. Messing in her kitchen was the main one. She was fully capable of loading the dishwasher and putting away the leftovers.

Her mother got that stubborn tilt to her chin. "I want to do it, Norah."

"I'll help her, Norah," Karl said as he stood up and started to gather up some bowls. The man was smart enough to read the signals right. "You and Ned go take that walk. I hear the harbor is quite gorgeous at night."

Ned stood up and reached for her hand. "Come on, Norah; we know when we're not wanted." He tugged her into the living room. "Better grab a sweater; it gets chilly once the sun starts to go down."

She knew when she was beat. Her mother never could surrender control of the kitchen. "Fine, but I'll want a chocolate ice cream cone from Bailey's if you make me walk all the way to the docks."

Ned rolled his eyes and winked at Karl. "If you stop complaining, I'll splurge for a double scoop."

"Fine. Let me get a sweater." She dashed upstairs and heard Karl and Ned both laugh.

Ned held Norah's hand as they slowly walked to the end of the dock. "See, isn't this nice." The sun had just about set, and Norah had put her sweater on while she was sitting in front of Bailey's enjoying her double scoop ice cream cone. He had a double scoop of butter pecan, and he'd avoided looking at Norah the entire time she was eating hers. There was something entirely too erotic about Norah licking her way around the cone.

"It's perfect." Norah was staring out into the harbor with its bobbing boats and the orange reflection of the setting sun on the water. "I keep promising myself that one of these days, I am going to get up early, drive to the lighthouse, and just sit there on the cliff watching the sun come up."

"Haven't you ever seen the sunrise?" He couldn't imagine a better way to start the day. In the construction business, the day started before dawn.

"Sort of, but only during the winter when it doesn't get light outside until later. I'm usually standing in front of a window cradling a cup of coffee in my hands and muttering about how cold it is and how warm the bed was." Norah took a step closer to him.

Ned moved his body so it blocked most of the ocean breeze from hitting her. Her billowing skirt was wrapping itself around his legs. He could even hear the charms on her ankle bracelet tinkling in the breeze. "You don't like winter?"

"Oh, I liked it as a kid. Snow days, sledding down hills, and Mom making me hot chocolate with marshmallows floating in it. What wasn't there to like about it?" Norah leaned into him. "Now, it means getting out of bed earlier so you can dig out the car and scrape the windshield. Then there's that really fun part—driving on ice surrounded by total morons who are driving either too fast or too slow. There is never a happy medium."

He had to laugh with her assessment. She was right on the mark. "You learn to keep the car in the garage, which will eliminate the scraping part, but the rest is pretty accurate." He wrapped his arms around her waist and rested his chin on top of her head. "We get hit with some pretty nasty storms, but on the coast here, we are actually warmer than the mountains to the west are."

"So what you are telling me is that I should be thankful my mother didn't want to open a hunting lodge out on Bear Mountain, right?"

"I'm very thankful your mother had a wonderful memory or two about her one trip to the Maine coast when she was first married." He placed a kiss on top of her head and hugged her closer. He knew it had been Norah's mom who had wanted to move to Maine as soon as the divorce was final. Norah had done a job search on the Internet, found the position at the *Hancock Review*, and landed the job with one interview. Finding and then buying the house next to his parents had been fate.

"Me too." Norah turned in his arms, reached up, and kissed him.

He loved her kisses. They stirred his body and his heart. How could one little woman slip into his heart so quickly? He broke the kiss by nipping her tempting lower lip. Norah Stevens was looking for trouble, and his usual iron self-control was slipping. He grabbed her by the waist and spun her in a circle.

Norah gave a shriek and then laughed as the world went spinning around. "Ned, put me down; I just had ice cream."

He could tell by the way her head was thrown back and by the wondrous smile curving her mouth that she wasn't about to be sick. Norah was enjoying herself. He lowered her to her feet and smiled down at her. "You have to stop kissing me like that."

"Why?" Norah's fingers were tangled in the front of his shirt.

"You know why." Ned watched the laughter slowly fade from her face as her fingers released his shirt. "I'm not pressuring you, Norah." He knew she wasn't ready to take the next step in their relationship. He just wanted to make sure she knew that he was, but he was willing to wait for her. For now.

"I know you're not." Norah took a step back, reached for his hand, and then started walking back toward solid ground. "What did you think of my column this week?"

"I still don't agree with it. Allowing oyster farming in some of the surrounding bays is just asking for trouble." It was the first thing he did on Wednesday morning—stop at the local Gas N' Go and pick up the paper. He sat in the parking lot enjoying a cup of coffee, and reading Norah's column, "Views From The Other Side."

"But it could be a financial windfall to some of the local fishermen, and it will supply food."

"What happens when an unusual storm hits those bays and upsets the whole farm industry despite all the precautions you listed nicely and neatly?" Ned looked down at Norah; he couldn't tell if she was for the oyster farming or against it. As was her style, she hadn't voiced her opinion in the column at all. Just the facts. "Those oysters will then be in the water. It's an ecosystem disaster waiting to happen. There's a reason those oysters aren't found naturally in those bays, and people can't go around playing God."

"No one said they were playing God."

"They didn't have to, Norah. You can't just relocate species and expect everyone and everything to live in harmony. It doesn't work that way."

"True."

He had a feeling she agreed with him on the subject, but she wasn't telling. "I have to admit, though, that some of your facts and figures are interesting. But there is still no way those permits will be issued."

"Preliminary meeting is next month."

"I know, and I'll be there." He didn't make his living from the sea, but he knew this decision would affect everyone. He wasn't going to let the issue pass just to put a few extra coins in some people's pockets. "So, are you going to give me a hint about what your column will be on this week? You're acting awfully secretive about it."

"Ah." Norah looked guilty, but in the fading light, it was hard to tell. "I think I'll let it surprise you."

Chapter Eleven

Ned pulled up in front of Norah's house and stared at her as she pushed the mower back and forth, cutting neat rows of grass. He had been so mad at her that he had actually seen red this morning. During the course of the day, the color hadn't faded much.

But darn it, she looked so incredibly sexy in her short little shorts and skimpy top and all sweaty from cutting the grass. How anyone could work up a sweat while using a self-propelled lawn mower was beyond him. Then again, she was wearing at least ten pounds of metal in the form of bracelets on her wrists. Just moving around would give her an all day workout.

He glanced down at the neatly folded newspaper lying on the seat next to him. Norah's column from this morning was turned face up for all the world to see. His little journalist had written about the logging industry, and not in very flattering terms.

No wonder she hadn't wanted to tell him what her next article was going to be. She had known he wasn't going to like it, yet she had written it anyway.

He drummed his fingers against the steering wheel. He was being unfair to Norah, and he knew it. It was her job to write that article, and while the facts she had quoted were right, they didn't tell the whole story. He wanted her to see the truth. His truth.

Daniel and Quinn had read Norah's column too but had wisely kept their opinions to themselves and let him work out his frustration. Considering he had set a record pace on the jobsite today, Daniel and Quinn had been too exhausted to say much of anything.

He was dirty and tired from putting in a twelve-hour day, and he wanted to strangle a certain little redhead.

Then he was going to kiss her senseless.

How could one barely five-foot-tall woman cause so many emotions all at once? Most of the time he had no idea if he was coming or going around her. One thing he did know was that he couldn't leave her with the impression he went around cutting down all the trees in the world and leaving Bambi and Thumper homeless. He considered himself very environmentally friendly. Just because he lived in a log home and worked at constructing them didn't mean he wanted to level all trees and make a dust bowl out of the world.

Norah made another pass with the mower and finally looked up and spotted him sitting there. It was hard to read her face as most of it was obstructed by the Phillies baseball cap she was wearing. She stopped pushing the mower and turned it off, but she didn't walk toward his truck.

It was time to pay the piper, and she knew it. The problem was, he was afraid to confront her. Afraid he would lose his temper and raise his voice. Afraid he would see that fear back in her eyes and know he was the one to put it there.

He took a deep, calming breath and let it out slowly while he counted to ten. Then he opened the door and got out of the truck.

Norah stood her ground and raised her chin a notch. He admired her bravery but was saddened that she thought it was necessary. He walked across the yard and stopped about three feet away. "Norah."

"Ned."

"I read your column this morning." He saw her flinch and felt like a heel. "It was interesting reading."

"Thank you." Norah's rings were tapping against the metal bar of the mower.

"You have anything planned for this weekend?" He shoved his hands into the pockets of his jeans and rocked back on his heels.

"Not particularly. Why?"

"You up for an overnight hike? There's a place out in Somerset County I would like to show you."

"What kind of place, and how much hiking?"

"It's an entire forest that was selectively clear-cut a couple years back." He could tell she was intrigued. "It will be an easy hike; I won't need any of my gear. Just a leisurely stroll up a mountain or two."

"We won't need sleeping bags or tents?"

"Those we will need; I was referring to my rock

climbing gear." He gave her a slow smile. "You up for the challenge, Rose Fairy?"

"I can stroll leisurely with the best of them." Norah gave him a wide grin. "What time are you picking me up?"

"I'll let you sleep late." His arms ached from not being able to reach out and hug her. She looked adorable. "I'll be here at five Saturday morning, and we'll be home after dinner on Sunday." He couldn't believe it. He was going to see Norah out in his world. His woods. Talk about a fish out of water.

"What do I need to bring?" Norah looked like she might be having second thoughts on this one.

"Wear jeans, a long sleeve shirt, and hiking boots." He was trying to make it easy on her. "Bring a change of clothes for Sunday, if you want, and maybe a sweatshirt and sweatpants to sleep in. Whatever you pack, you'll carry on your back along with a sleeping bag and a tent I have for you. I'll carry whatever supplies we'll be needing." He didn't want to bury her beneath a mountain of bottled water and cooking gear.

"Sounds easy enough." Norah looked him straight in the eye.

He leaned forward and gave her a quick kiss. "This doesn't let you off the hook. I'm still not happy with the column."

"Didn't think you would be." Norah visibly relaxed.

"I'll pick you up at five." He had a lot of work to do between now and then if he wanted to take the weekend off.

"I'll be waiting with bells on." Norah's smile was teasing.

He wouldn't put it past her. Considering the amount of jewelry she normally wore, bells wouldn't make that much of a difference. "Good. Since I'm packing everything, you're in charge of making a thermos full of coffee and something we can eat as breakfast while we drive."

"Consider it done."

He kissed her again because he couldn't stop himself. Kissing Norah was an addiction. He didn't pull her into a hug because he was disgustingly dirty from working all day. "Behave yourself till then, and if you have to write another column on the logging industry, call me. I'll give you the real story."

"I wrote the real story."

"One man's facts are another man's fiction." He quoted Nora's own words to her.

"I seem to have heard those words before."

"'Bye." He started back to the truck.

Norah stood there watching him with a wide smile curving her mouth.

"Oh, Norah?" He opened the driver's side door and looked across the hood at her.

"What?"

"Don't wear any perfume; the bugs will eat you alive."

By noon on Saturday, Norah was convinced she was going to die. *Leisurely stroll, my ass!* Ned's idea of a stroll was straight up the freaking side of a mountain. "How much further to where they cut the timber?" Her new hiking boots were killing her, but the seventeen-dollar socks that the sales clerk had sworn would prevent blisters actually seemed to be working. Now, if only her little piggies would stop aching.

"Are you ready for lunch?" Ned glanced over his shoulder at her and tried not to grimace at what he saw, but she noticed it anyway.

"Sure am; what are we having?" So she wasn't a raving beauty; sue her. She was so hungry she didn't care what she looked like as long as he fed her. With a sigh of relief, she lowered her backpack and plopped herself down on the nearest boulder. The rock was a little hard on the butt, but the nice-sized log about ten feet away looked dirty, and there was fuzzy stuff growing on it. There was no way she was sitting on that.

Ned gave a loud whistle and then lowered his pack. "Peanut butter and jelly sandwiches and an apple for dessert." He opened his pack and pulled out their lunch.

Flipper came charging through the woods from their left. The darn dog was covered in brambles, and he appeared to be smiling. Ned laughed at the sight, dug further into his pack, and pulled out an empty dog bowl. He poured some water into the bowl, and Flipper proceeded to lap it up, drenching everything within four feet of him.

Ned handed her the paper bag. "I packed you two sandwiches, thinking you might get extra hungry."

"Thanks." If she wasn't afraid her deodorant had stopped working about two hours ago, she would have kissed him. Instead, she reached for the bag and dug in.

Ned chuckled and sat down beside her. "You're not doing too badly for a first time hiker." He bit into his sandwich.

"I've done small hikes before." She unscrewed the cap from her bottle of water and took a long swallow. "You know, nature trails, scenic strolls around a lake, that kind of stuff." What she was doing with Ned wasn't strolling or even hiking. It was mountain climbing without the equipment. They had been heading straight up since leaving his parked truck in a pull-off area five hours ago. Five long and torturous hours ago.

Her thighs were never going to be the same.

"How come your boots look new?" Ned frowned at her feet.

"Because I just bought them last night." She tried to wiggle her toes, but they weren't budging. She wasn't sure if the boots were supposed to be that tight or if her feet had swollen.

"You went out and bought hiking boots?"

"You said I needed them." She thought they were big, clunky, and butt ugly, but they had been the cutest pair in her size. "The sales guy said I should break them in, but I told him I didn't have time. So we compromised." She pulled the hem of her jeans up, showing Ned her new pair of thick, expensive green socks. The kind of socks that experienced hikers wore. The kind of socks that would keep your feet warm until it reached forty degrees below zero. At anything lower than that temperature, she hadn't a clue about what would happen to her feet, nor was she ever going to find out. Winter vacations in the Antarctic weren't on her "Must Do Before I Die" list.

"I bought these, and I wore the boots around the mall and then home last night to soften them up some." They hadn't matched the green lace dress she had worn to work, but she'd figured what the heck, it wasn't like she knew anyone in Bangor. What were a few queer looks from strangers?

"Any blisters yet?"

"No, the socks are doing their job." She took another bite of her sandwich and moaned with delight. "I love strawberry jelly."

"That's good because we are having it for lunch again tomorrow."

"Great." She was feeling a little better now that she had gotten her breath back and was putting something in her stomach besides water. "You still didn't tell me how much farther to the clear-cutting."

"It's not clear-cutting; it's selective cutting, and you have been walking through it since we left the truck." Ned glanced around him. "This mountain has been harvested twice in the last ten years."

She looked around her in wonder. "Where?" It looked like a real forest to her. There were big trees, medium-sized trees, and even little baby ones. "What did they take?"

"Trees; straight, mature trees." Ned pointed to a crooked pine tree. "See how that one is bent and twisted. Now imagine trying to make a log for a home out of that."

"You can't." She smiled at the image in her mind. "So it stays."

"And seeds the ground around it with new, hopefully straight trees." Ned leaned back onto the boulder and put his face toward the sun. "Timbering, if done right, is a naturally renewable resource. Oh, sometimes it could use a little help now and again, but if we don't become too greedy, there'll be plenty of trees for our grandchildren not only to enjoy but also to use."

"You do know that not everyone thinks like you, right?" She liked Ned's perfect little world. Perfect little mountain. But the world wasn't a perfect place. She had triple checked those facts before putting into her column. She had known Ned, and quite a few other people, were going to challenge them.

"Yeah, but it would be a better world if they did." Ned laughed as he pulled his apple out of his bag. "Your facts were right, Norah. I can't argue them. I can only show you that there is another side to it. A side trying to keep people employed, trying to supply homes for those people, while keeping the forests green and thriving."

"So you brought me out to the middle of nowhere to show me crooked trees?" She had given quite a lot of thought to this overnight hike and what it would mean to their relationship. She was totally out of her element, while Ned was in his tracking through the woods and up a mountain. The man hadn't once pulled out a compass or a map. She, on the other hand, was totally lost. The only thing she did know was that the truck was parked downhill from where they were.

"Well, I would be able to point out some wildlife if you didn't scare them away with all the noise you make."

"What noise?" She glared at him and tried not to laugh. While he walked in front of her with barely a sound, she crashed through the underbrush, muttered obscenities at logs and rocks that were in her way, and in general, gasped for breath the entire hike. An elephant in a chicken coop would make less noise. "I only wore one bracelet." She held up her hand and wiggled her wrist. The copper bracelet didn't make a sound. "See, no clanging."

"I see." Ned reached into his pack and pulled out a treat for Flipper. "Here, boy, that's it until dinner. You're getting fat."

Norah looked at the hundred and fifty-pound, covered in black fur dog and shook her head. "How can you tell? Black is slimming, you know."

"Every time I turned around last weekend, Tyler was feeding him." Ned shoved the empty paper bags back into his pack and tossed his apple core into the woods. "Ready to go?"

She glanced in the direction she thought was up. The trees were so thick it was impossible to tell how much farther to the top. "Are we going all the way up to the top?"

"Not this trip." Ned strapped on his pack and helped her with hers. "I know a really good spot to make camp for the night. It's right near a stream where you can get cleaned up if you want."

"It's not too far, right?" She didn't know how much further she could leisurely stroll without breaking down and crying. She wanted a Jacuzzi and room service. Jill and Kay were absolutely right—backpacking wasn't conducive to romance. If she had been Kay or Jill, she would have made sure she made it to the top of this fricken' mountain just to shove her husband off.

"Just a little bit longer. You can make it." Ned gave a sharp whistle for Flipper, who had once again disappeared, and then headed up the mountain on some unseeable path.

She reached up, grabbed both straps of her new pack, and gave it a tug. The pack settled nicely against her back as she headed after Ned; she began singing about an ant and a rubber tree plant. In front of her, Ned's shoulders were shaking with laughter, but she didn't hear a sound.

Ned sat in front of the blazing fire and wondered what was taking Norah so long. He could hear Flipper barking nearby, but it wasn't his Lassie imitation of "come quick; Timmy fell into the well" bark. It was more like "look at me run back and forth through the stream getting Norah soaked, while I try to catch the spraying water with my tongue" bark. He didn't hear Norah yelling, so either she didn't care or she was already soaking wet.

The look of appreciation on Norah's face when he'd shown her the stream was well worth detouring around the mountain and not going to the top. He'd left her and Flipper by the shallow water with her backpack and told her to freshen up while he set up camp and got their fire going. If he hadn't added a couple of good-sized logs to the fire, it would have burned itself out by now. There wasn't that much of her to wash. Maybe he should go check on her. With the way Flipper was barking, there wasn't an animal around for a quarter of a mile.

Then again, his ear was still ringing from Norah's scream when a harmless little spider had made the fatal mistake of crawling up her arm. Norah had smashed the spider to smithereens, the whole time screaming at the top of her lungs. She had not only spooked every animal on the mountain, but she had also ruptured his eardrum. He'd nearly had a heart attack until he realized what the fool woman had been screaming about. He had all the confidence in the world that if Norah somehow managed to stumble across a snake, he, and the entire state of Maine, would know about it.

The sound of Flipper's barking growing closer alerted him to Norah's arrival before she came into sight. "Ned?"

"Follow Flipper; he'll show you the way." A moment later, Norah stepped into the small clearing, and his heart melted and his body heated. Norah hadn't just freshened up; she had totally bathed in the stream. Even her hair was freshly washed.

Norah was wearing pink-striped long pajama pants, a little bitty matching pink top, and a pink sweatshirt that she had left unzipped. A pair of pink flip-flops completed her slumber party in the woods outfit. She not only looked fresh and squeaky clean but like Barbie as well.

"Feel better?" He knew she wasn't used to hiking up mountains. But she had done him proud. She hadn't stopped, whined, or given up once.

"If the water had been a little warmer, I would have stayed in it longer." Norah dropped her pack by the tent. "Where can I put these so they will be dry by morning?"

Ned looked at her pair of wet socks. "Any blisters?" He got up and went in search of a branch.

"Not a one." Norah sat down on his sleeping bag, which was close to the fire and in front of the tent. She counted one tent. She leaned in close, and in the fading light, she saw that her sleeping bag had been unrolled inside the screened tent. There was barely enough room for it in the small nylon tent. If she sat up in the middle of the night, she would bump her head.

Ned followed her gaze as he jammed the end of

a branch into the ground near the fire. "You'll sleep in there; Flipper and I prefer to sleep out in the open."

"Under the stars and all of that?" Well, she now understood the sleeping arrangements. She had been thinking about them for the past few days. Ever since he'd invited her on an overnight hike.

"Nothing like it in the world." Ned took the wrung-out socks from her, gave them another good twist, and then hung them on the branch. "How about I go and clean up before it gets too dark. I'll put dinner on as soon as I get back."

"I could start it." She frowned at Ned's pack and wondered what he'd brought for dinner. She was starving, and there didn't appear to be a bucket of chicken or a T-bone steak in sight. She'd kill for a nice tall glass of iced tea with a slice of lemon floating in it.

"It only takes a couple of minutes to cook. I'll be right back." Ned reached for his pack, and Flipper came running to his side. "Stay." Ned pointed at her.

Flipper rolled his eyes and then plopped himself down under a nearby tree.

"He doesn't like me." She'd seen the look the dog gave her.

"Yes, he does," Ned chuckled, "but he likes splashing in the water more." Ned headed in the same direction she had just come from.

She looked around the surrounding area. The shadows were lengthening, and Flipper appeared to be snoring. Great; some protection he was. She eyed the top of Ned's sleeping bag for wayward spiders and found only a small twig. She was clean, comfortably dressed, and scared. Ned would have a field day with that one.

What was there to be afraid of? They hadn't seen an animal bigger than a chipmunk or another person the entire time they had been hiking. If a plane hadn't gone overhead, she might have thought they were the only two people left on the face of the earth.

She reached over and pulled her backpack next to her. It wasn't her fault she didn't shop at L.L. Bean or Lumberjacks-R-Us. She wasn't Kay or Jill. She dug into her pack and pulled out a flashlight and her small cosmetic bag. The flashlight had been her mother's idea, just in case she needed to use the little girl's bush in the middle of the night. The body lotion was hers.

She unscrewed the cap of her night moisturizer and began rubbing a few drops onto her face. She had taken the time to run a brush through her hair and clean her teeth down by the creek, but she had nixed the lotion. With Ned gone, she needed something to occupy her mind besides the thought of wolves, coyotes, and moose. Or was it mooses? Mices?

Two minutes later, she had the sweatshirt off, and she was slathering lotion on her shoulders and down her arms. She had taken Ned's words to heart, so she hadn't brought any sweet, flower-scented stuff with her. She had picked up travel size bottles of body wash and lotion that smelled like green tea at the mall after she'd bought the hiking boots and socks. She recapped the bottle, trimmed two broken fingernails with the clippers she'd packed, and then looked around again. No Ned, and it was getting darker.

A pile of wood and a hatchet were set neatly by the fire. She had heard Ned cutting it while she was bathing earlier. The man was a miniature version of Paul Bunyan and nature boy all rolled into one. He probably swung from vine to vine when nobody was looking. She reached out and put another log on the fire. She glanced behind her to make sure Chip and Dale hadn't coordinated an attack plan to take her out and steal the Tic Tacs she had in her pack.

Ned wouldn't have left her alone if there was any chance something would happen to her. She knew that, but she still wanted him to hurry back. There was a reason she'd never become a Girl Scout.

She rolled her pajamas up to her knees, kicked off the flip flops, and started to apply lotion to her legs and feet. The fire was nice and warm, but she couldn't really say it was cold out. She had a feeling that the temperature was going to fall during the night. Thankfully, the sleeping bag she had carried up the mountain looked soft and warm.

Ned entered the small clearing without her even hearing him. One minute, she was alone; the next, Ned was there. She gave a small squeal of surprise and dumped a little too much lotion onto her leg. "Geez, warn a gal the next time."

"Sorry." Ned grabbed a long stick and fixed the burning logs in the fire pit. "What are you doing?"

"My legs are dry." She noticed the way Ned was trying not to look at her legs. He was acting as if this was the nineteenth century, not the twenty-first. He had seen more of them the other day when she had been cutting the grass.

"You're supposed to be camping, Norah, not spending a night at the spa." Ned started to rummage through his pack, pulling out what he would need to make dinner.

"What do you mean, supposed to be camping?" She waved her arms at the surrounding trees and tent. "I am camping." She finished rubbing the delicious-smelling lotion into her feet. "I want to see where it is written in your camping handbook that I can't put on lotion."

Ned's lips twitched as he opened a huge can of stew and dumped it into a pot. "I don't have a camping handbook."

She looked into the pot and prayed she wasn't drooling. "Is that real stew?" Her stomach gave a low rumble. "Don't answer that; I'll eat it even if it's fake."

The amount of stuff Ned had fit into his pack was mind-boggling. Then again, the thing had to weigh forty pounds. She had offered to take some of the supplies, but Ned wouldn't hear of it and had only allowed her the sleeping bag. He'd even carried her tent.

"It's real stew, Norah." Ned pulled out a small metal frying pan, dumped a package of yellow flour into it, and started to add water. "It's a luxury out here, so enjoy it."

"Why so special?" She was watching whatever he was stirring turn into a thick, yellow paste. "What's that?"

"Corn bread, and I'm trying to impress you with my culinary skills." Ned placed the pan on a flat rock at the edge of the fire. "Am I succeeding?"

"I was blown away by the peanut butter and jelly." She stuck a finger into the batter and licked it. "For stew and corn bread, I might have to declare my undying love and devotion."

Ned chuckled. "God, you're easy."

"Nope, just hungry." She ran her fingers through

her drying hair to give it some body. She'd had that feeling you get when you've forgotten something this morning, but she hadn't figured out what it was until she'd started to wash her hair in the stream. She'd forgotten her styling gel. Tonight and tomorrow, Ned would see her hair in its natural state—à la flat.

"So now what do we do?"

"What do you mean?" Ned stirred the stew and moved it closer to the flames. He gave the pan with the corn meal a quarter turn and then pulled two metal plates from his pack.

The man had an entire kitchen in there. "This is it? You hike eight hours up the side of a mountain just to open a can of stew and sleep under the stars? You could do that in your backyard." No wonder Kay and Jill had been so frustrated with their husbands.

"It's more than that." Ned glanced around him. "It's the peace and quiet. Being surrounded by nature without another soul for miles. The tranquility."

She leaned back onto the sleeping bag and stared up at the evening sky. Daylight had faded, and the stars were just beginning to come out. "Okay, I grant you it's nice here." She hadn't really noticed the quiet until Ned had pointed it out. She closed her eyes and listened to the fire crackling and the night sounds of the forests. With Ned sitting three feet away, she felt safe. "I just wish we didn't have to hike so far to get here."

"Yeah, they could put a parking lot about three hundred yards away." Ned turned the frying pan another quarter turn. "Families could do bonfires and bring the popups and the trailers and their big ass generators for their refrigerators and heaters. Teenagers could have beer parties and take pot-shots at the deer."

"Okay, it wouldn't be the same." He didn't have to make it sound so depressing. "I concede the point. If it was easy to get to, more people would be here, and they would probably end up ruining it."

"It's because it is so hard to get to that people appreciate it more and take care of it." Ned dug Flipper's bowl out of his pack and filled it from the baggie of dog food he had brought. He set the bowl over by Flipper, who immediately jumped to his feet and started to eat.

"Maybe my boss would let me write a column on hiking in the wilderness."

"I'll be more than willing to supply you with any facts and statistics you need." Ned started to dish out the stew. He handed her a plate. "Careful; it's hot."

"Thanks, it smells delicious." Of course, liver and onions, her least favorite meal in the whole world, would have smelled like heaven. She took a small piece, blew on it, and then popped it into her mouth.

Ned sliced into the cornbread and dug her out a piece. "If you clean your plate, you get dessert."

"What's for dessert?" The cornbread tasted like butter-flavored cardboard, but it was filling.

"A pack of Ring Dings." Ned grinned. "They might be a little squished, but I figured you wouldn't mind."

She stopped eating and stared at him. What were the odds that he would know her favorite snack food? "What did you do—call my mother?"

"Nope." Ned continued eating his stew innocently.

"My mother called you?" Now that would be mortifying, but she couldn't picture her mother doing it. Her mother liked Ned. She told her so about five times a day. There was nothing subtle in her mother's attempt at matchmaking. Joanna was happy with Karl, and that meant her mother wanted everyone paired up and happy.

Ned shook his head. "Nope, haven't heard from her."

"So who told you I love Ring Dings?" Maybe someone at work had spilled the beans. After all, the whole place knew she kept a box of them in her bottom drawer.

"I think the word they used was addicted, not love." Ned polished off his stew and his bread.

"What? The entire town knows my diet?"

"Nope, just Hank and Beth down at the local Gas 'N Go. Beth swears you buy them nearly every morning with your coffee on the way to work."

"And they told you because?" She wondered if Beth had told him that she'd picked up a box of tampons there last week.

"They saw us having dinner the other night, and Beth wanted to make sure I knew your weakness." Ned wrapped up the rest of the corn bread and poured fresh water into Flipper's now empty bowl.

"What you are telling me is that a person can't have any secrets and shop at the Gas 'N Go."

"Or Barley's, or Krup's, or Claire's, or anywhere else in town. If there are any secrets in Misty Harbor, they aren't worth telling, or someone is paying a fortune to keep them quiet." Ned gathered up the dishes and the pots. "I'll go clean these in the stream, and be right back."

"What am I supposed to do while you're gone?" Evening wasn't falling; it had fallen. The woods were now in total darkness. "How about if I come with you?"

Ned held out his hand and smiled. "Come on, Rose Fairy; I'll make sure the bogeyman doesn't get you."

Chapter Twelve

The sleeping bag was soft beneath her, and the fire was warming her front, while Ned was snuggled up against her back. She lay there on her side, using her sweatshirt as a pillow, and stared, nearly mesmerized, at the fire. "I love all the colors that are in the flames and the way they move. It's almost like they are dancing."

Ned nuzzled the top of her head. "So, what do you think about hiking and the great outdoors now?"

"I think that if they put a Jacuzzi and a real bathroom up here, I'd never leave." She didn't know what Kay and Jill had been complaining about. She thought backpacking had a lot of romantic possibilities. Especially when your partner packed you Ring Dings and made you hot chocolate.

There was also something very seductive about lying beneath the stars and hearing nothing but the fire crackle.

"It would take away from the rustic ambiance."

"There's outhouse rustic, and then there's cave-man primitive. I prefer to live in the current century on certain things, like bathrooms."

"Point taken." Ned chuckled. "May I ask what happened with you, Kay, and Jill last Saturday?"

"What do you mean what happened? Nothing happened; we went to lunch and then did some shopping. Why?" As far as she knew, everyone had had a wonderful time.

Once Kay and Jill got into the swing of things, their inhibitions had been lowered, and then they had really had some fun in the mall. Kay dared Jill to buy a black thong; Jill countered with a red see-through teddy. It had been competitive shopping at its finest.

She had enjoyed the show, left it up to them as to what they should or shouldn't buy, and only voiced an opinion when she was asked. All she knew was that both women had been carrying a huge bag when they left the store, and the sales clerk had been beaming. Maybe Ned's brothers had gotten the credit card bills already?

"Something must have happened."

"Why do you say that? It was just a girl's afternoon out shopping."

"My brother John dropped a case of beer off at my place yesterday. Found it on the front porch when I got home from work with a note stuck to it."

"What did the note say?"

"Tell Norah thanks. It was signed John, and then he had drawn a smiley face. John isn't the kind of guy to draw smiley faces." Ned's fingers were slowly stroking the curve of her hip. "Want to tell me what I'm supposed to be thanking you for?"

"I have no idea." Oh, she had an idea, but she wasn't about to talk to Ned about his sister-in-law's choice of sleeping attire.

"What about Paul?"

"What about him? I haven't seen Paul since I was at your place when they came to pick up the kids."

"On Thursday night, he returned the chain saw he borrowed from me six months ago. He had it professionally sharpened for me." Ned's fingers trailed down over her thigh and then back up to her waist. "He too wanted me to convey his thanks. For some reason, he couldn't even stay for a beer or wipe the stupid grin off his face. He had to hurry home, and I'm pretty sure it was past the kids' bedtime."

She chuckled. Both of the Porter wives were bound and determined not only to seduce their husbands but also to bring a little romance back into their marriages. She had the feeling they were succeeding admirably. "I didn't do anything. Whatever Kay and Jill do in the privacy of their own homes is their business." She surely wasn't going to think about what they might be doing in their bedrooms with their poor, unsuspecting husbands.

Ned gently rolled her onto her back and smiled down at her. "I really don't want to know, do I?"

"Nope." She returned his smile. Lord, he was handsome tonight, all fresh from his own bath in the stream. Ned smelled like pine soap and the smoke from the fire. He'd managed to shave. She lifted her hand and stroked his smooth jaw.

"Are you the kind of guy that has to shave twice a day?"

"Depends." Ned turned his head and kissed the center of her palm.

"On what?" She loved the way his mouth smiled against her hand.

"What I'm planning on doing with my evening. If I'm going to be sitting home in front of the television or working in the office, then I don't bother." Ned's teeth playfully nipped at the base of her thumb.

"Tonight you shaved." She wrapped her free hand around the back of his neck. "What are your plans for this evening?"

"Kissing you." Ned's lips trailed over her wrist and to the sensitive area inside her elbow.

She had never known arms could be an erogenous zone. "I like a man with a plan."

Ned raised his head and looked at her. "Kissing you is very dangerous, Norah."

"How so?" She didn't see anything dangerous about kissing Ned. He made her feel safe.

"I don't want to stop." His thumb rubbed her lower lip, which was pouting. "You understand what I'm saying, don't you?"

She understood now. Ned was waiting for her to put the brakes on the physical side of their relationship like she had the other night when she had joined him for steaks and heated kisses at his place. Ned was going to have a long wait. "I came up here with you, didn't I?"

"This trip wasn't about us; it was about the article. There was, and is, no alternative motive, Norah. You're free to say and do anything you want. Anything you're comfortable with."

Ned was so sweet. A lot of men would have taken advantage of the romantic fire and seductive night. Not Ned. He was once again allowing her to call all the shots. Was it any wonder she was falling in love with him? "I'm comfortable with you." She reached up and kissed him. "I'm more than comfortable."

The heat between them exploded. Ned's mouth was gentle but hungry. She pulled him down on top of her and marveled at his size. Marveled that he didn't frighten her at all.

Ned caught most of his weight on his forearms as he broke the kiss. "Norah, I need for you to be sure."

"In one of the many little pockets on my backpack, you'll find a box of condoms I picked up last night at the mall." She ran her toes up his jean-covered leg and grinned. "I guess it's a good thing I didn't pick them up at the Gas 'N Go."

"You planned on seducing me?" Ned seemed both shocked and fascinated by her announcement.

"Oh yeah." Her fingers climbed their way up his chest. "Is it working?"

"Am I breathing heavy?" Ned was fighting a smile, but he was allowing her to trail her fingers wherever they wanted to go.

"Yes." Her fingers stroked his chest and dipped lower. Ned was definitely having a hard time breathing normally. She liked having the power to excite him.

Ned caught her hand as it dipped a little too low. "Then it's working."

"Good; you're easy." She loved the heat in Ned's

touch and gaze. She could see the reflection of the flames dancing in his brown eyes.

"Only for you, Rose Fairy." Ned's mouth lowered, and he whispered across her lips, "Only for you."

She welcomed his warmth. His touch. His sweet, hungry kisses. Mouth mated with mouth. Tongues danced, and the fire between them was finally allowed to rage out of control. Her hands tugged at his T-shirt. Ned broke the kiss long enough to pull his shirt over his head and toss it aside.

Her fingers wove their way through the dark curls scattered across his chest. His skin felt like fire beneath her touch. Warm, hard steel.

Ned's mouth skimmed its way down her throat and nuzzled at the swell of her breast. "I've dreamt about this moment." His hands slowly inched her top up her stomach, across her breasts, and then over her head. Ned's gaze was watching her eyes, not the skin he was exposing.

She was a little self-conscious about the size of her breasts. They were in perfect symmetry with the rest of her body, but considering the rest of her body was on the petite side, that wasn't saying much. No one was ever going to ask her to pose as a centerfold.

Ned's gaze lowered slowly as his hands rose and tenderly cupped Norah's breasts. He had never seen anything more perfect then her rose-tipped nipples silently begging for his attention. "You're beautiful." His mouth brushed one pouting nipple. His body was screaming at him to rush, to find heaven between her slender thighs. His mind was telling him to slow down. To savor it.

Norah moaned his name as he captured her nipple deep within his mouth. Her hands reached up and stroked his back, fanning the fire building within him. Her hips jerked upward, pressing against his jeans.

He nearly died when her fingers tugged at the snap on his jeans. "Easy, love; we have all night."

Norah shook her head and flattened her palm against the bulge in his pants. "I want you, Ned."

His hips jerked against her hand. His mouth captured hers in a kiss that showed her exactly how much he wanted her back. His fingers trembled as they slid under the waistband of her cotton pajama bottoms. He slowly slid them over her hips and down her legs.

Norah was breathing fast and driving him closer to the edge. He wanted their first time to be slow, gentle, and earth shattering. His self-control was slipping with her every moan, her every touch. He moved away and reached for the small side pocket on his backpack.

He fumbled with the box, causing Norah to smile. She was breathtakingly beautiful with the fire bathing her skin in golden light. She looked like a goddess. "I came prepared too."

"I see." Norah looked at the foil packet in his hand and then at his jeans, which were still on. "You need any help with that?"

"If you help, it will be all over before it starts." He couldn't believe how close to the edge he was. Norah made him feel like an untried school boy. He kicked off his jeans and made sure there was no way for Norah to touch him where he wanted to be touched the most. He didn't trust himself to act like a gentleman if she wrapped her fingers around him. He ran his fingertips lightly up her legs and over her thighs.

Norah closed her eyes and bit her lower lip. She was afraid she would disgrace herself and beg. She had never felt like this in her entire life, and Ned seemed bound and determined to take his good, old, sweet time. She didn't want that this time, sweet as it might be. She wanted Ned, and she wanted him now.

Her thighs fell open as Ned's fingers lightly stroked her. She was moist and ready for him. She had been ready for him for over a week. "Now, Ned."

Ned's lips trailed over her hip bone, and he chuckled against her stomach. "Patience, Norah, patience." His mouth nuzzled the underside of her breasts as his fingers moved in the same rhythm his hips were jerking.

Her hands stroked down his back and cupped his muscular buttocks. She opened her trembling thighs wider and arched her back as Ned playfully teased her nipples with his lips. She was out of patience, and the fool man wasn't listening to reason.

She reached between them and took him in her hand. Ned had already put the condom on, and he hissed and arched his back as she gently squeezed. Ned's hands grabbed her hips as she brought them up off the sleeping bag and wrapped her legs around his thighs. "We'll go slow the next time, Ned." She positioned the head of his penis against her opening. "Promise."

Ned slowly slid inside her warm, tight channel. He felt the way she clung to his every inch as he slowly pulled back out. It was as if she were trying to hold him deep inside her. To grip him tight and hold him fast. He plunged back in, and Norah came apart in his arms. Two swift thrusts, and he joined her.

Five minutes later, he was still trying to catch his breath while rehashing what had just happened. Norah was curled up beside him, fast asleep and using his arm as a pillow. Thankfully, in the heat of the moment, none of their clothes had been tossed into the fire.

Norah's red hair was dry, and it was going in every direction. Her lips were red and swollen from his kisses, and there was a becoming flush on her face. Her breasts had the same flush, and the diamonds marching up the curves of her ears caught the firelight and glistened. Maybe they were real diamonds after all. He reached out and lightly touched a rose-colored nipple. The nipple quivered, and a small smile curved Norah's mouth as she slept.

The only thing he was wearing was a stupid grin and a satisfied expression.

They had made love under the stars out in the open. He was half tempted just to spend the night where they were, but he didn't think Norah would appreciate it. Come morning, it was bound to be cold. He glanced toward the tent and slowly rolled to his feet. Norah didn't even budge.

Five minutes later, he had Norah tucked in between the two sleeping bags inside the tent. She had mumbled something incoherent as he carried her inside the low tent, almost dropping her twice. The fire was nearly out, their clothes were now folded neatly and placed at the bottom of the tent, and Flipper was snoring under a tree nearby.

All was right in his world.

He crawled into the tent, and zipped the screen panel closed. The light from the dying embers gave him enough to see by as he crawled into bed with his rose fairy.

Ned woke from either the most erotic lifelike dream he'd ever had, or Norah's fingers were really exploring his body in the most tantalizing way. He was afraid to open his eyes and ruin the moment. "If this is a dream, don't you dare wake me up."

A soft chuckle sounded against his chest. "It's not a dream." Norah's mouth trailed across his stomach, following the direction her fingers had taken.

His body, which was already hard and throbbing, grew painful. "Not that I mind, but can I ask what you are doing?" She was not just playing with fire; she was lighting the dynamite fuse.

"If you have to ask"—Norah raised her head and frowned down at him—"I'm not doing this right."

In the early morning light with her hair sticking out in every direction, she looked sleepy eyed and incredibly sexy. She even had a crease from using her sweatshirt as a pillow going down one of her cheeks. He thought she was the most beautiful woman in the world. "You're doing it right." His experience with women, while not vast by anyone's stretch of the imagination, told him not to pick a fight the first thing in the morning. Agree to whatever she wanted. "Ah, keep on doing whatever you're doing."

"I'm being slow and gentle," Norah's fingers wandered up his thigh. "Just like I promised."

Ned lay there wondering what he had ever done in life to deserve Norah and how fast they could get down off the mountain and back to his place. He wanted her in his bed, a real bed with a thick mattress and luxurious blankets. Not on the ground with only a sleeping bag between his bare butt and a pointy rock.

Norah's slow just might kill him.

Ned stood silently in the shadow of a tree and watched Norah. The look of wonder and excitement on her face went straight to his heart. Norah was barely breathing as she watched a mother deer and her fawn drink from the stream. Flipper, off scouting in a different direction, was missing the show. With Flipper galloping nearby, there wouldn't have been a show.

A moment later, both deer startled and ran into the woods. Norah turned to him with an expression of pure delight on her face. "Did you see them?"

"Yes." He looked to his left as Flipper came loping out of a thick stand of trees. His dog wasn't known for his stealth. "That's who scared them off."

Norah looked at Flipper, who dashed into the stream, spraying water in every direction. A herd of wildebeests would have kicked up less water. "Crazy mutt."

He laughed as his purebred, AKC-registered dog plopped himself down in two feet of water. Flipper rested his chin on a rock and lay there, letting the water flow around him. He couldn't argue with Norah's assessment. "He's just hot."

"If he'd stopped running around like an idiot, he wouldn't be hot." Norah joined him by the tree and handed him the metal dishes she had just finished washing. "There, the breakfast dishes are done."

"I told you I would do them." He had been busy folding up their tent when she and the dirty dishes had disappeared. By the time they had awakened the second time, breakfast had been more like brunch.

"You cooked, so it was only fair that I clean up." Norah reached up and quickly kissed him.

He couldn't grab her and hold the dishes. The little sneak. Norah knew exactly where her kisses would lead. The same place where her bathing in the stream this morning had led. Here he had thought he was prepared and optimistic by packing two condoms in his backpack. Thankfully, Norah had been a better Girl Scout than he had been a Boy Scout. The little minx.

Norah headed back to camp with Flipper at her heels. Not only had Norah slipped her way into his heart, but she had enslaved his dog as well. There was indeed something enchanting about his rose fairy.

He watched as she disappeared into the woods. For being such a little thing, she sure did pack a wallop. He had been wrong about Norah. It wasn't the physical size, strength, or bearing that mattered in a woman. The only thing that truly mattered was what was in her heart. Norah had given him her trust when they made love. It was the most precious gift he had received.

This morning in the clear, bright light of the shining sun, he had watched her eyes when they

had made love down at the stream. He had read
many emotions in their brilliant green depths—
desire, need, laughter, and satisfaction. Not once
did he glimpse the fear that had pulled at his
heart. While he was thankful for that, he was still
curious as to what had put that fear there in the
first place.

While Norah had trusted him with her body, she
still held a secret. A secret that he was afraid he
had to know the answer to. His love for her demanded an answer, and then he was going to right
whatever wrong had been done to her.

He knew he wasn't going to get the answer
today. They had a long way to hike to get down the
mountain. The good news was that it was all downhill. The bad news was that his truck was a good six
hours away, and he already wanted her again.
Backpacking off this mountain was going to be
damn uncomfortable.

➤ Karl James stood back and watched Joanna as
she slowly walked around his workshop. He was as
nervous as a turkey on Thanksgiving morning.
Very few people had been allowed in his workshop, and he hadn't worried about any of their
opinions. They hadn't mattered to him. Joanna's
opinion mattered. It mattered more than he cared
to think about.

Zsa Zsa, who was following in Joanna's footsteps,
sniffed at a pile of wood chips and sneezed. At
least, he thought it was a sneeze. With Zsa Zsa's
high-pitched yelping, it was hard to tell. Maybe it
was a hiccup. Sawdust was clinging to the Pomeran-

ian's brown hair as she made her way in and out of some of the bigger pieces of wood.

Joanna seemed more interested in her surroundings than in her dog. It was a first. Usually Joanna babied Zsa Zsa. A sneeze would have at least prompted a phone call to the vet. He didn't know if he should take Joanna's intense curiosity as a good sign or a bad. He was fascinated by the expressions on her face as she studied some of the finished pieces and the two he was working on.

The way she worried her lower lip between her teeth drove him crazy. The way she kissed drove him crazier. He'd be fifty years old in September, and he'd never wanted a woman as much as he wanted Joanna. And that is what scared him.

He had a sick feeling in the pit of his stomach that Joanna's secrets concerned her ex-husband and abuse. He'd seen the signs before. Joanna was just better at concealing them than most women. He was treading so carefully around her because he was afraid that he'd startle or scare her. It was like walking on eggshells and being constantly worried about what he might be cracking underneath his size ten sandals.

With all his contacts still in the FBI, he could pull in a favor or two and, within a matter of days, find out what had put the fear in Joanna's eyes. He couldn't bring himself to do it. He couldn't invade her privacy like that. Besides, something primitive down deep inside him needed her to be the one to tell him.

So he'd bide his time and pray he didn't smash too many eggshells.

This afternoon had been the perfect time to invite Joanna to see his workshop. Her daughter, Norah, was hiking with Ned Porter, and Joanna had the day off. Last night's late date had been short and frustrating. At least on his part. Joanna had seemed to enjoy the late night snack on her back porch after she had gotten home from work. He had supplied the food, while she'd supplied the good china and ice for the wine bucket.

They had had the house to themselves, yet he had left before the witching hour. Joanna hadn't been ready to take the next step in their growing relationship. He honestly didn't know if she ever would be. Time would tell, but if her kisses got any hotter, he didn't think he would be able to wait her out.

He glanced across the room to where Joanna was studying a piece he had just started this week. To the untrained eye, it wouldn't look like anything besides a six-foot tree trunk that someone had taken an ax to in a fit of rage. To the trained eye, it would look like a six-foot hunk of wood someone had taken an ax to. To him, he knew exactly what the tree was meant to be. What it was going to be. He couldn't resist asking, "Will you tell me what you see?"

Joanna gave him a fleeting smile before turning back to the marked up tree trunk. "I see that you've been busy and that Ethan is going to be very happy." Joanna glanced around the barn before walking around the trunk, inspecting it from all sides. "Do you want an opinion on everything or just this one piece?"

"Whatever you want to comment on." He loved to listen to her opinions. Joanna Stevens hadn't bored him yet, and that was saying something. He tended to get bored very easily with people. Twenty-five years in the agency did that to people.

He stood there and watched her study the piece of wood while nibbling on her lower lip. He liked how the sun was slanting in through the skylights, bathing Joanna in a crisp golden light. When he had refurbished the barn and made it into his studio four years ago, the skylights were the first thing he added. A top of the line heating system and lots of insulation were the second. Maine's winters were notoriously cold, and he wasn't fond of freezing.

If he hadn't met Norah, he would never have guessed Joanna was in her mid forties like she had claimed. He would have placed her in her late thirties, tops, and that was taking into consideration the few gray hairs he'd noticed. She was slim, beautiful, and classy. Today, she wore a khaki-colored skirt that almost reached her knees and a sleeveless black silk top. There were tan and black beads around her wrist and her throat. Her shoulder-length hair was twisted and pinned up, leaving her neck enticingly bare.

He had to wonder if Joanna was baiting him. She knew exactly how much he loved kissing that neck.

"It's a little cruder than your normal stuff." Joanna circled the rough sculpture again.

"I would say." He hadn't done anything more than chisel away at some of the bigger areas to give it more form in his mind. "Think Ethan could sell it?"

"If not, Christine's World of Art could probably get a fortune for it."

"That's not even funny." He shuddered at the

thought of having a piece of his work surrounded by gaping pornographic mannequins wearing black leather and chains. "Have any idea what it might become?" He was curious about whether Joanna could see what he saw.

"It's a person." Joanna picked up Zsa Zsa who was nuzzling her ankle. "First impression, female."

"Why female?" He moved closer and tried to see the carving through Joanna's eyes. He couldn't. He was surprised she knew it was a person but honestly shocked she had guessed the correct gender. When he looked at the bare wood, he saw a magical creature he had named Elainna, Queen of the Meadows.

"The form." Joanna hugged Zsa Zsa. "I get the impression of a lot of flowing. Flowing long dress. Flowing long hair." She gave him a shy smile. "So, how far off am I?"

"Right on the money." He moved closer and frowned at the splintered, barkless trunk. "Amazing." He didn't know if he should be impressed by her imagination or afraid of it. "Are you sure you've never had any formal training?"

"None. The closest I ever got to the art world before moving to Maine was hanging Norah's pictures on the refrigerator and making colored Play-Doh one time at a Brownie meeting."

"You were a Girl Scout leader?"

"No, I helped out at one Brownie meeting. Coordinating snack time I could do; it was the rest of the meeting I couldn't cope with. Someone had the bright idea to bring in live bugs and reptiles to use as models. Little Patty's lizard got loose and ate half the models before being corralled back into his cage." Joanna shook her head at the memory.

"It's a good thing Norah hated the outdoors and refused to join Girl Scouts the following year."

"Norah hates the outdoors?" He led the way out of the studio and toward the house. "I thought she went camping and hiking with Ned Porter this weekend?"

"She did." Joanna beamed. "Maybe she had a change of heart."

"Or maybe Ned didn't know what he was getting into." He chuckled at the thought. Ned Porter was the type of man who could survive in the woods for a month with nothing more than a pocketknife and the clothes on his back.

Joanna's soft laugh joined his.

They stepped out into the sunlight, and Joanna put Zsa Zsa down. He had invited Joanna for lunch, as well as a tour. While he didn't consider himself a gourmet cook, he did know how to make a mean turkey and cheese sandwich, if he did say so himself. "Are you ready for lunch?"

"Zsa Zsa's got to do her business." Joanna looked at his house on the other side of the gravel driveway. "Why don't you go get things ready? We'll be in in a minute."

He knew the neurotic Pomeranian didn't like to do her business when anyone but Joanna was around. "No problem; just walk right in." He'd humor Zsa Zsa for Joanna's sake.

He gave her a quick kiss and headed for the house.

Joanna watched Karl walk away as Zsa Zsa sniffed around some trees. She couldn't believe she was here with Karl. Last night, after their romantic dinner on her back porch, he had helped her dry the dishes. She had never noticed how tiny the kitchen was until Karl had shared it. The third time they had bumped into each other, Karl had declared he couldn't stand it a minute longer and kissed her senseless.

Senseless had never been so wonderful. She could have kept on kissing Karl throughout the night. One small hesitation on her part, however, and Karl had politely called it an evening and left. The hesitation hadn't stemmed from uncertainty on her part. She was more than willing to allow Karl to spend the night. She just didn't know how to bring up the subject of protection. Pregnancy wasn't her concern, but there was a whole host of other things that had to be thought about and worried about before starting a sexual relationship with a man.

She might have had only one sexual partner in her life, but she hadn't been living under a rock. She watched the news. So how did a woman bring up such a delicate subject without sounding like a twenty dollar whore?

Joanna was frowning at Zsa Zsa, who still hadn't made up her mind if she needed to go or not, when a beat-up old pickup truck pulled into Karl's driveway.

She moved to the side of the driveway and kept an eye on Zsa Zsa, who started to bark wildly. She bent down and picked up the dog. The man getting out of the truck was unsteady on his feet, and he didn't appear to be in any condition to be driving.

"Well, ain't you a fancy one." The man's words were loud and slurred.

She backed up a step, realized she was moving farther away from the house, and quickly stepped

to her right. Zsa Zsa continued barking and struggling in her arms. "If you came to see Karl, he's in
the house."

"I don't want James; I want my wife and boy
back." The man swayed on his feet for a moment
and then took a faltering step toward her. "He
stole them!"

She took another step to her right and almost
tripped over the root of a tree. Where in the world
was Karl? Couldn't he hear this man? "Karl didn't
steal anyone's wife or son." The man was not only
drunk but also delusional.

The man's frown turned into a snarl. "Maybe I'll
just take you and make you disappear like he made
my Marla."

She could feel her heart thudding against her
breasts. Her palms were sweaty, and Zsa Zsa was
trembling like a leaf. Or maybe that was her shaking so badly. "I don't know what you are talking
about." She doubted the man knew what he was
talking about.

"DePaul"—Karl's voice was sharp and direct—
"you looking for me?"

She closed her eyes and gave thanks that Karl
was stepping off the porch and heading their way.

"I'm not looking for you, James." DePaul took
another step closer to her. "I'm looking for my
wife and kid. You remember them, don't you?"

"They aren't here." Karl took a couple of cautious steps toward them.

She couldn't read the expression on Karl's face
because there wasn't any. Karl looked so calm and
cool, almost as if they were discussing the beautiful
weather they were having this fine afternoon. Only
his voice was different. This was a Karl she hadn't

met before. This was a Karl who was coming to her rescue and who would keep her safe. This was the FBI agent of twenty-five years.

She wanted to throw herself into Karl's arms. Only problem was, DePaul was standing between them.

"I know they aren't here!" screamed DePaul.

"John, you have to calm down." Karl kept his gaze on DePaul and barely gave her a glance.

"Who says?" DePaul staggered but managed to keep on his own two feet.

"It will be for your own good, John."

"Who in the hell are you to tell me what's for my own good?" DePaul staggered under the weight of his words. The man appeared to be in a murderous rage. "I'll tell you what's good for me."

DePaul gave her a look that sent a shiver up her spine and made the fine hair on the back of her neck stand up. "Since you took my wife, I'm taking your woman." DePaul lunged for her.

She never saw Karl move. One instant, he was a good twenty feet away from them, and the next he was in front of her, swinging.

Before her feet could even follow the command of "Run!" that her brain was screaming, DePaul was flying backward through the air. The sound of Karl's fist connecting with DePaul's jaw cracked through the woods.

She stared down at DePaul lying on his back on the ground. He was either unconscious or dead. She wasn't sure which.

"Joanna, honey." Karl's voice was soft and sweet as his fingers gently cupped her chin and turned her face away from DePaul. "I need you to go into the house and call the Sheriff's office. Do you think you can do that?"

She nodded. Zsa Zsa's head was buried between her breasts.

"Tell the Sheriff your name and that you're here with me. Larson knows where I live." Karl's expression wasn't calm now. He was worried about something. "Tell him that John DePaul was drunk and came looking for his wife again." Karl's fingers stroked the line of her jaw. "Do you think you can remember all that?"

She nodded and walked toward the house in a total daze. Karl James had laid the man out with one punch.

"Joanna?"

She turned and looked back at Karl. She didn't even glance at the man lying on the ground.

"Tell the Sheriff that we might need an ambulance this time."

She tried not to smile. "We might." She turned and walked into the house.

Chapter Thirteen

Karl watched as the Sheriff backed out of his driveway, finally leaving him alone with Joanna. John DePaul's sorry butt had been hauled away by an ambulance half an hour ago, with John screaming obscenities both at him and the EMTs trying to work on him. And he had been pretty sure he had broken John's jaw with that punch. Life was full of disappointments, however, and his hand hurt like a son of a bitch.

He glanced over at Joanna, who was sitting on his porch swing, calming drinking a glass of lemonade and enjoying the sounds of the afternoon. Birds were chirping, insects were humming, and in the distance, the occasional car went down the road. There wasn't a lot of traffic out in this neck of the woods. Zsa Zsa was sniffing around Karl's pitiful attempt at gardening that surrounded his house.

Joanna had handled the whole incident amazingly well. Too well he feared. After the ambulance had hauled DePaul out of there, the Sheriff had sat at the kitchen table getting both his and Joanna's statements as to what had transpired. Joanna had fluttered around his kitchen making sandwiches and squeezing half a dozen lemons into a pitcher. He wanted her to sit down, but she'd seemed more relaxed while rooting through his pitifully arranged kitchen cabinets in search of matching tableware and linen napkins.

If Joanna had been disappointed by his lack of linens and color-coordinated dishes, she hadn't said. He tended to pick up dishes when he needed them, never really giving any thought to what he already owned. Flea market finds were crammed in with the few pieces of his grandmother's fine china he had and thick earthenware mugs he had purchased from a local artist. He hadn't noticed until today that even his silverware didn't match.

He was a domestic disaster who didn't even buy paper napkins, while Joanna could give Martha Stewart a run for her money in the kitchen.

One had to wonder if Joanna was keeping busy as a way of ignoring or coping with what had happened. He couldn't believe he had decked DePaul right in front of her like that. Especially since he suspected abuse in her past. His only defense was that he had acted on instinct and adrenaline. DePaul had lunged for Joanna, and the next thing Karl knew, his fist was connecting with an unshaved jaw.

He hoped like hell that he hadn't scared Joanna too badly.

He gave a low whistle for Zsa Zsa and stepped

up onto the porch. Joanna gave him a soft, shy smile that melted his heart. There wasn't any fear in her eyes. He joined her on the swing.

"I like your home. It's peaceful here." Joanna started the swing moving. Zsa Zsa attacked a dead petunia in a pot by the front door.

"Thanks." He leaned back and tried to relax. He owed Joanna an explanation for DePaul. "John DePaul doesn't like me much." He gave the swing a little push and tried to figure out the best approach to this conversation. One that wouldn't have Joanna clamming up.

"He claimed you stole his wife and son." Joanna didn't seem upset by that claim.

"I didn't steal Marla or little John Junior." He wondered how big a can of worms he was about to open. "Marla needed some help."

"And you rode to her rescue?" Joanna gave him a big smile. "You make a habit out of doing that?"

"I didn't rescue her. I helped her and her son out of a tough situation, that's all."

"What situation was that?"

"DePaul thought a marriage certificate entitled him to a few free smackarounds about every weekend or so." He watched Joanna's face. "Marla thought differently, but she was such a little, bitty thing, and she didn't have a family to turn to for help. Marla didn't stand a chance. After John Junior was born, things turned from bad to ugly."

"Did he hit the baby?" Joanna's voice broke at the horror of the situation.

"Not directly, but he hit Marla so hard once that she fell into the bassinet. Thankfully, she was able to prevent Junior from getting hurt. That was the night I learned about the situation."

"So where are Marla and the baby now?"

"The baby is now a toddler, and her divorce should be granted in another month or so."

"You didn't answer the question."

He had been hoping she wouldn't notice. He sighed and shook his head. "I'm not allowed to say. Marla doesn't want anyone to know because she's afraid it will get back to DePaul and that then he'll come after her and try to take his son."

He reached out and held Joanna's hand. "I can't blame her, Joanna. DePaul isn't too stable, and the Protection From Abuse she had taken out on him was like waving a red flag in front of a charging bull. DePaul sees it as a challenge."

"So why does DePaul keep coming after you?"

"Stupidity." He chuckled at the thought. "I'm the only one who knows where Marla and his son went. I guess he figures if he keeps asking and I keep knocking him on his butt, that one time I just might feel sorry for him and tell."

"Don't you dare." Joanna frowned at him. "You wouldn't, would you?"

"Never. Marla and her son are settling into a new life. It's hard, but they'll make it just fine. They have already made friends. Good friends."

"How did you know what to do for her?"

"Marla wasn't the first woman I helped; she was more like number six or seven." He shrugged and tried to play down his role in Marla's new life. He didn't like the gleam of hero-worship he saw in Joanna's eyes. He wasn't a hero. A hero would have prevented Marla from being hit the first time. A hero would have helped Joanna when she had needed it.

"The first time I helped someone, it took a lot of

phone calls, favors, and running around to figure it all out. Now I know who to call and how to get the woman, and children if there are any, out of there with a minimal of fuss and red tape."

"What you are telling me is that in your spare time, you help abused women?" The expression on Joanna's face was one of excitement and awe.

"No, what I'm telling you is that even after retiring from the agency, I'm still fighting for the underdog. Just in a more behind the scenes capacity. DePaul never should have found out I helped Marla, but one of the deputies opened his mouth, so Sheriff Larson goes out of his way to try and keep DePaul in line."

He wanted Joanna to understand why he had decked DePaul, but he didn't want to make a big deal about him helping out Marla. To him, it wasn't a big deal. He looked on it as community service. Instead of beautifying the community, he gave a woman who needed a helping hand a beautiful new start in a different community.

Personally, he would have preferred to load up all the deadbeat and abusive husbands, haul their asses out into the middle of the Atlantic, and let them play with the fishes without the benefit of a boat. But there were laws against that. If he ever found a way around those laws, he was renting Bob Newman's tuna boat and doing some offshore dumping.

Joanna laid her head against Karl's shoulder, kicked off her sandals, and curled her feet up beneath her. She hadn't doubted for a moment that Karl would charge out of the house to rescue her from John DePaul. She had been a little concerned about his timing in the beginning, but once she'd heard his voice, she'd known everything was going to work out. Now that she knew the reason behind DePaul's visit, she wished she would have let Zsa Zsa down.

It was amazing how fast a person could go from falling in love to being in love. After Karl had left last night, she had lain in her lonely bed and wondered why she was alone. She didn't want to be alone, but the company of just any man would not do. She wanted to be with Karl. Only Karl. At that point, she realized she had been falling in love. She had held that wondrous knowledge close throughout the night and dreamt of a future.

The moment she heard that Karl helped women who were total strangers to him out of abusive relationships, she knew she wasn't falling in love. She was in love. There was no falling about it. She loved Karl James, and she wanted to shout it to the world. His reaction to her discovery was going to prove interesting.

"May I ask you a question, Karl?"

"Anything." Karl's feet were slowly pushing the swing back and forth.

She studied his bare knees. Today, Karl was dressed in Army green shorts with a dozen or so pockets and a gold paisley button-down shirt. His rope ankle bracelet was still around his ankle. She thought he had the sexiest knees. "Why did you leave last night?"

Karl stiffened for a moment, but the swing didn't miss a beat. "You weren't ready, Joanna." He kissed the top of her head. "I'm not going to push you into anything you aren't ready for."

She didn't know if she should laugh or cry. Karl thought she wasn't ready for them to have a physical relationship. She was more than ready. "What makes you think I'm not ready?"

Was she giving off some kind of signal she wasn't even aware of? The rules couldn't have changed that much. Surely she would have picked up on that while watching television and reading. She knew females in this generation were more liberated and open-minded when it came to sex. Short of ripping Karl's clothes off in her kitchen last night or begging, she really didn't know what else she could have done.

"Sweetheart," Karl said, "it's okay."

"No, it's not. I want to know what I did." She sat up straight and looked right at him. Last night, she had held her tongue and had ended up enduring a lonely, frustrating night.

"You were hesitant, Joanna." Karl looked like he would rather be discussing bioterrorism than their relationship. "There, are you happy?"

"No, I would have been happier last night if you had stayed." She couldn't believe her slight hesitation had caused all of this. "Do you want to know why I hesitated when you were unbuttoning my blouse?" She'd also had her tongue halfway down his throat, and her butt had been on her kitchen counter. Karl had been standing between her thighs, and there hadn't been a doubt in her mind about where the night was heading. "I was embarrassed."

"About what?"

"I was trying to figure out the proper way for a lady to ask if the gentleman has a condom with him." There, she'd said it. Her face might be beet red, but she had just stepped into the twenty-first century.

"You wanted to know..." Karl groaned and buried his head in his hands. His shoulders were shaking, but she couldn't tell if he was crying or laughing.

Neither of those reactions made her feel better. "I take it ladies aren't supposed to ask that question?"

"They do if they are smart." Karl looked at her. "I had two of them with me last night and an entire box sitting in my nightstand drawer."

The fire in his gaze made liquid heat pool in her stomach and slowly descend to the junction of her thighs. Karl wanted her as much as she wanted him. She prayed her mother in heaven wasn't listening to this particular conversation. "How many are in the box?"

Karl's laughter startled a few birds and caused Zsa Zsa to stop attacking the dead plant. With a wild cry, he jumped off the swing and swung her up into his arms. "Enough to get us through today at least."

She let out a small cry as she was crushed against his chest.

Karl immediately loosened his hold. "Sorry."

She smiled and wrapped her arms around his neck. "Don't be." She reached up and kissed him.

Somehow, they made it into the house without falling over Zsa Zsa, who was weaving her way in between Karl's legs every step. Her skirt was tossed on the newel. Karl's sandals were kicked off at the foot of the stairs. His gold shirt lost a button or two beneath her impatient fingers. Karl's fingers had more finesse. Her silk blouse landed on the runner in the upstairs hallway, but at least all the buttons were still on it.

Karl backed her into his bedroom before breaking that first wild kiss. "God, Joanna, you're beautiful."

She did feel beautiful, but she also felt wanton, hot, and desirable. Her trembling fingers went for the waistband of his shorts. "I'm not hesitating now."

Karl backed her against the bed, and her black lace bra went sailing to the left, while his shorts hit the floor. The soft cotton of the patchwork quilt was cool beneath her back as he lowered her to the bed. Karl's mouth was hot against her breasts.

Hands roamed and demanded to feel, to touch everywhere. Karl's fingers were impatient as he slid her black panties down her legs. Her fingers shook as she slid his wild print boxers over his buttocks and down his legs. Karl yanked open the drawer of the nightstand and fumbled in a box.

She laughed at the sight of Karl trying to rip open the foil package. It took him three tries.

Karl did a lousy job of frowning. "You think this is funny?"

"No, I just have never seen you so worked up about anything before. You are usually very laid-back and calm." She ran her big toe up his calf and playfully tugged on a chest hair. "I thought FBI agents were cool under fire."

"I'm not an agent any longer." Karl rolled the condom on and backed her into the center of the bed. "And in case you haven't noticed, the only thing that is about to go off isn't a gun."

She glanced down his chest and over his stomach to where his sheathed arousal was standing at full attention. "Oh, I noticed." She ran her fingers down his chest. "It's a little hard not to."

Karl grinned. "Sweet talker." He leaned down and captured her mouth in a kiss that heated her blood and melted the last of her inhibitions. With her ex-husband, she had always allowed him to set the pace. While Vince hadn't been a selfish lover, he hadn't been one to allow a woman to take control. Today, she wanted control.

Joanna placed both her palms on Karl's chest and pushed him over. She knew he went willingly because there was no way she could physically dominate him. She straddled his hips and wiggled.

Karl groaned and closed his eyes. "Oh, Joanna, you might not want to do that."

"What? This?" She wiggled a little more and watched as Karl's hips arched off the bed. "Why?" She leaned down and teased his mouth with the tip of her tongue. Her nipples brushed against the silky hair on his chest, and the head of his penis nudged at her opening. "Don't you like this?"

She wiggled back and felt him slip an inch or two inside her. Karl's eyes opened as his hands grasped her hips. "What do you think?" Karl's voice was a low growl, and his breathing was fast.

She sat back farther and took him all the way in. Karl stopped breathing as she arched her back and closed her eyes. It felt so good. So right. She bit her lower lip and prayed she wasn't about to embarrass herself. Weren't women supposed to last for more than two seconds?

Karl's fingers trembled against her hipbones. "You have to move, Jo."

She was afraid to move. If she breathed too deeply, she was going to climax. "Can't." She was in a hell of a predicament. Her whole body was screaming at her to move, while her heart was telling her to slow down, to make this first time with Karl special.

"Why?"

"Too close." She squeezed her eyes tighter and felt herself squeeze the entire length of Karl tighter.

"Good, at least I'm not alone." Karl thrust his hips upward, and she went over the edge.

Someone shouted, and she could only pray it had been Karl because ladies certainly didn't shout during a vigorous round of lovemaking. Then again, ladies weren't supposed to make love vigorously, and they surely weren't supposed to be on top.

She fell face first into the pillow next to Karl's and silently giggled as she realized she wasn't a lady after all.

Karl lay in bed, loving the feel of Joanna curled up beside him. He especially loved the fact that she was naked and warm beneath the sheets. Tantalizing fingers were tracing some imaginary pattern across his chest. For the first time in his life he wanted to ask, "So, was it good for you?" He needed to know it had been not just good for Joanna but great. Their lovemaking had not only been perfect for him, but it had also knocked his socks off and blown a hole right out of the top of his head. He'd never experienced anything like that in his life. That didn't just fascinate him; it also scared him spitless.

What in the world was he going to do about Joanna Stevens? Handcuffing her to his bed for the next twenty years wasn't an option. He really wasn't sure if she was ready to start a long-term, seriously committed relationship. The amazing part of all of this was that he was. He was in love with Joanna—he not only wanted her in his bed every night, but he also wanted to wake up with her in his arms every morning.

Statistics indicated that more than half of his lifetime was over. Spending half a lifetime with Joanna wasn't going to be enough. He was running short on time.

His fingers toyed with the ends of her silky brown hair. In the late afternoon light, some of the strands of hair were golden blond, some were a dark shade of brown, and a few were gray. He liked the gray the best. It matched his.

"Want to tell me about your ex-husband?" He refused to even think that it was jealousy tugging at his heart. He didn't want to think about the man Joanna had spent most of her life with and who had fathered her child. But he needed to know. He needed to know what, rather who, had taught Joanna to fear.

"Vince?"

"How many ex-husbands do you have?" He chuckled at the thought. He was in love with a woman he didn't know very much about.

Joanna yanked a chest hair. "One."

"Ouch." He grabbed her fingers and brought them up to his mouth. "Stop that." He kissed the tip of each finger before releasing her hand.

"What do you want to know?" Joanna snuggled closer.

"Whatever you want to tell me."

"We were high school sweethearts who got married at twenty and were parents by the time we were both twenty-one. We were young and in love and too stupid to realize life wasn't a storybook."

"I knew you had Norah when you were young, but hearing it makes me realize you were nothing more than a kid yourself." He couldn't imagine becoming a father at twenty-one. Who would want to? There was a whole world out there ready to be explored.

"Oh, we were young, but Norah was, and is, the best thing that ever happened to me. We bought a little house in a quiet neighborhood. Vince worked with his father at the local gas station, and I took care of Norah and the house."

"So what went wrong in Norman Rockwellville?"

"We almost lost Norah during the delivery. Labor lasted too long, and there were all kinds of complications." Joanna's fingers stilled for a moment. "But she made it. At five pounds, three ounces, she was on the small side, but she was healthy."

"And you? How healthy were you?" He could hear the emotion in her voice, and he knew that delivering Norah hadn't been easy.

"I made it." Joanna's fingers trembled against his chest. "When Norah was two months old, I had to have a complete hysterectomy."

He placed his hand over top of hers and squeezed. "I'm sorry." He had the feeling Joanna might have liked to have more children. "How did Vince handle that?"

"At first, he was very supportive. He helped around the house when he could. Took Norah for walks in her stroller and even changed a diaper or two."

"And later?"

"Vince wanted a son. You know, the stupid belief that a man needs a son to pass the family name to.

Vince worked with his father, and he was fully expecting to take over the garage when his dad retired. He did too. Vince is a very gifted mechanic." Joanna turned her hand over and threaded her fingers through his. "Vince just wanted a son to pass the business on to."

"He blamed you for not giving him that son, didn't he?" He stomach turned at the thought.

"It was my fault, Karl. I couldn't have any more children, while he could still father them."

"That's bullshit, and you know it." He reached down and cupped her chin. He forced her to look at him. The sheen of tears in her eyes tore at his heart. "The man should have gotten down on his knees and given thanks that he still had you and a healthy daughter."

"At first he did, Karl." She reached up and tenderly stroked his jaw. "As the years went by, the resentment grew and ate at him. All his friends started their families, and it seemed every one of them had boys. Lots of little boys, which we would never have. Vince took over the business from his father when he got sick and eventually died. Vince started to drink about then."

He'd known it. "So when did he start to hit you, Joanna? Before Norah was in high school? College?"

She cringed. "She was around fifteen or so. Vince came home from the bar drunk, and one thing led to another. Next thing I knew, I was telling my daughter I'd accidently run into a door."

"And she believed you." He could see it all in his mind. Joanna proudly standing by her man because she felt as if she had let him down by not giving him a son. It was the typical pattern for abuse. Blame the woman.

"She was fifteen, and I became an expert at hiding the truth. I fell down the basement stairs. I tripped over the back porch step. Norah started calling me 'Klutzy the clown' after Krusty the Clown on *The Simpsons*."

"Why did you stay with him?" He'd dealt with abuse and knew all the reasons.

"I loved him." Joanna glanced away. "Stupid reason, but there it is. Ninety-nine percent of the time, he was a good man, a good provider. He never touched Norah."

"So why did you divorce him? What changed?"

"Norah graduated from college and had a job at a local newspaper and her own apartment in town. One night, she stopped by unexpectedly and saw her father smack me. She attacked her father, and Vince turned and hit her." A tear rolled down Joanna's cheek and fell onto his chest. "Norah was knocked over by the blow."

He reached out and captured a second tear on his fingertip. "What did you do?" He had to keep reminding himself to breathe. Joanna and Norah were fine. They were both safe and fine now.

Joanna gave him a funny little smile and said softly, "I picked up one of my good table lamps and whacked him in the head." She shrugged as if the whole incident weren't important.

Because Karl was holding Joanna in his arms, he could chuckle about it now. "Good for you."

"Yeah, well he knew never to lay a finger on Norah," Joanna said. "Vince pushed me back, and I ended up with a cracked collarbone. Norah was on the phone to the police before the stars stopped swimming in my head, and that was the end of everything."

"Did you press charges?"

"Darn straight I did. I loved that lamp." She teasingly kissed his chest before wiping her eyes with the sheet. "You know what my biggest regret is?"

"What?" He wanted her to say something about not having a heavier lamp.

"That Norah had to suffer because of my stupidity. Norah received a blow from the one man in her life she should have trusted to keep her safe—her father. With that one blow, Vince destroyed Norah's trust in men."

"I can imagine." He pulled Joanna closer and silently vowed he would make Vince Stevens pay for what he had done to both Joanna and Norah.

"Oh, you should have seen her before that night, Karl. Norah laughed all the time, she was outgoing, and she'd never met a stranger. She could have had a date every night of the week if she wanted to, and most nights she did." Joanna laughed at the memories. "I couldn't keep her boyfriends straight."

"Norah seems to be handling it well."

"Oh, she is just starting to date again. I think Ned Porter has a lot to do with it. Ned's the first guy she has gone out with in two years."

Vince Stevens had a lot to answer for in life. "Ned's a good guy, Joanna. He won't hurt her."

"I know that." Joanna worried her lower lip. "Do you know why I agreed to have lunch with you that first time?"

"I'm irresistible?"

"You are that." Joanna reached up and quickly kissed him. "But the truth is, I went out with you to show Norah life goes on. That all men aren't the same as her father, and that I wasn't afraid any longer."

"So?" He didn't like the thoughts that were spinning through his mind. "You thought I was safe or something?" Great, he was a teach my daughter a lesson date.

"You were the total opposite of safe. I knew you could be dangerous, but I couldn't resist your laidback charm or your ponytail." Joanna sat up, bringing the sheet along with her. "But something went wrong."

"What went wrong?" He sat up, not caring that the sheet no longer covered him. Joanna was prim and proper enough for the both of them. How in the hell had the afternoon turned from perfection to this?

Joanna's teeth worried her lower lip, and there was a slight tremble in the hand that was clutching the sheet to her breasts. "I fell in love with you."

He opened his mouth to argue, to tell her that they could work out whatever problems she was imagining, when her words registered. "Oh, Joanna, now you really have to marry me."

"What?" Joanna screeched.

He tugged the sheet away from her breasts and grinned. "What kind of example would it be for Norah if we just lived together?"

Joanna was still sputtering when he laid her flat on her back and began kissing his way to heaven.

Chapter
Fourteen

Norah was watching one of the forensic crime shows on the television and enjoying a cup of tea when her mother finally left her bedroom and joined her on the couch.

"So, how was the hiking," Joanna curled her feet up under her and added, "and Ned?"

She'd known her mother would get around to asking about Ned. "Hard and fine." She placed her empty cup onto the coffee table, grabbed the remote, and turned off the TV. The surfeit of autopsy tables currently being aired on television had killed the shock value. Now all the shows seemed interchangeable and depressing.

"Whoever thinks hiking for the weekend is relaxing is crazy. I'm exhausted, and I ache in places I didn't even know I had." Soaking in a tub filled with hot water and bubbles for half an hour had relieved most of the aches.

"Did you get to see the trees?"

"Yes, Mom, I saw trees and then more trees, and when I was tired of looking at them, Ned pointed out more trees." She had to chuckle at how naive she had been before hiking up that mountain. She really had expected to see huge patches of the forest gone. Harvested by the big lumber corporations and bulldozed into oblivion.

"Ned wasn't upset about the article, was he?"

"Of course he was, but instead of yelling and ranting like the lobster fishermen did, he proved his point by making me climb a mountain." As wonderful as the weekend had been, a few photos with aerial views would have proven his point nicely. Then they could have spent Saturday night in his bed instead of rolling around naked in the great outdoors. She had an insect bite in a place that she would be arrested for scratching in public.

"The exercise and fresh air will do you good." Her mother settled herself more comfortably.

Usually by this time of night, her mother was in her pajamas and ready for bed. Tonight, she was in a pair of jeans and a blouse. She knew her mother had taken a shower because she had heard the water running. It was almost like her mother was planning on going out again. "Well, the next time Ned wants to take someone hiking up into the clouds, I'll volunteer you."

Joanna chuckled. "Not in this lifetime, sweetheart. I don't do tents, bugs, or squatting behind bushes."

Camping wasn't quite that bad, but she didn't think her mother would appreciate a play-by-play description of everything that had transpired. Some things a daughter just didn't share with her mother. "It had its good moments, and for some reason, food just tastes better cooked over an open fire. Even the instant coffee was great."

"That's nice." Her mother seemed preoccupied and nervous. "I got to tour Karl's workshop today."

"So you said." When her mother had come home about an hour ago, all she'd talked about was Karl this and Karl that. "Mom, can I ask you a question?"

"Sure, anything." Joanna was sitting here trying to figure out a way to tell her daughter she was about to leave again. Karl was waiting for her and Zsa Zsa to return to his house for the night. If Karl had had his way, she wouldn't even have gotten to come home to pick up the things she would need in the morning. As it was, she'd had a difficult time explaining to him why he shouldn't drive her home and talk to Norah with her.

"You and Karl are getting pretty serious, aren't you?"

"Yes." She didn't think now was the time to tell Norah that Karl had asked her to marry him and that she had said yes. Her daughter was just beginning to get used to the idea of her and Karl dating. Marriage was in their future, but she wasn't sure if it was going to happen as fast as Karl was planning. "What do you think of Karl?"

"He's great, but more importantly, he makes you happy." Norah grinned at her. "You either used a really good soap in that shower, or you're glowing."

She tried not to blush. "Maybe the water was a little too hot." She knew exactly what had put the glow in her cheeks.

Norah snorted. "Try another one, Mom."

She decided to change the subject. "So you don't have a problem with me dating Karl?"

"Nope." Norah pulled her feet up onto the couch and wrapped her arms around her knees. "You have a problem with me dating Ned?"

"Nope." She was so thrilled that her daughter was getting back into dating that she really didn't care who she was going out with. But if she had to chose someone for Norah, Ned Porter would definitely be at the top of her list.

"So how do you look at a man, Mom, and know he would never hurt you? Never turn on you like Dad did?"

"You can't, sweetheart." Joanna felt like crying. It was her fault that her daughter carried this weight. If she had left Vince after the first time he had hit her, Norah never would have known. Her daughter never would have had that trust between a father and a daughter shattered. The trust between a man and a woman. "People change, Norah. When we were first married, your father never even raised his voice at me, let alone his hand."

"So what changed?"

There was no way she was telling her daughter that her father resented that she was born a girl instead of a boy. That he resented the fact that his wife couldn't give him any more children. That she couldn't give him that son he so desperately wanted. Vince and Norah had never been as close and as loving as most fathers and daughters. It hadn't been Norah's fault; she had tried. Vince had just never appreciated what he did have because he was too busy regretting what he couldn't have.

"Life, I guess. In hindsight, your father had all the signs of being a potentially abusive husband from the beginning. He had been raised in a house where the man's word was law. Your grandmother was a shadow of a woman, and she probably had been abused herself."

"Just because a person comes from an abusive home doesn't mean they will become abusive themselves."

"You're right. It doesn't always happen like that." Joanna wanted to take the pain out of Norah's voice. She wanted a magic pill or magic words that would make everything better. It wasn't going to happen. "Your father never became abusive unless he was drinking and drinking heavily."

The last couple of years of their marriage, Vince had been drunk a lot, but over time, she had become an expert on avoiding him and the arguments.

"How do you have the strength to go into another relationship, Mom? Aren't you afraid?"

"No, I'm not afraid, Norah. You have to have faith and love."

"And do you have faith in Karl?"

"Yes, and I'm also in love with him." She studied her daughter's reaction, wondering how much she should tell about their relationship and about Karl's proposal.

Norah grinned. "Does he know?"

"He does now." She felt like a teenager discussing her boyfriend with her best friend. Norah was not just her daughter; she was also her best friend. Women over forty shouldn't be giddy, but she was. Love did strange things to people.

"What would you do if Karl changed and became like Dad?"

"Not all men are violent and abusive, sweetie. Only a small percentage are, and I know now that I have the strength to walk away from any relationship that turns abusive." She reached out and squeezed her daughter's hand. "Thanks to you."

"I didn't do anything."

"You did more than you realize." She gave her daughter a smile that contained every ounce of love she felt. "You have that same strength too, Norah. If you look deep enough inside, you will see that strength and not be afraid."

"And if a man ever raised his hand to me?"

"Pray you have ugly table lamps that you won't regret bashing over his head."

Norah laughed just like Joanna had known she would. "Mom, one of these days, I'm going to go on eBay and see if I can't locate a lamp just like the one you destroyed. I'll buy it for your Christmas present."

"I won't need it with Karl." She had never been more certain of anything in her life. "Speaking of Karl, I've got to get going." Joanna stood up and nervously smoothed out her top.

"Go where?" Norah knew her mother had been up to something.

"Karl's." Her mother headed into her bedroom and walked back out with a packed tote bag and a dress on a hanger. "I wrote his home phone number and his cell phone number down and put them by the phone in the kitchen, just in case you need to reach me."

"You're going to Karl's now?"

"Yes." Her mother scooped up Zsa Zsa. "I work until five tomorrow; I'll be home sometime after that." Joanna headed for the front door. "Good night."

Norah slowly got to her feet and stared at the door her mother had just closed behind her. She wondered whether she should run after her mother, demand that she get back into the house, and then ground her or should she just laugh? This role reversal was the pits.

Her mother was a mature woman who was old enough to make her own decisions. Her mother had obviously chosen to spend the night with Karl. She wasn't even going to think about what they would be doing.

And she had turned down Ned's invitation to spend the night at his place because she didn't want her mother thinking about what they would be doing. Well, if her mother was old enough to make her own decisions on where she would be spending the night, so was she.

Norah smiled the entire time as she climbed the stairs, threw some stuff into a bag, and headed for Ned's.

Fifteen minutes later, she was petting Flipper and taking her bag out of the backseat when Ned stepped off his front porch. "Norah?" Flipper had been her welcoming committee.

"You were expecting someone else?" Now that she was here, she felt a little foolish. Maybe she should have called first to see if the invitation was still open.

A bare chested, barefooted Ned took the bag out of her hand. His worn jeans were tight, low on the hips, and incredibly sexy. "I thought you were staying at your place tonight."

She closed the door and tried not to blush at being so forward. "You changed your mind?"

Ned leaned down and kissed her. "Never."

She grinned. "Good." Ned's hair was still damp from his shower. He smelled like soap, and he hadn't bothered to shave. "I've missed you," she called over her shoulder as she followed Flipper and walked toward his house.

"I dropped you off two hours ago." Ned held the screen door open for her and his dog. "A long two hours." Ned shut and locked the front door behind them. "What took you so long?" He dropped her overnight bag and tugged her into his arms.

She laughed as he swung her up and headed for the stairs. "Um-m-m . . . Ned?" She nuzzled his stubbled jaw as she wrapped her arms around his neck and hung on for dear life. "My pajamas are in that bag."

"You're not going to need them." Ned took the steps two at a time and carried her straight into his bedroom.

Norah kept her arms locked around his neck as he lowered her to his bed. Her mouth teased his as she felt the softness of his mattress take their weight. Now this was more like it. While she had loved their night on the ground, there was something to be said for a Posturepedic and clean sheets.

Ned gave her lower lip a gentle, playful nip. "I've got to go shave." He tried removing his weight from on top of her.

She wasn't letting him up. "No, you don't." Her lips nibbled their way across his stubbled jaw. "I like you just the way you are." She kicked off her sandals and wrapped her legs around his thighs.

Ned groaned as his hips nestled their way between her thighs. "You're a dangerous woman, Norah."

The thickness of his arousal pressed against her center and caused moist heat to gather there. "Are you complaining?" Her hands stroked down the smooth, warm skin of his back, and her fingers tunneled their way under the waistband of his jeans.

Ned's hips jerked against her as he arched his back and moaned, "Never."

Her lips pressed against his chest as her fingers moved around and tugged at the snap on his jeans. "Know what else was in that bag?" She didn't want Ned to leave her, but sometimes in life, you don't get what you want. They needed that protection.

Ned tugged her tank top over her head. "I have some up here." His mouth skimmed down her throat as his fingers released the front clasp of her bra.

The gentle tugging of his lips on her nipple nearly sent her over the edge. She tried to pull Ned back up into the cradle of her thighs. Their difference in heights was proving to be a challenge, one she was determined to conquer. She arched her back as Ned took her hard nipple into his mouth more fully. "Get them."

"Them?" Ned chuckled as he released her bud. "You might be giving me more credit than I deserve."

Her fingers finally released the stubborn snap. "I think you will rise to the occasion." She trailed a fingernail down the metal zipper and grinned as he instinctively jerked against her hand.

Ned retaliated by pulling away from her while

removing her shorts and panties in one downward swipe. He opened the drawer on the nightstand and took out a box.

She chuckled as Ned dumped the entire box out and then triumphantly held up a gold foil packet. "Think you're special, don't you?" The grin on his face stole its way into her heart. She knew Ned was special, very special.

"Nope." Ned removed his jeans and underwear. "But I do happen to know you're one very special lady."

"I am?" In the pale light coming in from the hallway, she watched as he rolled on the condom. Ned was a physically large man, and every inch of him was in proportion to his height and the breadth of his shoulders.

Ned slowly lowered himself on the bed next to her. He gently cupped her chin. "I love you, Norah." He kissed her lightly. "That makes you one very special woman."

Tears filled her eyes. "You do?"

Ned frowned and tenderly wiped at the tear rolling down her cheek. "This upsets you?"

She shook her head. "It makes me very happy." She looked into his brown eyes and saw the truth there. Ned did love her. She wanted to remember this moment, this slice of time for the rest of her life.

"Why?"

"Because I happen to love you back." She watched as joy and wonder lit Ned's rugged face. She reached up and scraped a fingernail down his jaw and then outlined his smiling mouth.

He captured her finger. "I really need to shave, Norah. I don't want to mark you all up."

"What you really need to do is kiss me." She snuggled up closer as Ned sucked her finger into his mouth. She felt the pull of his mouth clear down to the junction of her thighs.

Ned grabbed her hand and released her finger. His lips nibbled on the inside of her wrist where her pulse was thudding wildly. "Now that, I can promise you, I'll do."

She slid her leg in between his and pressed her thigh against his swollen desire. She liked the contrast between their legs. Hers were smooth from just being shaved, while his were hairy. The jutting of his arousal nudged her stomach. "What else can you promise?"

She had a feeling that Ned was really close to the edge. She was half tempted to see how far she could push him before he tumbled over the ledge.

Ned rolled her onto her back and grinned down at her. "I can promise to make you scream." He captured both of her hands and raised them above her head. Ned's mouth trailed down her neck, and rough whiskers nuzzled the valley between her breasts.

She liked this game. She wiggled her hips and laughed with delight. "Betcha you can't."

Twenty minutes later, Ned held her close and chuckled softly. Norah was almost asleep. "I do believe I won that bet hands down."

Norah's fingers pinched his side.

"Ouch!" He rubbed the spot. "Well, I did." He couldn't believe how loud she had screamed when he'd finally allowed her to climax. Of course, there was no way he was admitting that he had been the one who couldn't hold out another moment longer.

"It's not polite to point that out to a lady." Norah turned her back on him, bunched up a pillow, and then buried her face in it.

"A lady wouldn't have begged me to do those things you wanted me to do." He pulled her into his arms and grinned as her bare little bottom wiggled against him. Norah had blown him away in more ways than one.

"Cretin." There was a smile in her voice.

He kissed the back of her neck and chuckled when she squirmed some more. "This cretin has to get up at four in the morning."

Norah groaned and tried to pull the pillow over her head.

"What time do you want me to set the alarm for you?" His hand stroked the gentle curve of her hip. "I don't expect you to get up with me."

"Seven?"

"Seven it is." His lips nuzzled the back of her neck again just to feel her wiggle. "Help yourself to the shower, food, coffee, and anything else you might want."

"Where do you keep the family silver?"

He playfully swatted her bottom. "Brat." He could feel her shoulders shaking with silent laughter. "You'll be here for dinner tomorrow night?" He needed to get up and go downstairs to shut off the lights and let Flipper out one last time. For now, he was content to stay where he was until she fell asleep.

"My mom's expecting me. Why don't you come over there for dinner?" Norah gave a big yawn. "About six, six-thirty?"

"I'll be there." He still didn't know why Norah had changed her mind and decided to spend the night. Not that he was complaining. It was going to be a little awkward seeing her mother tomorrow night, but there was no getting around that one.

Joanna Stevens would just have to understand and accept the fact that her daughter was going to be spending an awful lot of nights over here if he had any say in the matter. In fact, he wouldn't be surprised if it turned into a permanent arrangement complete with a hall rental and a name change.

Norah looked down at the notepad in her lap and wanted to cry. It wasn't fair. Her latest assignment was guaranteed to push Ned's buttons. Ned might accept an attack on his job and livelihood, but he'd come up swinging against an attack on his brother's dream.

"I take it you didn't know Matthew Porter wants the property?" Millicent Wyndham frowned.

"No one made me aware of that fact before this interview." She had to wonder if Thomas Belanger, her boss, had known when he'd assigned her the next topic for her "Views From the Other Side" column. Tom knew she was dating Ned.

"I'm the one who called Thomas and asked for this particular article to be written." Millicent slowly stroked the Siamese cat lying across her lap. "You've done some wonderful columns, Norah. You're factual and informative, but more importantly, you make people think. The residents of Misty Harbor need to think about not only their future but also the town's future."

"So you think having a huge hotel built right next to the lighthouse is a good thing?" She couldn't believe this. All week long everything between her and Ned had been going great. She'd spent more nights in his bed than in her own. Oh and what nights they had been.

The cat jumped down and stalked away. "I don't recall saying that." Millicent carefully poured them each a cup of tea. "Just about every person in town is against the hotel being built. I just want to make sure they fully understand what they might be giving up." Millicent held up the sterling silver spoon. "Sugar?"

"Two, please." She glanced down at the blank notepad in her lap. So far, she hadn't written one word.

Millicent held up the creamer. "It's real cream, not milk."

"No, thank you." The antique silver tea set before them probably cost more than her car. "How about we start from the beginning. How does one go about owning a lighthouse?"

"Working lighthouses, which are getting fewer by the years, are operated by the U.S. Coast Guard. Misty Harbor Lighthouse, while it still can work some of the time, isn't operational. Modern boats are equipped with advanced electronic navigational aids. They don't require lighthouses to guide them into the harbors."

"So the lighthouse is just for show?"

"Tourists expect lighthouses on our coast. They hold a lot of sentimental and historical value." Millicent handed her a porcelain cup and saucer with miniature pink roses all over it that was filled with hot tea. "Back in 1960 when the lighthouse was no longer required, it was given to the town. Problem was that the town couldn't afford its up-keep. It sits on twenty acres of wild and windy terrain. The town wanted to sell it for the tax revenue it would bring. To prevent it from being destroyed by someone rich enough to tear it down and build a house up there, my late husband, Jefferson, purchased it."

"So you've been paying the property taxes on the land and the lighthouse all these years?" Millicent Wyndham, who appeared to be in her late sixties or early seventies, was Misty Harbor's town monarch. She didn't appear to be hurting for money, but it still seemed like a lot of expense to her for nothing in return.

"Yes." Millicent took a sip of tea and then held the cup and saucer elegantly in her hand. "Jefferson and I never had any children of our own. We considered Misty Harbor our child and tended to spoil the residents. A fact I'm now worried about."

"From what Thomas told me, a hotel chain contacted you and offered to buy the lighthouse and the surrounding acreage."

"True. I hadn't considered selling it until I received that letter. Matthew made it known years ago that when I was ready to sell, I was to think of him first."

"I'm sure it must be worth quite a lot of money." Twenty acres on the coast of Maine. Her mind had a hard time wrapping itself around all those zeros. "So, why the change of mind after all these years?"

"I'm getting older." Millicent gave her a polite smile when she began to protest that statement. "I'll be seventy-four in a couple of months, and no one lives forever." Millicent placed her almost full cup back on the tray. "Which leaves me with the task of dividing up my worldly possessions and making a will. Since I have no immediate family, it's only logical that the town will be my major beneficiary."

"So why not leave the lighthouse to the town?" Made perfect sense to her.

"If I did that, the town would lose out on a big chunk of taxes and be saddled with the added expense of lawn care, maintenance on the building and plowing. It would become a burden."

"I hadn't thought of that." She put her cup back on the tray and started taking notes. There definitely was a column here.

"Jefferson and I already donated the land that is now the town square, the huge gazebo, and the playground. Everyone in town gets to enjoy it, and the maintenance and upkeep are figured into the town's budget. One of the local churches built most of the playground equipment. The volunteer firemen built the gazebo, and they repaint it when it's needed. Even the Women's Guild does a lot of the flower planting and gardening."

She scribbled faster. "I've seen the town square. It's gorgeous." A few quick notes were added. "That was very generous of you and your late husband."

"We didn't do it to be generous, and I would really rather you didn't mention it in your column. I'm more concerned about the offer I received from the hotel chain. It's a substantial amount of money, plus as part of the agreement, they will promise not to tear down the lighthouse. They even offered to restore it and make it accessible to their guests. It would be a big draw."

"Makes sense." She wondered if Millicent's mind had already been made up and if she was using her column to explain her decision to the town.

"I could use the profits from the sale to help fund another college scholarship for one of the local kids. I set one up a couple months ago, but I'm sure two scholarships wouldn't hurt."

Norah sat back in her chair and ignored the pad on her lap. "You've already made up your mind, haven't you?" No sense doing the column if it was a done deal.

"No." Millicent smiled and relaxed. "In this folder"—she picked up the folder that had been lying on the coffee table next to the tray and handed it to Norah—"are copies of what the hotel chain sent me."

Norah quickly flipped through the pages. Most were letters. There were a few drawings.

"They've been doing their homework, Norah. Facts, figures, and projections that will make your head spin. All it did for me was give me a head-ache."

"I like facts, figures, and even projections." She glanced at a pencil drawing of what a world-renowned hotel chain thought a three-story, one-hundred-room hotel should look like when it was built next to a five-story lighthouse. She wasn't im-pressed.

"Tom's a good friend of mine." Millicent smiled as her cat jumped back up into her lap. "There was a condition on you doing this column for next week's edition."

"That would be?" She wasn't fond of conditions, especially when they pertained to her work.

"The following week you must write the other side of the story. You must tell Matthew Porter's story."

"I didn't even know Matthew wanted the property and the lighthouse." She couldn't imagine where Matthew was going to come up with that kind of money.

"He's made no secret of it, Norah. He wants to restore the lighthouse himself and open it up to visitors. He also wants to rebuild from the original plans the lighthouse keeper's house. Matthew has already acquired those plans and a few ancient photographs to work from."

"Is he going to live in the house?" She had no idea where Matthew was living now.

"I believe so. I think on the other end of the property, he wants to build his workshop and storage for his business."

"Will he be able to afford the taxes and all if he does that?" Maybe there was a way around this.

"That you'll have to ask him." Millicent continued to pet her cat calmly. "My biggest concern is what the town will be giving up if I sell to Matthew. In the paperwork I gave you is the hotel's projection of the additional tourist dollars that would flow into Misty Harbor."

"I take it they are substantial?"

"Very. We're talking a big hotel with a well-known name. One who would bring in a higher class of tourist who has deeper pockets. Every shop, tour boat, and restaurant in this area would profit from them."

"Heck of a dilemma." She wouldn't want to be in Millicent's shoes trying to decide what to do.

"Yes, it is." Millicent played with the tiny silver

cross she wore around her neck. "That's why you have to tell both sides of the story. From what I've seen of your work, you're fair and factual, and you don't express your own opinion."

"This ought to be fun." *Not!*

"I could have asked Tom to write an editorial about the sale of the property."

"Why didn't you?" Maybe if she found out why she hadn't, she could convince her to change her mind. Tom would probably do a better job of it. He understood the economics of the area.

"Rumor had it that you were seeing Ned Porter before you wrote that piece about logging."

"True."

"Yet you wrote it anyway. In my book, that took guts. I've known the Porter boys all their lives. They stick together like glue, and they aren't going to appreciate the column in which you explain the pros of the hotel chain buying the property."

"Are you trying to talk me out of this?" Ned was going to be livid.

"No, I'm expecting you to show the same guts now. Some of the residents are going to be awfully upset no matter which way this goes. It's a hot issue."

"Your friend Tom has a habit of giving me hot issues to cover."

"Someone has to do it." Millicent chuckled softly. "I think Tom chose well."

"Some days, I think I should have gone with my second career choice."

"Which was?"

"Crash test dummy."

Millicent's loud, unexpected laugh disturbed the cat, which sprinted out of the parlor with his tail in the air. "I can see now why our Ned is so taken with you." Millicent frowned at the formal tea set and stood up. "Let's forget the tea and the formality, and go into the kitchen. It's been a while since I had such delightful company, and besides, I have some of the most delicious butter pecan ice cream."

Chapter
Fifteen

Ned was so mad he didn't know if he was going to spit or go blind. How could Norah do this to his brother? Granted, she might not have known that it was Matthew's dream to restore the old lighthouse and rebuild the house that had once stood beside it before she had written her column. But surely she had discovered it as she researched and verified her information. Three quarters of the town knew Matthew wanted that piece of property if and when Millicent Wyndham decided to sell.

Yesterday, ninety percent of the town had been opposed to having some massive, one-hundred-room monstrosity built on the cliff that overlooked the harbor. This afternoon, half of them were wondering where to line up to fill out job applications, and the other half were rubbing their hands together in anticipation of the windfall that they thought was about to be bestowed upon them. Norah had a lot to answer for.

No wonder the little minx had been acting

funny all weekend. She had even come up with an excuse as to why she couldn't spend last night in his bed. She just didn't want to be there in case he read the article before she went to work. He honestly didn't know what he would have done if he hadn't been sitting at the jobsite on the opposite end of the county when he'd finally been able to read her column.

A tiny part of himself was relieved though. It all made sense now. When Norah had started acting a little different over the past week or so, he couldn't figure out why. He had actually started worrying, thinking that Norah might be having second thoughts about their relationship.

He was the one having doubts now. Not about their relationship but about her sanity. Had she purposely been trying to ruin what was between them or to push him over the edge? Norah knew how much his family meant to him. The Porter boys might have tried to kill each other when they were younger, but now they would die for each other.

Ned drove into town and headed for Norah's. He knew he should take the time to go home first, take a shower, and cool off. But he needed to see Norah now. He wanted to hear her explanation of why she hadn't told him about the article before it hit the stands.

That was what hurt the most. She hadn't trusted him enough to tell him. He knew that writing that piece hadn't been her idea. Tom Belanger and Millicent Wyndham were old friends. He could see why Tom had assigned Norah that particular topic. But why hadn't Norah told him? Did she think he

would have tried to persuade her not to write it, or
at the least, slant it in Matthew's favor?

He muttered a curse as he turned up Norah's
street. She would have been right to worry about
that one. He would have tried and been extremely
disappointed in her if she hadn't listened. And she
would have hated herself for compromising her
journalism ethics. Norah hadn't been hired to write
opinion pieces or to manipulate the facts. She had
been given that column to write the other side of
the story.

If he kept up this line of thinking, he would be
thanking Norah for ruining Matthew's chance at
obtaining his dream. Norah had him so confused
that he didn't know if he was coming or going.

He pulled up in front of Norah's and saw her
standing by the Jeep's door. She either had just
gotten home, or she was leaving. By the guilty look
on her face when she spotted him, his guess would
be that she had been running to hide.

That guilty look just made him madder. He got
out of the truck and slammed the door.

Norah flinched at the sound of the slamming
door. She had been dreading this moment for
over a week. She watched as Ned stalked up the
driveway. Ned was furious. The keys to the Jeep
were in her hand. She had been two minutes too
late to make her escape. Coward that she was, she
had been hoping to be with her mother and Karl
by the time Ned finally tracked her down.

Millicent had told her she had guts. She only
hoped her new friend was right.

"I'm not apologizing for writing that article,
Ned. Every word, fact, and prediction is a direct

quote and true." She raised her chin a notch and looked up into his stormy face. She actually felt better going on the offensive. "It was my assignment and my job. I'm sorry if I hurt Matthew's chances of buying the property, but the town needs to know what they might be losing. Millicent Wyndham was the one who requested I write that piece." She left out the fact that next week's column was already written. A copy of Matthew's side of the argument was neatly folded in her purse.

Ned's jaw clenched. "I'm not accusing you of falsifying a single word, Norah."

"Then you're mad that I didn't take Matthew's side." Millicent had been insistent. The first week's column would cover the hotel's side. The second week's would be Matthew Porter's. "Don't you think the town has the right to know what the hotel could offer?"

"This isn't about what the hotel has to offer, and you know it!"

She blinked in confusion. Ned was so livid his face was beet red. His voice rose like thunder and nearly shook the ground beneath her feet, but amazingly, she wasn't afraid. She realized that while Ned was furious as hell with her, he would never hit her. She smiled up at him.

Ned's eyes grew round, and the vein near his temple stood out in sharp contrast to his molten, red face. "You did it on purpose, didn't you?" He crowded her against the side of the Jeep and shouted, "You wrote that article to see how mad I would get. You wanted to push me to the edge, didn't you?"

She relaxed further and tried not to smile. Ned

looked like he was going to blow a gasket. She really hadn't meant to get him quite this upset.

"What did you think I would do, Norah? Hit you like one of your old boyfriends?" Ned's voice rose with each slowly pronounced word. "I . . . don't hit . . . women!"

Norah felt her smile fade. "None of my boyfriends ever hit me, Ned." She fumbled with her keys as humiliation washed over her. "It was my father."

Every ounce of color faded from Ned's face. In shock, his lips formed two words, but no sound emerged. "Your father?"

She turned, opened the door, and climbed into the Jeep. Before Ned could regroup and question her further, she drove away. She just needed to be alone for a moment.

Ned couldn't believe it. One instant, Norah was standing in front of him; the next, she was gone. She couldn't drop a bombshell like that and then just drive away. Her father had hit her?!

Here, he had been thinking a boyfriend had put that fear into her eyes. Fear he hadn't seen in weeks. He hadn't once thought it might have been her own father. Her mother didn't seem to be afraid of men. Joanna Stevens was even dating Karl James.

There was something different about Karl. He wouldn't quite call him dangerous, but there were some hidden depths there. Rumor had it that Karl had been a leader of some notorious motorcycle gang out on the West Coast. Ned didn't believe that particular rumor, but there was something more to Karl than met the eye.

Ned drove down Main Street looking for Norah's battered old Jeep. Misty Harbor wasn't big enough for his rose fairy to vanish completely. Joanna's car hadn't been at the house, nor was it parked by the gallery where she worked. He headed for Karl's.

Five minutes later, he pulled into Karl's driveway. Joanna's car and Karl's truck were both parked there, but not Norah's Jeep. Maybe Norah's mother would have an idea of where her daughter might have gone. He didn't like the fact that Norah was alone after he had practically screamed himself hoarse at her. He needed to apologize. He needed to hold her.

He climbed out of his truck as Karl and Joanna stepped out of the house and onto the porch.

"Ned." Karl was holding Joanna's hand.

"Where's Norah?" asked Joanna, looking toward his truck.

"I was hoping you could help me with that one." He walked to the porch and joined them. "We had an argument, and she drove away. Now I can't find her."

"About her column in this morning's paper?" Joanna's gaze was on his face.

"Yes and no." He ran a hand through his hair in frustration. "I understand why she wrote that article, and I even have to agree with some of what she said. Of course, I didn't get around to telling her that part."

"What part did you get around to telling her?" asked Karl.

"The part where she did it on purpose just to see how mad I would get." He held Joanna's concerned gaze. "I kind of yelled at her." The understatement of the year if ever there was one.

"What was she doing when you were yelling?" Norah's mother's look of concern turned into confusion.

"She was smiling, which only made me madder so I yelled louder." He still hadn't figured out why she had been smiling.

Joanna laughed. "She was testing you, Ned. I'm not sure if it was consciously or subconsciously, but my daughter wanted to get you so mad that you didn't know what to do."

"She wanted to see if I would hit her or not."

Joanna cringed. "I'm afraid so." Joanna sat on one of the porch rockers and told Ned about the night Norah's father had hit her.

Ned listened with dawning horror and anger. How could a man treat his wife and daughter like that? As Joanna finished the story, he glanced at Karl, who was standing next to the rocker. Karl's expression was frighteningly calm.

"I shouldn't have yelled at her." He needed to find Norah right away. Somehow, he had to make this okay.

Joanna laughed softly. "Ned, if you are planning on having any kind of relationship with my daughter, you'll be raising your voice a lot more in the future. It's perfectly normal and healthy to argue, disagree, and occasionally raise your voice."

"Especially if Norah takes after her mother." Karl leaned forward and kissed Joanna's cheek. "In case you haven't figured it out yet, Ned, the Stevens women are a little headstrong and stubborn."

Ned chuckled as Joanna blushed. "I hadn't realized that Norah got that particular trait from her mother's side of the family."

"I'm afraid so," Karl said.

Ned glanced up into the early evening sky. The sun was going down, and it would be dark soon. "Joanna, do you have any idea where Norah might have headed off to?"

"Not a clue." Joanna stood up. "I don't think she'll be gone long. Especially if she was smiling when you were yelling. She probably just needed some time alone to work her feelings out, that's all."

"Okay." He headed for his truck. "Thanks."

Karl joined him by the side of the truck. Joanna was sitting on the porch swing out of earshot. "Relax, Ned. I'm sure she's fine. As Joanna said, she was smiling."

Ned wanted to rip something apart. "Do you happen to know where Norah's father is now?" There had been a whole lot of the story Joanna hadn't told him. He hadn't been born yesterday; he could fill in the blanks. Not only had Vince Stevens hit his daughter, but Joanna had suffered at his hand as well.

Karl slapped him on the back. "Relax, Ned; the situation is already being handled."

"How?" He wanted particulars. He wanted to be able to close his eyes at night and know Vince Stevens had suffered for what he had done.

"I called in a couple of favors." Karl's chuckle was a lighthearted sound.

He looked at Karl. Maybe the rumors were true, but he couldn't imagine what a motorcycle gang on the West Coast was going to do about it. "What are they going to do—chain him behind a chopper and drag him down the highway?"

"Damn rumors." Karl chuckled. "I have never been a member of a motorcycle gang, Ned. It's nothing quite that glamorous or interesting."

"So what favors did you call in?"

Karl studied him for a moment. "I don't want it to get around, but I'm a retired FBI agent."

"A Fed?" Karl didn't look like any Fed he had seen, but then again, he didn't know any personally. "You're kidding, right?"

"Afraid not." Karl chuckled. "I like being an old gang member better. It gives a guy a lot more color, don't you think?"

Ned chuckled along with him. "Agreed, but you still didn't tell me what kind of favors you pulled in."

"Let's just say Vince Stevens is going to find himself hounded by the law for every little thing for a very, very long time." Karl grinned. "I do believe last week he even got a jaywalking fine."

Ned was still laughing as he drove around town trying to spot Norah's Jeep. He definitely never wanted to have Karl mad at him.

Fifteen minutes later, he finally spotted her Jeep in the place he should have looked first. It was parked in front of the lighthouse. He could see Norah sitting on a rock staring out over the ocean. One of the long skirts she favored was blowing in the breeze like a beacon. Considering the color of yellow it was, he should have spotted her up here when he had driven through town the first time. Ships out at sea could have spotted her.

He parked his truck next to her Jeep and

walked to where she was sitting. He was half afraid to face her because if she was crying, he'd probably throw himself off the cliff for causing those tears. He sat down next to the rock and looked out over the ocean.

He knew she had heard him pull up, but so far, she hadn't said a word. Night was falling and turning the ocean dark. The cries of the gulls and the pounding of the water against the rocks below comforted him. They were familiar sounds. Sounds he had known all his life.

"I've been looking everywhere for you." He finally broke their silence. He gathered his courage, turned, and looked at her.

Norah's smile was the most beautiful thing he had ever seen. "I've been right here."

He didn't see any signs that she had been crying. "I'm sorry I yelled at you."

Norah slid off the rock and joined him on the ground. "It's okay, but the next time, I'm yelling back." She leaned forward and kissed him.

Ned pulled her up onto his lap and held her close. "There's not going to be a next time." He never wanted to fight with her again. His heart couldn't take it.

Norah chuckled against his chest. "Yes, there will."

He pulled back and looked down into her laughing green eyes. "Your mother warned me about you."

"My mother?"

"I stopped at Karl's looking for you. She told me about the night your father hit you." He tenderly cupped her cheek. "I can't promise I'll never raise my voice at you, but I can promise never to raise my hand."

"I don't need your promises, Ned." She turned her head and pressed a kiss in the center of his palm. "I know you won't. Haven't you realized why I was smiling at you when you were yelling?"

"You're certifiable?"

"No." She chuckled. "I was smiling because I realized that I wasn't afraid any longer. There you were yelling, towering over me, and turning red in the face from screaming, and I wasn't afraid."

How was it possible to feel even worse? He brushed her lips with his mouth. "I'm glad you weren't afraid. A wife shouldn't be afraid of her husband. Ever."

"A wife?" Norah's lower lip started to tremble.

"You are going to marry me, aren't you?" Ned stroked her lower lip with the pad of his thumb.

"You haven't asked."

"A technical detail." Ned laughed and rolled her under him. The evening breeze smelled of the ocean and the freshly cut grass beneath them. Norah's body was soft and yielding beneath his. "I love you, Norah Stevens. Will you put me out of my misery and marry me?"

"Misery, huh?"

"Norah?" He could see the laughter and happiness lurking in her eyes, but he wanted an answer. He needed to hear her say it.

"I guess, since you asked so sweetly."

Ned lowered his mouth and captured her acceptance.

* * *

Norah waited for Ned to get out of his truck. He had followed her home from the lighthouse. It was a safe, secure feeling seeing his headlights in her rearview mirror. They were getting married. She still couldn't believe it. Of course, the grass stains on the back of her blouse and skirt would convince everyone they might have to, but at least they had controlled themselves enough to come tell her mother before heading to his place.

"Hey, handsome." She stepped into his arms as he joined her on the walkway.

"I still haven't had a shower yet. I'm not exactly clean, love."

"This will take what, five minutes here, five minutes at your parents. If you behave that long, I'll scrub your back in the shower when we get back to your place." She wanted to tell her mother they were getting married, but she also needed to tell her that everything was okay. She had looked deep within herself and found the strength, faith, and love to trust Ned fully.

Her mother would understand.

She kissed Ned and hugged him tightly. "I love you."

Ned hugged her back. "Stop that, or we are never going to make it into the house."

Norah laughed and tugged him up the walk. "Five minutes, tops."

Ned rolled his eyes as if he didn't believe her.

An hour later, Norah couldn't believe it. Her mother had taken the announcement of their impending marriage well. Her mom and Karl had congratulated both of them and then had surprised her and Ned by announcing their own engagement. Norah had no idea how often a mother and daughter got married in the same year, but she was betting it wasn't that common.

Joanna had been so excited that she had called Peggy and John Porter over to hear the news and celebrate. An impromptu party was organized. John and Karl ran out for pizza, Ned ran to his parents' house for a quick shower, and her mother raided their refrigerator for everything edible. Peggy used the phone to call the rest of her boys and their families. Within half an hour, the house was jammed with people. Porters were wall to wall.

Norah found Matthew in the dining room scarfing down some of her mother's brownies. "Hi, Matt."

Matt smiled. "Hello, future sister. I knew you and Ned were going to make a great couple." Matt seemed mighty proud of himself.

"You did?" Ned had told her why Matthew had asked her out at the barbeque weeks ago.

"Sure did." Matt took another bite of the brownie.

"You read the paper this morning?" Matthew didn't seem upset by her column. Maybe he hadn't read it yet.

"Sure did." Matt raised one eyebrow and took another bite.

"You aren't mad?"

"Oh, for about an hour I was." Matt stood up, came around the table, and gave her a hug. "Then I reread your column. I was determined to prove you wrong and to point out every mistake." Matt nugged her tighter. "Strange thing was, I couldn't find any. You wrote the truth, Norah, and I can't be mad about that."

"It's only one side of the truth, Matthew." She dug into the pocket of her skirt and pulled out a folded piece of paper. "I'm sure you're wondering what happened to all those answers you gave me last week when I interviewed you."

"I figured they weren't important, or you would have used them."

She had called Matthew late one night and chatted his ear off. Once she had gotten Matthew to talk about his dream, there had been no shutting him up. She handed Matthew the folded page. "Here's an unedited version of next week's column. I used your answers in it. Millicent wanted the town to hear and understand both sides of the issue before she decides what to do."

Matthew unfolded the paper and started to read. "Does Ned know about this?"

"I haven't told him yet."

"Told me what?" asked Ned as he came up behind Norah and wrapped his arms around her waist. His chin nuzzled the top of her head.

"I wrote a second article about the lighthouse property. It's going to be printed in next week's edition."

Matthew kept reading. He gave a low whistle. "Does Millicent know about this?"

"Tom Belanger gave her final approval on both columns. She has a copy of all my facts and where I obtained them from. I can tell you she was mighty interested in them." She had a feeling Millicent was going to sell Matthew the property, but it was only a hunch. She couldn't relieve Matthew's mind yet.

Ned tried to read over Matthew's shoulder. "Hold it still; I can't read it."

Matthew moved away and grinned. "You get to read it when everyone else does next week."

Ned glanced at her. "Is he serious?"

She laughed and moved further into his arms. "Don't worry, Ned." She reached up and kissed him. "You're sleeping with the reporter; I'm sure there must be some way to get the information out of her."

Matt groaned. "Will you two get a room?"

Ned wiggled his eyebrows and planted a loud kiss on her mouth.

"Yuck," cried Tyler, who had just joined them. "Gross."

Ned leaned down and ruffled his nephew's hair. "You'll change your tune once you grow up."

"Ned, stop corrupting my son," Kay said as she handed Tyler a plate with a slice of pizza on it. "Here you go, Ty."

Jill, who was cradling a sleeping Amanda, stepped into the dining room. "Norah, do you think your mother would mind if I laid Amanda on her bed? I would ask her, but Karl seems to be monopolizing all her attention." Jill's smile was contagious.

"No problem." She kissed Ned again just to hear Tyler complain. "Come on; I'll help you get her settled." She headed for her mother's bedroom.

Jill laid the baby in the center of the bed. Kay, who had followed them into the room, took the sham-covered pillows and blocked one side of the baby so she couldn't roll off the bed. Jill grabbed the other two pillows and barricaded the other side.

"I thought she didn't roll over yet?" Amanda was nearly lost in the middle.

"She doesn't, but we've learned never to trust them. Babies always do the unexpected. Remember that."

"I don't think I need that information quite yet." She and Ned hadn't even discussed children.

Kay laughed. "Well, John and I had our first discussion on the subject while I was in labor with Tyler. He chose that particular moment to inform me he wants at least three kids."

"What did you say to that?" She tried not to laugh at the look on Kay's face.

"I told him that I'd give him a son and a daughter, but the rest were up to him." Kay grinned. "He hasn't gotten pregnant yet."

"Cruel, Kay, cruel." Jill gently covered the sleeping baby with a blanket. "Paul and I both want four."

Kay snorted. "If Tyler and Morgan give me another day like today, I just might give them to you. You won't even have to go through labor."

Norah laughed along with them. "I'm glad you both are going to be my sisters-in-law."

Kay and Jill both hugged her. "We are the ones who are thrilled that you're joining the family. Think of all the shopping trips we can take together," Jill said.

Norah shook her head at the thought. "I've created two monsters, but I did notice that Paul and John still haven't stopped smiling since our last trip."

Jill and Kay both blushed, which caused her to

stifle a laugh so that she wouldn't disturb the sleeping baby. "I don't know how you two were doing it."

"Doing what?" Jill asked in confusion.

"Hiking, camping, or whatever you want to call it." Norah grinned and headed for the door. Jill and Kay could probably hike across the country and never break a sweat. She should be the last person on earth to give them any advice on the subject, but she couldn't help herself. "I happen to find hiking very conducive to romance."

Kay and Jill were still laughing when she joined Ned in the living room.

"What are they laughing about?" Ned asked.

"I haven't the faintest idea." She moved into his arms. "I was just giving them some pointers."

"Pointers on what?"

She smiled and simply said, "Hiking."

ABOUT THE AUTHOR

Marcia Evanick lives with her family in Pennsylvania. She is currently working on her next contemporary romance set in Misty Harbor. Marcia loves to hear from readers, and you may write to her c/o Zebra Books. Please include a self-addressed, stamped envelope if you wish a response.

BOOK YOUR PLACE ON OUR WEBSITE AND MAKE THE READING CONNECTION!

We've created a customized website just for our very special readers, where you can get the inside scoop on everything that's going on with Zebra, Pinnacle and Kensington books.

When you come online, you'll have the exciting opportunity to:

- View covers of upcoming books
- Read sample chapters
- Learn about our future publishing schedule (listed by publication month *and author*)
- Find out when your favorite authors will be visiting a city near you
- Search for and order backlist books from our online catalog
- Check out author bios and background information
- Send e-mail to your favorite authors
- Meet the Kensington staff online
- Join us in weekly chats with authors, readers and other guests
- Get writing guidelines
- AND MUCH MORE!

**Visit our website at
http://www.kensingtonbooks.com**

By Best-selling Author
Fern Michaels

Available Wherever Books Are Sold!

Contemporary Romance By
Kasey Michaels

__Can't Take My Eyes Off of You
0-8217-6522-1 $6.50US/$8.50CAN

__Too Good to Be True
0-8217-6774-7 $6.50US/$8.50CAN

__Love to Love You Baby
0-8217-6844-1 $6.99US/$8.99CAN

__Be My Baby Tonight
0-8217-7117-5 $6.99US/$9.99CAN

__This Must Be Love
0-8217-7118-3 $6.99US/$9.99CAN

__This Can't Be Love
0-8217-7119-1 $6.99US/$9.99CAN

Available Wherever Books Are Sold!

Visit our website at **www.kensingtonbooks.com**.